Snowflake

Snowflake

A Novel

Louise Nealon

HARPER

An Imprint of HarperCollins*Publishers*

HarperCollins books may be purchased for educational, business, or sales promotional use. For information, please email the Special Markets Department at SPsales@harpercollins.com.

Originally published in the United Kingdom in 2021 by Manilla Press, an imprint of Bonnier Books UK.

FIRST U.S. EDITION

Library of Congress Cataloging-in-Publication Data has been applied for.

ISBN 978-0-06-307393-7

21 22 23 24 25 LSC 10 9 8 7 6 5 4 3 2 1

To my parents, Tommy and Hilda,
for their wisdom, love, and support.

The Caravan

My uncle Billy lives in a caravan in a field at the back of my house. The first time I saw another caravan on the road I thought that someone—another child—had kidnapped him on me. It was only then that I learned caravans were meant to move. Billy's caravan never went anywhere. It was plonked on a bed of concrete blocks, right beside me from the day I was born.

I used to visit Billy at night when I was too afraid to go to sleep. Billy said that I was only allowed out of the house if I could see the moon from my window and if I brought him wishes from the garden. On the night of my eighth birthday, the sight of a round, fat moon sent me straight down the stairs and out the back door, the wet grass on my bare feet, the thorns of the hedge grabbing me, pulling me back by the sleeves of my pajamas.

I knew where the wishes hung out. A coven of them grew close to the caravan on the other side of the hedge. I picked them one by one, satisfied by the soft snap of stem and sticky juice of severed end, the bump of one fluffy white head into another. I cupped my hand around them as though protecting candles from the wind, careful not to knock off a single wisp of wish and lose it to the night.

I twirled the syllables around my head as I collected them— dandelion, dandelion, dandelion. Earlier that day, we had looked up the word in the big dictionary underneath Billy's bed. He explained that it came from the French term—*dents de lion*—lion's teeth. The dandelion began as a pretty thing and the petals of its skirt were pointy and yellow like a tutu.

"This is its daytime dress but the flower eventually needs

to go to sleep. It withers and looks tired and haggard and just when you think its time is up"—Billy held up his fist—"it turns into a clock." He uncurled his fingers and produced a white candy-floss dandelion from behind his back. "A puff-ball moon. A holy communion of wishes." He let me blow the wishes away like birthday candles. "A constellation of dreams."

Billy marveled at the bouquet of wishes I presented to him when he opened the caravan door. I picked as many as I could find to impress him.

"I knew it," he said. "I just knew that the moon would come out for your birthday."

We filled an empty jam jar with water and blew the cottony heads of the dandelions into it, their feathers floating on the meniscus like tiny swimmers lying on their backs. I closed the lid on the jar and shook the wishes, celebrating them, watching them dance. We left the jar on top of a dank stack of newspapers to stare out of the caravan's plastic window.

Billy heated a saucepan of milk on the hob of his gas cooker. His kitchen looked like a toy I hoped to get for Christmas. It always surprised me when it worked in real life. He let me stir the milk until it bubbled and formed little white sheets of skin that I pulled away with the back of a spoon. He poured in the chocolate powder and I whisked the spoon around and around until my arm hurt. We tipped the steaming brown stream into a flask and brought it up to the roof to watch the stars.

It took days for the dandelion seeds to fully submerge in the jar. They clung to the surface, hanging from their ceiling of water until it seemed like they either gave up or got bored. Just when the world thought they were goners, tiny little green shoots appeared like plant mermaids growing tails underwater. Billy called me to come over and marvel at the stubborn little yokes, the wishes that refused to die.

❄

Today is my eighteenth birthday. I'm a bit nervous knocking on Billy's door. I don't really visit him at night anymore. The outside of the caravan is cold against my knuckles. It has a lining of rubber along the sides like a fridge door. I dig my nails into the squishiness and tear a bit away. It comes off in a smooth strip like a sliver of fat off a ham. There is a shuffle of papers and the squeeze of steps across the floor. Billy opens the door and tries his best not to seem surprised to see me.

"Well," he says, making his way back to his armchair.

"Sleeping Beauty," I greet him. He didn't get up for milking this morning and I had to do it for him.

"Yeah, sorry about that."

"On my birthday and all," I say.

"Oh fucking hell." He grimaces. "It's a wonder St. James didn't leave you in the *leaba*."

"He didn't know. Mam forgot to tell him."

"We're an awful shower. What one is it anyway? Sweet sixteen?"

"Egotistic eighteen."

It's a small victory to see his face scrunch into an amused grin. I wait until he turns his back to fill the kettle.

"The offers for college came out today," I say.

He turns off the tap and looks back to me. "Was that today?"

"Yeah. I got into Trinity. I'm starting next week."

He looks sad. Then he grips his hands on both sides of my shoulders and lets out a sigh. "I'm fucking delighted for you."

"Thanks."

"Fuck the tea," he says, waving the idea away. "Fuck the tea, I'll get the whiskey."

He rummages around in the press. Plates rattle and a tower of bowls topples over. Billy attempts to knee the avalanche of crockery back into place. I want to clean up the mess to have something to do, but then he stands up, emerging from the press triumphant with a bottle of Jameson.

"Happy birthday, Debs," Billy says.

"Thanks." I take the bottle of whiskey from him like it's a prize in a raffle.

We're both standing awkwardly. I really don't want it to be my idea. I'm supposed to be an adult. I can't beg for things to happen anymore.

"There's a clear sky up there tonight," he says, finally.

"It's also fucking freezing," I say.

"There's a hot water bottle in the press if you want it." Billy reaches up to the door in the ceiling and pulls down the fold-up ladder to the roof. He stomps up the steps in his boots, trailing his sleeping bag behind him like a child going to bed.

I boil the kettle. The odd contents of the caravan peer at me. A wooden model of an old-fashioned aeroplane dangles over his bed. A tiny man is sitting on it as though it's a swing, a pair of binoculars in his hands. We christened him Pierre because he has a mustache.

The hot rubber of the water bottle warms my hands. I climb the steps of the ladder two by two until the night wind splashes my face. It feels like being on a boat. We crawl into our cocoons of sleeping bags and lie down on the galvanized metal sheet that covers Billy's home. The roof is cold and slippery under my hands. It feels like lying on a block of ice.

We look at the sky as though it depends on us to hold it up there.

The view from the roof of the caravan is the only thing that doesn't get smaller the older I get. We can hear the cows' hooves swishing through the grass. They come mooching over and sniff around the place to see what's happening. I inhale the dank, musty sweat of the caravan off the sleeping bag. Billy smells of cigarettes and diesel. The sleeves of his jumper dangle over his fingerless woolen gloves. A hedge of stubble prickles around his mouth and reaches across his cheekbones to join up with the hair behind his ears.

"You have a story for me," Billy says.

"I don't feel like a story."

"You do," he says. "I'll pick a star."

I pretend to be unenthusiastic and fidget with the zip of my sleeping bag. I tuck my hair behind my ear and wait for him to land on a star.

"Can you see the North Star?"

"No, it's only the brightest star in the sky."

"It's not, actually. The Dog Star is the brightest."

"You told me the North Star was."

"Well, I was wrong."

"That's a shocker."

"So you see it? I've shown you it before?"

"Only a couple hundred times, Billy, but you told me it was the brightest star in the sky."

"It's the second brightest."

"And I'm supposed to figure out the second brightest star?"

"It's the one with the W near it."

"Yes, I know, it's the one that *seems* like the brightest . . . but it's not."

"I'm just checking we're talking about the same one. Fucking hell. So, you see those five stars that make the wonky W near it?"

I squint up at the sky and try to connect the dots. I used to pretend I was able to see what Billy saw. I hate the effort of trying and still not being able to make things out. As far as I can tell it's like reading braille, only using lights that shine from billions upon billions of miles away. There are too many—the crowd of them all staring back at me is overwhelming.

The older I get, the more of an effort I make. Billy breaks the stars down into pictures and stories, and makes it easier to distinguish between them. The W is one of the easier ones to spot.

"Yeah, I know it," I say. "The one that looks like a rocking chair."

"Exactly," he says. I look over at his index finger pointing up, tracing the stars together in smooth, straight lines. "Cassiopeia's chair."

"I remember her."

"Right so—tell me about her."

"You know the story, Billy," I say.

"I haven't heard you tell it before."

I sigh to buy some time. The characters are beginning to congregate in my mind.

"Go on then," Billy prompts.

"Cassiopeia was a queen in a past life—the wife of Cepheus," I explain. "He's up there too. Cassiopeia was gas. She was lovely like, but people thought she was strange. She wore her hair loose and went around in her bare feet all the time, which people found shocking because she was supposed to be royalty. She gave birth to a daughter called Andromeda and she brought her up to love and respect herself—a radical idea, back in the day. Her free spirit was mistaken for arrogance. Word got out that there was this hippie queen going around barefoot, loving herself and teaching her daughter to do the same. Poseidon wasn't having any of it. He decided to remind humans that they could not run the show. So he sent a sea monster to destroy her husband's kingdom. Cassiopeia was told that the only way to save the kingdom was to sacrifice her daughter, so she did. She chained Andromeda to a rock at the edge of a cliff and left her for dead."

"The bitch," Billy says.

"Well, she had no choice. It was either that or let the monster kill everyone."

"The Greeks were fucking nuts. Can I guess what happened to Andromeda?"

"You can."

"Rescued by prince charming?"

"Of course," I say.

Billy passes me the bottle of whiskey. It burns my throat.

"Perseus killed the sea monster on his way back from slaying Medusa, and Andromeda was obliged to marry him out of courtesy," I say.

"Classic. And what happened to Cassiopeia?"

I point up to her. "She's up there in her rocking chair. Poseidon tied her to it so that as she circles the North Pole, she is upside down. She's stuck in that chair, spinning until the end of time."

"Jesus," Billy says. "Spending half your time upside down. It might make you see the world differently."

"I'd just be dizzy."

"Maybe you would at first, but you might get used to it."

"I'm happy with gravity, thanks."

"Happy enough for me to push you off this roof?"

He shoves my sleeping bag so hard that I roll over and scream. "You prick, Billy! That's not funny."

"Not a fan of the birthday bumps?"

"Stop it," I say, but I'm happy and warm inside. I think about my story and take another swig from the bottle. The first sip of whiskey has already sent me spinning up toward the sky.

Commuter

It's my first day of university and I've missed the train. Billy insisted that I'd make it. He was late finishing up the milking before dropping me off at the station. So now I'm going to be late. I don't know what I'm late for, exactly. Maybe I should try and make friends. I'm nervous that all the good ones will be gone by noon. It's orientation week and I have seen films set on college campuses. If I'm going to bump into my future best friend or lover, it will happen on my first day.

I've only ever been to Dublin in December. Billy brings me up to see the Christmas lights every year. My first memory of Dublin is waiting to get the bus home from O'Connell Bridge with Billy when I was five or six. When the bus finally came, it was a relief just to get onto it to shelter from the lashing rain and the wind that was turning umbrellas inside out. Billy tapped the driver's window and showed him a ten-euro note. He folded it up and tried to squish it down the coin slot like he was doing a magic trick.

The driver looked at him. "What am I supposed to do with that?"

Billy took out the note and made way for the passengers behind us to pay their fare. "Sure you've plenty of change there, boss," he said, nodding at the clinking sound the coins made.

"Do I look like a slot machine?" The driver stared at us until Billy backed away.

We got off the bus and back into the rain. We always got the train after that.

It was strange to see Billy around people he didn't know.

He wasn't as sure of himself. When he made me hold his hand, I didn't know if it was for my benefit or his.

Still, we found a way to navigate the city that suited us. The years melt into each other so that they become one: we would stop by the GPO to pay our respects to Cúchulainn and the lads, then walk across the bridge and up through Dame Street as far as Thomas Street to the bakery where a scary woman with skin like a pastry sold us fifty-cent sausage rolls. Billy once offered a cigarette to a homeless man along the canal. We sat down on a bench with him and had the kind of easy conversation some people make at the church gate after mass.

On Grafton Street, we watched a puppet in the window of Brown Thomas teasing a shoe with a hammer and nail. Toy trains went chugging around their predestined paths. Billy asked me what I wanted to be when I grew up. I pointed at a busker painted as a bronze statue and said I wouldn't mind being one of them because their job was to make people happy. Either that or a priest. He smiled and said, "Good luck with that."

Billy always wanted me to apply for Trinity. "The only college worth going to. Fairly up their own holes though." He pointed at the high stone walls and spiked railings at the side entrance on Nassau Street but we never went in. I don't think he realized that it was open to the public. I always thought of Trinity as a reverse *Shawshank Redemption* situation, where you had to bribe Morgan Freeman with cigarettes and tunnel your way in.

Last year, when my school brought us to a careers fair, Morgan Freeman wasn't manning the Trinity stand. Instead, a gray-faced woman in a navy pantsuit gave me a brochure, eyed my scruffy uniform, and told me that it took a lot of brain power to get into Trinity. She was wrong. It didn't take much brain power at all. You don't have to be smart to get into Trinity. You just have to be stubborn.

✳

I lose my ticket on the train up. I only realize this at the ticket barriers at Connolly station. I go over to the box marked IN-FORMATION and tell the man behind the glass window what happened.

"Where did you get on at?" he asks.

"Maynooth."

"How much was the ticket?"

"I can't remember."

"Can I see some identification please?"

"I don't have any."

"What's your name sweetheart?"

"Debbie. Eh, Deborah White."

"Are you over eighteen?"

"Yeah."

"Well Deborah, you've got yourself a hundred euro fine." He points to a small sign at the bottom corner of the window that reads FIXED PENALTY NOTICE and slips me a sheet of paper through the tray. I scan it: *Up to twenty-one days to comply—if the penalty goes unpaid—may be subjected to a court appearance—may face a fine of up to a thousand euros upon conviction.*

"I lost my ticket," I say.

"Love, if you bought the ticket you'd remember how much it cost."

"But I genuinely can't."

"I don't know that. Show your fine to yer man at the barrier there and he'll let you through."

❊

I enter Dublin on my own for the first time as a convicted criminal.

❊

I find myself following a woman on her way to work. She is wearing a pair of runners with a pencil skirt and tights, take-away coffee in one hand, briefcase in the other. She's walking as if she's trying to catch up with the rest of the day. I keep my distance a few paces behind her. We cross a wide bridge that vibrates under the weight of all our footsteps, bouncing under our feet as though it's trying to cheer us up.

I get as far as O'Connell Street before I pluck up the courage to ask a guard to point me in the direction of Trinity. He laughs at me and I blush, hating myself. I set off in the direction he sends me with a new resolve to look like I know where I'm going.

I wait by the railings at the front gate for a while before entering. I watch people going in and out of the mouse-hole that leads into the college and wonder why they made the entrance so tiny. It reminds me of a disturbing episode of *Oprah* I eavesdropped on when I was six years old. When my grandad was alive, daytime TV was his kryptonite. After eating his dinner in the middle of the day, he'd sit down and watch either *Oprah*, *Judge Judy*, or Anne Robinson on *The Weakest Link*. On this particular episode of *Oprah*, a psychologist with floppy hair said that walking through doorways causes a brief lapse in memory. The audience of women gasped and nodded, remembering the times they left a room to do something only to stand there cluelessly scratching their heads.

I refused to leave the sitting room, convinced that now that

I knew what the doorways were up to, they would wipe my memory clean. I clung to the armchair, burying my head in the crease of the cushions, kicking and biting Mam's hands when she tried to pull me up. In the evening, I gave up the fight and she dragged me into the kitchen to eat my tea. I crossed the threshold wondering how long it would take for me to forget who I was.

This doorway feels like it has the power to do something similar. It doesn't matter who I am. Once I walk through that door I will be changed. I'm not prepared for this. It feels like I should have a funeral for myself.

I make it look like I'm waiting for someone in case anyone is watching me. I look at my phone and my watch and scan the curious parade that passes by. Androgynous grunge, preppy blazers, cropped capri trousers, Abercrombie and Fitch jumpers, Ralph Lauren T-shirts, tote bags adorned with badges for obscure political campaigns.

A girl wearing a yellow raincoat gets off her bike. It's one of those vintage bicycles with a wicker basket at the front. I have no idea how she is pulling off the raincoat. Black hair. Fringe. Freckles. Nose-piercing. She looks happy—excited, but not in an embarrassing way.

I am wearing my best pair of jeans and one of Billy's check shirts with the cuffs rolled up. I look like I'm going out to dig potatoes. I watch the girl disappear through the hole to the entrance into the front square. I take a deep breath and follow her.

❄

Standing under the banner that heralds Freshers' Week, I am painfully aware of how fresh I am. I don't know what I was expecting—maybe a designated corner for the purpose of making friends. I'm used to knowing a person's name, their dog, and what their da is like drunk before I risk speaking to them. There are stalls and tents full of people who seem to know each other already. English accents clip the cobblestones. I wander around like a self-conscious ghost waiting for someone to notice me.

"Hello!"

"Jesus."

"Sorry, I didn't mean to frighten you." A bearded avocado is talking at me. "I'm with the Vegan Soc and we are playing a word association game to try and debunk the myths surrounding veganism. So, like, if I say vegan, what's the first thing you think of?"

"Hitler."

"Excuse me?"

"Hitler was a vegan. At least, people say he was. It was propaganda, probably. Or bullshit."

"OK, interesting. You still associate the term with that factoid even though it was proven to be false."

"Something about Hitler sticks in the mind."

"Would you ever consider going vegan?"

"I don't know. I live on a dairy farm."

"Dairy farming takes babies away from their mothers," he says. I can't tell if he's joking or serious. "Cows have been modified over centuries for human consumption. They are Frankenstein's monsters, every single one of them."

"But Frankenstein only had one monster," I say.

He pauses to think about this for a moment until he comes to a conclusion in his head. "Exactly," he says, pointing his finger at me as though he has crossed a finishing line and won the conversation.

"What's your name?" I try.

"Ricky."

"Ricky," I repeat. "I'll try to remember that."

"You won't." Ricky looks like he is going to say something and then stops himself. "Go vegan," he says instead, and fist-pumps the air.

❄

I join the end of a queue to look like I'm doing something.

"Is this the queue for registration?" The girl in the yellow raincoat is talking to me.

"I think so," I say.

"Great, I need to do that today. What course are you doing?" she asks.

"English," I say.

"Oh great, me too. Are you in Halls?"

"Ha?"

"Halls. College accommodation?" she asks.

"No, I live at home. About an hour away."

"Oh, you're a commuter! How are you finding it?" She says it like she is genuinely interested in my well-being.

"Well, I've only done it once so far."

"Oh right, yeah, that was a stupid question." She pauses. "I'm Santy, by the way."

"Nice to meet you, Santy. You've a cool name."

"Thanks very much. My parents are big on Greek mythology."

"Oh." I've never heard of a Greek called Santy.

"What's your name?" Santy has the type of green eyes I've only seen in music videos.

"Debbie."

She laughs. "Sorry, it's just—you just pointed to yourself."

"Did I? Sorry, I'm not used to introducing myself."

Santy is from Dublin, but she doesn't speak like the Dublin kids in the Gaeltacht who sounded so posh they may as well have been foreign. She sounds normal. Grounded. Unspoiled. There has to be something wrong with her.

"Santy!" A girl wearing a beret walks toward us. She is short and stocky, wearing expensive glasses and carrying a brown leather satchel.

"Hiya! Debbie, this is my roomie, Orla. She's from Clare."

"Nice to meet you," I say, giving the girl a firm handshake. Anyone else from the country is my competition. There's only room for one gobshite from the back-arse of nowhere. I needn't have worried though. Orla sounds like a member of the royal family.

"What are we doing today?" she asks Santy.

"I need to register," Santy says.

"Great, me too." Orla pulls a folder out of her satchel. "I think I have everything."

"Are we meant to bring stuff with us?" I ask.

"You don't have the forms?" Orla asks.

"What forms?"

"You're supposed to register online. You got an email."

"I haven't seen it yet," I say. "Our Internet at home is shite."

"Oh dear." Orla looks embarrassed for me. "There's really no point in queueing if you don't have the forms."

Santy tilts her head to the side and looks at me like I'm a stray dog she's found in her back garden. "It's OK, you can do it any day this week," she says. "All they're going to do is give us condoms and a rape whistle."

"Do the boys get rape whistles too?" Orla wonders.

"I suppose so," Santy says. "It would be sexist not to give them to everyone."

"Do you know where I could find a computer?" I ask.

"Have you checked the library?" Orla clearly thinks I'm an idiot.

"Oh right yeah, sorry," I say, and apologize my way out of the line.

"It's that way," Orla says, pointing in the opposite direction.

"Thanks."

I pretend to walk toward the library. I open up my purse and count up coins to buy a ticket for the train home.

Not Maud Gonne

I dump my bag in the kitchen and go straight out to the yard. I find Billy in one of the pens about to bottle-feed a newborn calf. He clutches a big plastic carton with a tube hanging out of the hole where the lid should be. He sees me watching and takes exaggerated steps as he sneaks up on his victim. She scarpers as soon as he lays a hand on her.

"Come here ya little bollix," he says, grabbing the calf by the tail and pulling her back to him.

"Bitch," I correct him. "She's a girl. It's the same with the cows, you're always calling them bastards but they're women."

"The day I have to worry about the gender identity of cows is the day I lie down on the flat of my back for a bit of euthanasia." He shoves the plastic tube into her mouth and down her neck, then turns the bottle upside down and holds it above his head. The beestings trundles out of the bottle into the calf's stomach. I wonder if she is able to taste it.

"You look shook," Billy says.

"I am."

"How'd it go today?"

I shake my head and feel myself go red.

"That bad?"

"Why did you never tell me there was a Greek called Santy?" I ask.

"Ha?"

"A girl I met. Her name was Santy."

"Good for her," he says.

"I thought you knew all of them."

"The Greeks? A whole ancient civilization? I'm flattered."

"You talk about them like you do."

Billy shoves his cheek out with his tongue like he's trying to work out a sum in his head. "Let me get this right. You're thick with me for not telling you something I thought you already knew."

"No, I'm thick with you because you talk like you own everything."

"Wow-wee. That's some accusation."

I hop the gate and sit cross-legged in the straw. "And now I sound like a gobshite."

"You do. This girl . . . Her name didn't happen to be Xanthe, no? X-a-n-t-h-e. That's a Greek name."

"Oh fucking hell." I collapse into the straw. Blood rushes to my head. "I kept calling her Santa Claus's nickname."

"Well, now you know."

"How can I have lived this long without knowing anything?"

" 'I know that I know nothing.' Socrates. By the way, other people know about him too. I'm not sitting on him."

I pick up a strand of straw and twirl it in my fingers. It goes from being two blurry strands into one strand when I open and close my left eye. "I hate being stupid."

"You're not stupid. Just, maybe, naïve?"

"Well, that's condescending."

"There's nothing condescending about it. Naïve is a great word. You should look it up."

"Give it a rest."

"Naïf, from *nativus* meaning natural or innate. It has the same roots as the French verb *naître*—to be born." He pulls the tube out of the calf's mouth. It trails across the straw like an umbilical cord. "We're all naïve. There's no other option."

"It must be exhausting being so profound."

"I've taught you everything I know," he says, clanking the gate open.

"I think that's the problem."

"Are you making me my tea?"

"Do I have a choice?"

I hold out my hand and he pulls me up from the straw.

Outside the shed, we pass three dead calves piled on top of each other.

"Notice anything strange about that one?" Billy says, poking the one in the middle.

"It's dead?"

He turns the calf over with his boot. "Its legs are in the middle of his belly."

"It's like Chernobyl out here," I say. "What was wrong with the other two?"

"They were too big. The bull gives calves too big for the girls to push out. I did my best but those are the casualties."

"Oh." I nod, and try to be in control of how I feel about that piece of information, as though knowing something about the problem could lessen it somehow.

※

I take out ham, tomatoes, and butter from the fridge and toss them onto the table.

"When I say vegan, what's the first word you think of?" I ask.

"Hitler," Billy says.

"Same."

"Although, he probably wasn't."

"Yeah, I know."

I start chopping the cherry tomatoes in half. "I didn't apply for my grant on time."

"Why's that?"

"I'm allergic to reality."

"You're going to have to get over that. Is there a way I can pay your fees for this year?"

"You can't afford to be doing that."

He fills up the kettle by the snout. "You can't afford not to go to college. You want out of here."

"I'm not ready."

"What do you mean you're not ready? You should be itching to get out."

"Well, I'm not," I say. "We don't even have proper Internet."

"I can't really get a signal from the roof of my yoke," Billy says.

"I've no money to get a laptop."

"Is that what this is about? You can't go to college because our broadband is shite?"

"It's not just that, it's loads of things. Like, who's going to look after Mam?"

"That's not your job."

"See you say that, but someone has to keep an eye on her. That someone is not you."

"To be fair now, you're not great at it either." He sits down at the table. "Since when were you Mother Teresa? You're looking for excuses to stay when you should be raring to get out of here."

"Just for the year. I'll take a year out. I can defer my course and go back next year. Do it properly."

"There's never a right time to start anything."

"There is. I want to live in town."

"Hang on." He puts his hand up and swallows his gobful of sandwich. "Let me get this straight. You come home traumatized after spending a few hours in the place, and now you want to move there?"

"I'll apply to stay in college accommodation."

"In a city that just scared the shite clean out of you."

"I'll save up this year. You don't have to pay me as much as James."

"No fear of that. I don't pay him enough for all the work he does in the yard, never mind the time he spends baby-sitting your mother. That's all done pro bono."

"Just give me enough to move out next year."

"To throw away on paying rent to live in a box in town?"

"It's what people do," I say.

He licks his index fingers and picks up the crumbs of brown bread like a child. "I'll see about getting you a caravan."

"Is that a yes then?" I ask.

"It's a fart in the wind is what it is."

"Well, I'm not going back anyway. I can't."

"You can and you will."

"You can't make me."

"Ah Jesus, Debs, listen to yourself. Do you realize how spoiled you sound? A day in Dublin has done this to you."

I hold back my head, trying to force the tears back down. I've always cried easily. I hate myself for it, which makes me cry even more. I let out a few sniffles.

Billy sighs, embarrassed by my tears. "Come on now, less of that. Chin up, snowflake."

"Don't call me that."

"*Don't call me that*," he mocks me.

"You're such a child," I say, but it's done the trick. I've stopped crying. I wipe the tears away with the sleeves of my shirt.

"Debs." He waits until I look at him. "The city frightens you. Don't let that stop you. Get to know it."

"Do you know that my only experience of town is hanging around Collins Barracks and the GPO with you?" I ask.

"My stint at trying to radicalize you. You're no Maud Gonne."

"Neither was she. An English-born Irish revolutionary muse. How'd she swing that one?" I dunk a fig roll into my tea.

"Her father was a Mayo man. It was hardly her fault she was born in England. Anyway, she broke free of her naïvety."

I catch the wet biscuit in my mouth just as it's about to fall into the tea. "She allowed herself to be mythologized."

"And that's a bad thing?"

"I think so."

Billy stands up and slip-slides in his socks toward the back door. "You're going to college this year," he says. "If I have to foot the bill, so be it." He bends down to put on his boots. "Learn how to drive and I'll sort out the Internet," he says, and slams the door behind him.

Saoirse

Our house is tucked into a bend at the foot of a hill. We call it Clock's Hill because that's the name of the man who lives in the bungalow at the top of it. I don't know what his real name is, or why everyone calls him the Clock. The Clock cycles past our gate every day on his way to the shop to get the paper. He never says hello. He smells like turf from ages ago and is the only man I know who smokes a pipe. Sometimes, James enlists him to stand in a gap when we're moving cattle and then I feel obliged to talk to him because he's old and lonely. He doesn't say much, but sometimes tries to guess my age. He always thinks I'm much younger than I am and looks at me skeptically if I bother to correct him.

Our cattle dot the fields on either side of the road that rolls down from the Clock's house to the village. The steeple of the church peeks over the top of the trees. The hedges are trimmed to accommodate the view that is framed by the branches of two oak trees on either side of the road. A sign that reads FÁILTE is nestled on the inner bend of the hill opposite our house, welcoming people as they pass through our village on their way to somewhere else.

We used to have a wooden sign that hung on the wall of our entrance. Billy made it for my seventh birthday. I really wanted a horse but Mam said I wasn't allowed. I got to name the house instead, which definitely wasn't a thing. Billy made it into a thing because it didn't cost any money. I called it what I was going to name my horse: Saoirse, after the rush of freedom I imagined I would get from galloping down the hill and into our yard.

The name lasted for a few months until a car crashed into

our garden in the middle of the night. It was a blue car with a raised spoiler on the back that swung off on impact and hurtled over our hedge. It was going too fast down the hill and slipped on a patch of black ice on the bend, spinning out of control and smacking straight into the sign that read SAOIRSE. A nineteen-year-old boy died. Sometimes, for his anniversary, his family leaves a bouquet of white lilies at the wall of our entrance. We watch them wither away in their dirty plastic wrapping.

The night the car crashed into our wall, I had a dream. I was a boy in the dream and I was driving a car. I can't remember much about the dream itself but I remember how it ended. I didn't see the sharp bend at the bottom of the hill until the last second. I locked hard and then I felt the ice underneath the tires and it was graceful, really. And then a beautiful thought went through my head. The world spun me around like the way a woman unexpectedly makes you twirl on the dance floor and you feel a little silly, a bit emasculated really, but it doesn't matter because it's only a bit of craic and you think she might fancy you anyway . . .

Mam says that I woke up screaming before we heard the car crash into the wall. I was inconsolable. It was my fault that the boy died. He had hurtled his way into my head and I had stopped him from going to heaven. He was in too many pieces, like the wreckage of his car that we kept finding in the garden. I kept bursting into tears. I would howl out in bed. Mam tried her best to comfort me.

I started going out to the caravan at night. One time, Billy lost his patience with me. I told him that I couldn't sleep because the boy was still inside me. He slapped me across the face so hard that, even now, I'm not sure it happened. "That car crash had nothing to do with you," he shouted, and then, with his face in his hands, he told me that he wasn't angry with me. He was angry with my mother.

We never replaced the *SAOIRSE* sign. Billy forgot about it and I didn't dare remind him. There are still nights that I sit up in bed too afraid to go to sleep, waiting for the next car, the next ghost to crash-land into our garden on their way to oblivion.

Slut Stings

I look outside the kitchen window and see my mother in our back garden completely naked dancing in a bunch of nettles. Their stalks reach up to her chest like a crowd of palm leaves waving in adoration. Her spine twists and the tops of her shoulders take it in turns to kiss the space underneath her chin. Her hands trace half-moon circles around her as though she's wading through water. It doesn't look like she's getting stung at all until she moves out of the bush and it becomes apparent that she has set herself on fire.

By the time the lads come in for dinner, she has made herself bleed from scratching the stings. Billy pretends not to notice. Once, when he was drunk, he called them slut stings.

When Mam hands James his dinner, he reaches out and strokes the red rash with white bumps splashed across her skin.

"What happened to you?" he asks.

"I got stung by some nettles."

"Some? You're stung all over. Did you fall into them?"

"No, I jumped."

"What?"

Mam assures him that she stung herself on purpose.

"Why on earth would you want to do that?"

"There is serotonin in them. That's why they sting—they're natural needles that inject you with a happy chemical. It's good for you."

"Is that right?"

"Yeah."

James considers this for a moment and then nods. "Fair enough."

"Jim-bob will happily dive headfirst into a bed of nettles with you, Maeve," Billy says without looking up from peeling his potato.

"Well, I wouldn't say that now."

"I can think of better ways of doing drugs," Billy says.

"The two Ps, Billy: pleasure and pain. There's a reason why they are paired together," James says.

"Only in his case it's two Hs: hammered and hungover," Mam adds.

It really isn't that funny but James's laugh makes the table shake.

"As we all know, there are as many types of alcoholics as there are stars in the sky and I'm glad I'm the social kind. Others have enough serotonin to be staying in and downing bottles of wine in bed—"

"Jesus Billy, take it easy. It was only a joke," James says.

"Well, sometimes a joke is the most serious thing you can say."

That's how dinnertime is. Mam and James versus Billy and me. Always the same teams, picked before we sit down to eat.

❋

I could never fathom the idea that my mother gave birth to me. It seems much more likely that I rose up from the slurry pit like some sort of hellish Venus, or that I came out of the arse-end of a cow. It would make sense if James was my dad because he loves Mam, but he was only six when I was born. James was stitched into his John Deere overalls when he came out of the womb and was born into a family without any land. He was a sixteen-year-old pulling pints in his mother's pub when Grandad passed away. Billy asked James to come work for us. He turned out to be a godsend, milking cows, fixing fences, and pulling calves at all hours of the night. And Mam, who was devastated after her father died, perked up whenever he was around.

James is only six years older than me. He was the first face I imagined into the pillow I kissed at night. I used to make poor attempts to hide from him when he came in for breakfast in the morning. There were limited places to hide in the kitchen. My legs stuck out when I wrapped myself in the curtains and there were only so many times I could go underneath the table and try to avoid touching his legs and feet, squealing when a big hairy arm swooped under the table to grab me. I once tried hiding in the coat stand in the back hall, but it was too far away from the kitchen and he forgot to find me.

I love James in a Disney prince kind of way. I am used to separating the fantasy of him from the reality. James isn't bothered by the reputation that precedes my mother. He doesn't care about the whispers and nudges down the pub when he goes home with her at closing time to spend the night in her bed.

Their age-gap isn't as obvious as it should be because Mam looks young for her age and James looks older. Billy says that James went through puberty in an afternoon. It's true. One moment he was a boy and the next he was a grown man. He's six foot seven and captain of the local hurling team. We go to all of his matches and watch the sliotar fall from the sky into his outstretched hand like a gift from God.

※

I never knew who my father was but I think I know where I was conceived. There is a Stone Age passage tomb in one of our fields—a national monument with a sign from the government warning that defacement of the area is punishable by law. It's a place where teenagers go to drink cans. There is a sign on the way into the field that reads: KEY AVAILABLE FROM MR. WILLIAM WHITE. TURN LEFT AT CROSS, FIRST CARAVAN ON THE LEFT. Billy is the local historian who gives the occasional archaeological enthusiast a guided tour of the mound. The trusted keeper of the keys, he often leaves the gate open.

There are two stone steps that mark the entrance from the road and a path to the mound itself, which is fenced off from the rest of the field. The neat dome of grass swells up from the earth. A heavy metal door leads into the passage tomb where crushed cans and the occasional condom wrapper adorn the ancient burial ground. Names are etched into the sacred stones, the curvatures of *Suck my dick* immaculately carved alongside megalithic zigzags and spiral inscriptions.

The monument is called Fourknocks, which comes from two Irish words, *fuair* meaning cold and *cnoic* meaning hills. My mother has been absorbed into the folklore of Fourknocks. In the summer of 1990, the passage tomb was where boys went to lose their virginity. Mam's only stipulation was that she would not have sex with the same boy twice. Nobody mentions the stories around me but they know that I know them. Billy, the local historian, told me.

Tabernacle

My mother has been asleep for most of her life. Mornings lie beyond her realm of existence. Her alarm goes off at midday. It plays "Downtown" by Petula Clark on repeat. She wakes up in time to make dinner for the lads at two o'clock. After dinner, she goes back to bed. Today is Sunday, the only day of the week that Mam needs to wake up early for ten o'clock mass.

I put the blade of the butterknife into the lock and twist until I hear the click. The door creaks open. Petula Clark's voice is released into the rest of the house. I turn off the alarm and watch Mam come groaning back to reality.

"Morning," I say.

"Morning."

"Will I get your coffee?"

"Yes please."

I've learned that making Mam coffee is the most effective way to make sure she doesn't go back to sleep. By the time I come back with a mug of Maxwell House, she is sitting at her desk wrapped in her writing blanket.

Mam sits down at her desk to record last night's dream in an old school copybook. She uses blue pens and gets upset if she can't find one. Mam has been writing a book about dreams since before I was born. She tells people that she's a writer, but she's never been published. She has no interest in submitting to journals or competitions, which is probably a good thing.

We call Mam's bedroom the Tabernacle because the door is painted gold and she locks it with a key like the one the priest uses at mass. Mam would be happy enough to let the entire world fall down around her as long as she had her own space. The Tabernacle could be an art installation or a dressing room in an underground theater. Sometimes, I jimmy the lock open while she is asleep just to look at it.

Walking into that room is like stepping into the middle of a pop-up book. She rips out pages from books and sticks them to her bedroom walls. Leaves upon leaves of paper make a collage of poems, novels, and philosophy books—all of them about dreams. She places them side by side as if she's trying to link clues.

The sheets are stuck together with masking tape. It's satisfying to peel the sheets away from each other. They make a sound like lips smacking together before opening, somewhat reluctantly. Lift a flap of paper and another layer of dream lies underneath. Pull open the cover page to one of John Field's nocturnes and the entire manuscript tumbles out of the wall.

A mobile of tin shells inscribed with spirals hangs suspended from the ceiling by braids of hair. The shells have a celestial gleam. I expect them to jingle when I touch them but instead they make a disappointing rattle like a beautiful woman with a horrible voice.

Mam keeps a faded biscuit tin filled with postcards and clippings of paintings from art magazines under her bed alongside a crate of mini-bottles of white wine that James regularly swipes for her from his mother's pub. A small blue skull made of lapis lazuli sits on her windowsill. A navy lamp stands on the dresser at the foot of her bed like a fat lady with a wide-brimmed hat. Its light casts Mam's shadow across the wall—her elongated silhouette reaching out to cradle a sleeping body that is just out of reach.

Mam rarely ventures outside the house, except to go to mass, the supermarket, or the social welfare office. Billy makes sure that she draws the dole every week. He calls it her arts grant. He's in charge of Mam's bank account. We've learned the hard way that giving Mam access to money causes carnage. Billy drives her food shopping once a week and stays in the car while she shops. There are days when she'll come back to the car with a smoothie and a doughnut and no groceries at all and he has to send her back in.

Mass remains the only occasion Mam makes an effort to be normal. Grandad was very religious. When he was alive, we all used to kneel down in the sitting room to say the rosary every night. He was also extremely proud. He liked his family to look well at mass, so Mam has come to associate religion with style. She already has her outfit picked for this morning's mass. She will have a shower and spend at least an hour and a half getting ready.

Before her shower, Mam goes outside in her bare feet. She takes careful, deliberate steps through the grass like she's stepping onto a stage. Then she closes her eyes, puts her hands by her side with her palms facing outward, and gathers long, slow breaths into her lungs—inhaling fresh whiffs of reality and exhaling her own mystery.

Aisling

I used to sleep in the Tabernacle with Mam. After the nine o'clock news, Grandad sent us up to bed. We changed into our pajamas and brushed our teeth. I wasn't tall enough to reach the sink so I spat my toothpaste into the toilet bowl.

We turned the bed into a tent by pulling the blankets up over Mam's head. She used to read me a pop-up book of *Alice's Adventures in Wonderland*. I loved Alice. The white apron that went over her blue dress showed off her tiny waist. When I pointed to her on the page, my finger was fatter than her. She looked like a Disney princess.

When Alice saw the white rabbit, Mam made bunny ears out of her fingers and threw a rabbit shadow on the wall. It flickered in the lamplight like magic cast by an old film projector. My least favorite page was the last one, when the adventure ends and Alice wakes up on the bank beside her sister. I peeled off the back page to expose the cardboard underneath.

Mam's reading of *Alice's Adventures in Wonderland* would eventually veer off course. This usually happened when she read Alice's worry: *"I wonder if I've been changed in the night? Let me think: Was I the same when I got up this morning? I almost think I can remember feeling a little different. But if I'm not the same, the next question is: 'Who in the world am I?' "*

"Alice is not herself because she has disappeared," Mam explained. "When Alice falls down the rabbit hole into Wonderland, she falls out of herself. It happens to us all. When we fall asleep, we fall out of ourselves."

I was never sure if this was a good or bad thing. The way Mam described the dreams reminded me of trying to follow Billy's hand when he pointed to a star.

"That's Orion's belt," he'd say. I'd look up at the sky solemnly, seeing nothing but mulling over the phrase Orion's belt. I never saw Orion or his belt but the mystery was enough. It was better.

The mystery of the dreams was enough for me too. I tried to follow Mam's logic but she let go of my hand along the way.

✳

Mam used to tell me a bedtime story about a speck of dust called Aisling who didn't believe in snow. Every night when Aisling fell asleep, cold water came and turned her into a snowflake. When morning arrived and the sun came out, Aisling melted back into dust before she woke up, completely unaware that she had changed into the thing that she didn't believe in in her sleep. She felt something cold tugging at her, but the memory was numb and frozen over. She dismissed it as a fragment of a dream.

Mam ended the story by running to the freezer in the utility room. I followed her downstairs in my pajamas, my bare feet slapping the linoleum floor. The chest of the freezer hinged open like a coffin and smoke rose up like mist. We scraped our fingernails along the side to gather snow. Mam told me that we would need a microscope to see the snowflakes properly, even though they were right under our noses.

"Like the way Billy needs a telescope to see the stars?" I asked.

"Yes," she said. "Except it's the opposite. The telescope helps us see things that are far away by bringing them closer. The microscope helps us to see things that we can't see properly because we are too close to them. It creates distance between us. Perspective."

"Would Aisling believe in snow if she had a microscope?" I asked.

Mam thought about that, and then told me another story, about the first man to photograph snowflakes. "They called him the Snowflake Man. He caught snowflakes on black velvet and photographed them with a microscope attached to a camera lens. He was able to capture the image of the snow crystals' structure before they melted. But a photograph is not the real thing." And then she said, very seriously, "There is no way to catch a snowflake. And I haven't met anyone who is able to catch a dream."

Cover Girl

I can go a whole day in the city without talking to anyone. I frequently disappear on the train, in the Arts Block, on the streets of Dublin. I sit alone in lectures. I go as far as getting coffee from a vending machine to avoid interacting with people. After spending my first couple of days trying and failing to find friends, it feels better now that I've made a conscious decision not to talk to anybody at all.

I constantly need to pee so I spend half the day scoping out toilets to squat in and take a break. The bathroom is where I go to recharge, let myself cry, and pull myself together just enough to define my edges so I seem solid on the outside. My shoulders ache from carrying my backpack. I spray deodorant on sticky, sweaty armpits and between my boobs while reading graffiti on the walls. Most of them are anonymous cries for help. I feel this thrust of responsibility thrown onto me by the cubicle. A scribble on the toilet dispenser threatens suicide. There are other less urgent musings: *Is it weird that I don't enjoy sex?* Underneath is written: *Tighten your cervix and relax girl!* I wonder how that works.

On my way out of the toilets, I bump into a girl coming in. She throws out a lively "Sorry!" before bumbling past me. The force of the collision has scared me. I feel so insubstantial that I imagine myself easily being knocked out of my body and into hers.

"Wait, Debbie!"

It's Xanthe. I didn't recognize her without the yellow raincoat.

"Hi!"

"Are you free for a coffee?"

"Now?"

"Only if it suits?"

"Em, yeah?"

"Great, I'll just go pee."

*

Xanthe emerges from the bathroom looking like a woman in a perfume ad. She's wearing wide-legged trousers, a blue knitted jumper, and a flat cap that could have come out of Billy's caravan but somehow manages to bring the look together.

"How's the commuting going?" she asks as we slide into the slipstream of people going down the stairs.

"Grand," I say.

"How long does it take for you to get to Dublin?"

"It's about forty minutes by train. But we live, like, a twenty-minute drive away from the train station, so about an hour altogether."

"So you're out in the proper countryside?"

"Yeah. I live on a farm."

"That's amazing. What kind of animals do you have?"

"We only have cows. It's a dairy farm. My uncle owns it."

"Do you ever work on it?"

"I milked this morning."

"Oh my God! How long does it take?"

"Around an hour and a half."

"Do you milk them on your own?"

"Yeah, but James kept an eye on me while he was cleaning out the sheds."

"Is James your uncle?"

"No, James just works on the farm. My uncle wouldn't get out of bed. He was out last night."

"Haha, out on a Tuesday?"

"Every night is a night out for Billy."

I follow her out a side entrance I've never noticed before. An ambulance flies past. I go to cross the road but she is still standing at the curb, looking at me.

"What?"

"Did you just bless yourself?"

I blush. "Oh yeah. It's a habit."

"It's really cute."

I want to tell her to fuck right off.

"Sorry, that's condescending," she says.

"You're grand."

"It's a nice thing to do, is what I mean."

"I'm not really religious," I say.

"I know. I mean, I don't know. I'll stop talking now."

We cross the road into a café. The place is so packed with students and tourists that there's condensation on the windows. The coffee machine sounds like a building site.

"I'll go grab us a table," Xanthe shouts.

I'm not sure where the queue starts.

"Are you in line?" a woman asks me.

"Sorry, no," I say, and move to the side.

Xanthe is in my ear. "I got us a seat over there."

"Great, thanks. Do you know what you want? Do you want to go ahead of me?"

Ordering food is an ordeal. I'm starving. I want lunch, but it's too expensive. Xanthe orders herbal tea so I go for tea and chocolate cake. I apologize to the girl at the till for not having a loyalty card.

✳

I push my slice of cake over to Xanthe. "Do you want to share?"

"No thanks."

"Seriously, help me eat it."

"I can't. I have a nut allergy."

"Oh."

"Yeah. I used to be one of those people who didn't believe in allergies. I thought they were for weak people. Turns out, I'm weak."

"Do you like peppermint?" I say, pointing at her tea.

"No, actually."

"Then why did you order it?"

"I'm trying to get into herbal tea because they're meant to be good for you."

"Herbal tea reminds me of the daisy perfume I used to make when I was a kid. Smushed flowers in water. Even back then, I wasn't stupid enough to drink it."

"That makes me feel a lot better about spending a fiver on this."

"Are you joking?"

She points to the chalkboard above the counter.

"Daylight robbery," I say.

✳

An hour into the conversation, I've given Xanthe my life story.

"Your mam is going out with a twenty-four-year-old?"

"Yep."

"What age is she?"

"Thirty-six. She had me when she was eighteen."

"Wow. And your dad must be young too?"

"She never told anyone who my dad was."

"Not even you?"

I shake my head. "I'm not even sure she knows, to be honest."

"She sounds amazing. Wait until you decide to get married. It will be like a culchie version of *Mamma Mia*."

Xanthe overuses the word amazing. She doesn't like talking about herself. The only thing I know about her is her nut allergy.

"What happened to your fingers?" she asks, as though she's sensed I'm about to catch her out with her questions game.

I hold out my left hand. "A childhood accident," I say. "I got them caught in a door."

❋

Every spring, Mam picks reeds in the field beside our house and makes St. Brigid's crosses for the whole parish. At the beginning of February, she brings a wicker basket full of crosses to mass and the priest thanks her from the altar.

When I was seven, I tried to help her. The field where the rushes grow is called the swamp—a childhood, in-between place where my boots squelched and I was never sure if the grass surrounding me was land or lake. I used to imagine hippos submerged in the mud behind a clump of reeds.

Mam snipped the reeds with scissors, tied them in bunches, and put them into a hessian sack. I trailed along behind her, trying to pull the reeds up myself, but they were too stubborn to move. Usually, the more I tried to please Mam the less patience she had with me, but she tolerated me this time because Grandad was moving fences nearby. When I asked if I could help she let me drag the sack of reeds after her.

We went back inside the house with the rushes. I tried my best not to make any noise but even my silence annoyed her.

"Go outside and play, Debbie."

"But I want to help."

"I don't need any help."

"Please, Mammy, I'll be very good."

"I haven't time to teach you how."

"I already know how, we made them in school with pipe-cleaners." I smiled at her, triumphant.

She picked rushes off the table and started to walk toward her room, carrying the bundle into her chest like a baby.

"I want to help, Mammy, please." I started crying and she began to run. I chased her down the corridor, put out my hand to stop her from closing the door, but she slammed it. A black pain shot up my hand.

I lost the tops of two fingers that day—the middle and ring fingers of my left hand. Billy brought me to the hospital. When we arrived back home, Mam didn't acknowledge my injury, but she made me a cup of tea. Later that night, she slid a letter under my pillow while I was sleeping. It was disguised as an apology, but really, she explained how the situation was my own fault.

Mam brought the St. Brigid's crosses to mass that Sunday and the priest thanked her from the altar. People took one home on their way out of the church. The crosses were put over doorways to protect houses from harm.

Where Water Dreams

Mam twisted James's arm into bringing us to the beach. It's windy and raining. A day for ducks. She would never entertain the idea of going to the beach on a sunny day. The worse the weather is, the more excited Mam gets about swimming in the sea. Zeus's lightning strikes the idea into her head and his thunder eggs her on. Today is wild enough for Mam to want to go and harmless enough for James to agree to bring her.

"Turn left. Left!" Mam says, turning on James's indicators for him.

"You mean my other left? As in right?"

"No, left!"

"Do you want to drive the car, Maeve?"

Mam pushes James's hand away from her knee. They're both in bad form now. The only thing Mam and James ever fight about is Violet. Violet is a '98 purple Toyota Starlet. Billy went to see a man about a dog one day and came home with Violet instead. Mam says novenas for her every year when the car test comes around. She always manages to scrape a pass and James comes home with the certificate in his hand, patting her bonnet and beaming like a proud father. Mam likes Violet. She just doesn't like to drive her.

James's dog, Jacob, can drive the car better than Mam. Jacob sits on James's lap while he's driving, panting happily with his tongue lolling and his head out the window. He is an idiot beyond belief. He's supposed to be a sheepdog. James was all talk of the great servant Jacob would be when he was a puppy, but as he grew up he just got fatter and lazier. If he was human, Jacob would be a male model—you know, the ones who don't even have to try. His attractiveness isn't ruined by a poor diet and exercise regime. He's got good genes. There is a bit of husky in him and his coat is thick and glossy—black and white with a tinge of brown. He also has huge golden eyes.

But my God does he fuck up on a colossal level. He once chased the cows out of the field in the middle of the night, scaring them so much that they broke two electric fences and ended up stomping around the graveyard, shitting all over headstones and flowers. When Billy woke me up that night saying that the cows had broken into the graveyard, I imagined the heifers trying to squeeze their hips through the side-gate, their eyes bulging in embarrassment like larger ladies getting stuck in a turnstile. You still can't say a bad word about Jacob around James though. He defends him almost as much as he defends Mam.

Ever since I can remember, James has been teaching Mam how to drive. Technically, Mam knows how to drive a car. She knows a lot about cars in the same way some people are obsessed with world wars: she can talk about them in an abstract way but doesn't necessarily want to be in one. Lift the bonnet and she is able to name every part and what it's doing there. Ask her to turn on the ignition and she freezes. She gets defensive. James calls it an irrational fear. She calls it a reasonable one. Every now and then they have the same argument.

"Maeve, if you're so frustrated by the way I drive, why won't you drive the car yourself?"

"You don't get it."

"So why can I drive and you can't?"

"You are able to see the lines between things. I'm not. When I look out the windscreen, I can't see the lines that separate one thing from another. Things melt together in my brain."

Mam only drove the car to mass once. It was only two hundred meters but it was a big moment for her. She parked the car outside the church and gave James a massive hug. He kissed the crown of her head.

After mass, as she was turning into our gate, she overshot the corner and crashed the car into the wall, smashing into the exact same place where the nineteen-year-old boy died. We sent Violet down to the mechanic and she bounced back, but Mam never recovered. James stopped giving her lessons after that.

My stomach sinks when we get to the car park. I hate the effort of the beach. I balk at the thought of sand between my toes. Mam, on the other hand, rolls around in the sand. Throws it on top of herself. A few days after going to the beach she'll put her hand down her pants and smile when she discovers sand hiding in her arse crack.

The only thing that can surpass Mam's passion for sand in her arse crack is her love of the sea. She babbles about how amazing your body is to be able to adjust to the temperature of the ocean. As soon as the water hits her toes, her lungs wake up. She recites the names of the levels of the sea as she descends into the water. "Sunlit zone, twilight zone, midnight zone, abyss . . ." She waits until she is ready to dunk her head under to whisper, "The hadal zone of Persephone, the winter queen."

Mam says that she loves swimming in the sea but she doesn't actually swim at all. She can't. She just stands in it. James made the mistake of buying her swimming lessons for Christmas last year. He tried to hide his disappointment when she only lasted one swimming session and came home sulking. The instructor didn't like her, she said.

"And we had to wear condoms on our heads—those latex yokes that yanked hair from my scalp. The water was dead. And everyone was staring at me."

"Then don't go back," I said.

"Do you think James will understand?"

"Of course," I said, though I wished that he wouldn't.

I hoped it would be something they would fight about. But of course James understood. He even found it endearing how she hated other people seeing her in a swimming suit. That was another thing. Mam had to buy a swimming suit for lessons. When she swims in the sea, she goes in as naked as the day she was born.

❋

James is on at me to come in with them, but the thought of going skinny-dipping with Mam is just too much. I try not to watch her strip off, but I can't pull my eyes away from her flat stomach, the dimples at the base of her spine, the curve of her back, her weirdly perky breasts. She has scant pubic hair—fine and blond like the hairs on her arms.

James doesn't go in naked. Not until he gets into the sea, anyway. I don't know what happens in there, whether she rips the shorts off him or not. They kiss. She wraps herself around him. He loves it.

❋

I come to the beach for the shells. The windowsills of our house are littered with beach booty—cockles, razor shells, scallops, clams, whelks, periwinkles . . . There's a bowl of cowries in the bathroom. Mam saves the best shells for the windowsill of the Tabernacle—a striped Venus, spindle shells, and tellins that open up like tiny porcelain butterfly wings. I once stole a pelican's foot from the Tabernacle and put it under my pillow. When I woke up the next morning it was gone. All that was left under the pillow was the tiniest trace of sand. I imagined the tooth fairy prying it from my closed fist and returning it to the Tabernacle where it belonged.

We found a queen conch once. Mam said that if I put it against my ear I would be able to hear the ocean. Then she told me that what I was really hearing was the sound of my own pulse—the sea inside of me.

The tide is out. Mam and James are only knee-deep in the water but the waves are the crashing kind—collapsing walls that try to knock them off their feet. I lower my gaze and start to comb through the clutter. Some of the shells are as thin as eggshells; others as thick as teeth. I skim over the razor shells, mussels, and cockles—the pawns of the sea. If I was younger I would have my arms full by now—each and every cockle was a marvel—but I've become more of a connoisseur, only stooping to inspect the most curious. Some aren't shells at all. Fragments of glass from beer bottles are taken in by the sea and cleansed of their generic beginning. I think I found a bone once. I was afraid to show it to Billy in case he told me it was something more normal.

I'm thinking about the boy who stands at the back of mass. Sitting down is too much of a commitment for him. He's cooler than that. He prefers to loiter, making a point of his agnosticism. I flirt with him at mass. I mean, try to flirt. I sneak glances at him. Whenever I succeed in making eye contact I panic and look away. It's stupid and terrifying. Embarrassing, really.

We were in the same class in school but I never talked to him. I still make a point of avoiding him. Whenever we are forced to interact I have a fear that I'm breaking something between us, like I'm afraid to trespass into reality. I'm not even being original in fancying him—everyone does. So I'm angry with him for turning me into a cliché, even though we've never had a proper conversation.

We used to lean our school bags against each other every morning next to our lockers. I liked the thought of them lying next to each other all day. It was comforting. I miss it now that school is over. Billy always said the Leaving is a sad name for an exam. Finishing school is a strange kind of grief.

It's the boy I never talked to who I miss the most. The fantasy of him stays inside the school walls, decaying like a memory mausoleum. The only way that I can resurrect the daydream is by seeing him at mass and transporting him to places like here, the beach. I look out at Mam and James and try to imagine him and me. I can't bear to talk to him in real life but I strip naked for him now in my mind's eye. I kiss him in the sea.

I bend down to pluck a white feather from the sand. It's small and fuzzy. I wrap it in a tissue and put it in my pocket like I'm giving myself a secret to keep.

❋

I sit on a towel on the stonewall and hug my knees into my chest. The wind sucks the hood of my jacket to one side of my head and makes me feel like I'm in a tent. Mam and James come out shivering and reaching for towels. James rushes to get the stuff from the car.

"How was it?" I ask.

"Amazing," Mam answers.

"Fucking freezing," James shouts.

He brings the big shopping bag out of the boot. Triangle ham sandwiches in tinfoil with cheese-and-onion Tayto. A teapot. A packet of chocolate digestives. Two flasks of hot water. He fills the teapot and sits Mam's woolly hat on top of it like a tea cozy.

I avert my eyes away from Mam getting dressed and crunch up the Tayto in the middle of my sandwich. She zips up her fleecy jacket. Last to go on is the woolly hat that has been toasted by the teapot.

"Are there good shells down there, Debs?" James asks.

"They're OK."

"I spotted some nice dog whelks," Mam says.

"They were badly bashed around though."

"Remember the time I got called into school about the beach story you wrote?" Mam asks.

"Yeah." I'm surprised she remembers. I'm looking forward to hearing how she'll twist it into an amusing anecdote for James.

※

I was around eight years old when Mam caught me with a handful of shells at the beach. I asked her if I was allowed to keep them and she said only if I learned their names.

"Names are magic," she said. "It's important for things to have names—otherwise they don't exist. Can you imagine if I called you Fiona or Louise?" I shook my head, my eight-year-old self terrified at the thought of other mes.

The week after we went to the beach, Mam was called into the school to talk about a story I wrote entitled "My Summer Holidays." In my heartwarming adventure, I spent my days at the beach collecting and identifying shells until my mother called me to say we were going home. Every time my mother called me by a different name, like Fiona or Louise, I was split in two and my misnamed counterpart would walk into the sea. By the end of the story, the body count was considerable. The teacher had pointed to a word on the page and asked me to pronounce it. "Suicide," I said, proud of myself for knowing a big word.

Mam came home from the meeting with my teacher with a smile on her face. She made us both a cup of tea and talked to me about the story as if I was an adult.

"The girls—they should walk into the ocean," she said. "Not the sea."

I nodded.

"The ocean," she repeated. "Don't call it the sea—that's vulgar. Give it its proper name. Call it the ocean."

"Ocean," I tried.

"See how much better that is? You can taste the sound of it in your mouth."

That night, she left a letter under my pillow. She had written it in an excited scrawl. I read it so often that I know the words off by heart, though I'm not entirely sure what they mean:

Ocean. Say it out loud. You can taste the sound of it in your mouth. The word ocean comes from the name of the Greek Titan Oceanus, a great body of water that wraps himself around the earth. No matter where in the world water is, it eventually finds its way back home to its own body where it can be rocked to sleep in the steady breath of its waves. The ocean is where water dreams.

When we fall asleep, we go to a place where words dissolve and become meaningless, like rain dropping into the ocean. As soon as rain hits the ocean it is no longer called rain. As soon as a dreamer enters a dream there is no longer the dreamer. There is only the dream.

Blessings

When we arrive home from the beach, James goes out to milk and we spend an hour and a half getting ready for Cemetery Sunday. Everyone descends on the graveyard for the annual evening outdoor mass. It's an event that is both a novelty and an effort—a cross between a silent pilgrimage and the world's most boring outdoor concert. We stand over our dead relatives for an hour and have a nosey at how well or poorly the other graves are kept.

The headstones are staggered in neat rows. At the top of the hill, there's a large wooden cross—four meters by two—apparently, the precise size of the one lugged up Calvary. It used to be a crucifix with a life-size Christ on it but some shitheads robbed him, leaving behind a lone left hand nailed to the cross.

It's the priest's first Cemetery Sunday and it shows. His feet are wobbling on the makeshift altar that has been set up on a trailer attached to the back of a Ford Transit van. He's being a good sport though. Father John is a slight Filipino priest. The community took an instant liking to him because he is affable and able to hide his intelligence, sort of like a holy Louis Theroux. The football team managed to get him down to training. He turned out to be a nippy corner-forward. He seems happy out drinking with the lads on Saturday nights and playing along with the running joke that he'll see them at mass in the morning.

The Blessings of the Graves is always a shit show, but this year's is especially bad. The choir are trying to pass off Leonard Cohen songs as hymns. "Hallelujah" is blaring out through dodgy speakers. They're on the verse about your one tying him to a kitchen chair. James nudges Mam and whispers something and they both laugh quietly, their shoulders shaking.

Of course, people have clocked that James is standing at our family's grave and not his own. He finished up milking late and our grave is closer to the gate so he just slipped in beside Mam. His mother, Shirley, has a face on her like a slapped arse, but she'd never say anything to him.

I'm jealous of Mam standing beside James. He seems like gravity itself standing all tall and broad-shouldered with his big, strong hands. Hands like shovels our Jim-bob, Billy says. Billy is the only one who shortens James's name. Jim, Jimmy, Jim-bob. If he calls him James it's sarcasm, usually to get at Mam. It's a power thing, I think. Listening to them talk, anyone would think that James was the one who owned the farm. He's the one who gives the orders and calls the shots. Men who call to the back door are never looking for Billy. Always James. Before James, they looked for my grandfather. Billy prefers it that way. When anything goes wrong in the yard, it's not his fault.

We're standing at my grandparents' grave. I'm named after my grandmother, Deborah. It's weird seeing your name written on a headstone. I was told that my grandmother died in her sleep. I learned of the overdose later. It was never said outright, but it was implied by things Billy said when he got drunk and sentimental.

Then I heard the story about what the church sacristan, Betty, said to Billy one night in the pub around closing time. Betty is a nervous, small woman who isn't able to hold her drink. Billy was trying to knock a bit of craic out of her, but then, out of nowhere, she shouted that Debbie White was the devil's whore and should not have been buried anywhere near consecrated ground. Billy squared up to her and said that if she breathed another syllable about his mother, she would have to pick a window for him to throw her through. They still call him Pick-a-Window down the pub.

Father John is going on tour now, descending from the steps of the trailer to sprinkle the graves with holy water. Ninety-year-old Mrs. Coughlan has been carted up graveside in her wheelchair with a full duvet snuggled up to her chin. She looks as though she's ready to be tipped in beside her husband.

Billy isn't religious. This is the only mass of the year he attends in order to pay his respect to his parents' grave. He makes sure that the grave is kept clean and the flowers watered. He gets them a poinsettia for Christmas. For now, a pot of yellow primroses graces the gravestones. Primroses were my grandma's favorite flower.

I'm not here for my grandparents. I'm here to catch a glimpse of the boy who stands at the back of mass. I saw him walking in with his family. He's wearing a Waterford jersey and jeans. His skin is too tan for an Irish summer. He must have been away. I look in the direction of his grandfather's grave. He's hidden behind a gravestone, but I can just about make out his elbow. A holy elbow, if ever I saw one.

It's like he senses that I'm looking at him because he shuffles into view and I look away. I end up catching the eye of my old piano teacher instead. She smiles and looks back down at her feet. I feel bad for not smiling back. Audrey Keane has the nicest bathroom I have ever seen. I used to spend half of my piano class going to the toilet. She must have thought I had severe bladder issues. I remember digging my index finger into the wax of the scented candles on top of the toilet cistern and putting my waxy finger under the tap, marveling at the way I couldn't feel the water through the wax.

Billy stopped taking me to piano lessons after someone told him that Audrey Keane had gone to rehab. It is socially acceptable to be an alcoholic in our parish as long as you don't get treatment for it. Being fond of the drink is a form of survival around here. If Audrey had kept quiet and continued to drink at home, people would have still sent their kids to piano lessons. Audrey's problem was admitting that she had a problem, and the problem was with alcohol, the one thing everyone loved.

I couldn't imagine my piano teacher drunk, no matter how hard I tried. I'd lie awake in bed at night trying to reconcile the image of the soft-spoken, elegant-fingered, immaculately dressed lady patiently showing me how to play the scale of C major with the bleary-eyed, potbellied men I knew from the pub. After rehab, she put less effort into her appearance. She let her hair go gray. I think it suits her. I wonder how long she's off the drink, or if she's off it at all.

The moon is out early. The crescent has slipped into the sky like a coin rolling out of its slot. I feel a drop of rain on my cheek and I curse the weather for breaking before mass is over. I wait for more but it doesn't come. It feels significant—a tiny piece of cloud falling from the sky, like a blessing.

Damsel in Distressed

I lose my student card, my wallet, or my phone at least once a day. It's always the same. I tap my pockets. Then I check my coat. I empty out my bag. My thoughts race, my brain goes into overload, and I can't breathe properly. I feel my face grow hot. I get a lump in my throat, my hands shake, and I tune out of everything. I run, or walk quickly, toward I-don't-know-where. I've missed lectures because I was looking for my student card. I didn't eat for an entire day until I found my phone in the lost property department of Connolly station. I hugged the barista who found my wallet in the bathroom of a Starbucks. The reunions are emotional, especially after a long separation. I look at them and promise that this time will be different. I will cherish them. Like an unreliable father, I swear that I will never, ever leave them again.

※

The guy at the security desk should know me by now, but I still have to point to myself in the lineup of missing student cards displayed on the inside of the window.

"I'm that one," I say. I look like a child in my photo.

He slides it under the window into the tray.

"Thank you so much," I say. "I won't let it happen again."

He takes a sip of his coffee and turns to chat to the guy beside him.

As soon as I feel the plastic card in my hand, I am able to breathe again.

I start to walk over to the balcony by the sliding door, but a lecture has just finished and I have to stop to let a stream of people pass. They're laughing—all of them—having the best time, while I bumble about on my own, panicking and losing shit.

I don't even know why I panic. There's nothing to panic about. I spend all of my time losing things and finding them again. I'm starting to think there's some part of me that is doing it on purpose. I'm caught in a vicious cycle. It's the most mundane form of self-sabotage.

I go to the bathroom for a break. I join the queue and catch a glimpse of myself in the mirror. There are blue shadows under my eyes. I'm exhausted from constantly giving out to myself. I've been sleeping a lot more since I started college, but it's the kind of sleep that makes me more tired. I'm beginning to rival Mam in the sleep department. I got fourteen hours last night and I still want to go to bed as soon as I get home.

I put my hands to my face to cool down my cheeks. A woman comes out of a cubicle. I barrel my way toward the free space and blot out the rest of the world. I sit down on the toilet seat and wait to feel OK again.

❄

The benches outside the arts block are reserved for cliques, smokers, and precocious pigeons looking for food. Even the pigeons intimidate me.

"Debbie!"

It has to be Xanthe. My only friend. Friend? Acquaintance? Person who knows my name? I turn around but can't see her.

"Debbie!"

"Oh, hi!"

She's sitting on one of the benches with a guy. His arm is around her.

"Debbie, this is Griffin."

"Nice to meet you, Debbie." Griffin offers his hand and I shake it. I stand there awkwardly until he gestures to the other side of the bench. "Have a seat."

I slide into the bench. It feels like an interview.

"First year?" he asks, pointing to my *Norton Anthology of American Literature.*

"Yeah."

He nods. "You know you can get that in a secondhand shop for like, a tenner?"

"Seriously? I'm just after paying an arm and a leg for it in Hoggis Fidges!"

They laugh.

"Or whatever the fuck you call it." I blush, knowing I got the name wrong.

"You could always return it."

"The effort of that. In fairness, they were really nice in there. And I got a few stamps on my loyalty card."

"Very true. Every time I go in there I want to buy the whole shop. There's nothing like the smell of a new book," Xanthe says.

Griffin sniffs my bag. "Smells expensive," he says, tapping the ash off his cigarette.

"Are you doing English too?" I ask.

"Oh God no, I plan to get a job after college. No offense. Final year Physics for me."

"Sounds like fun."

"It is."

"Griff is a genius," Xanthe says. "He got Schols."

"What's Schols?"

"They are scholarship exams I sat in my second year. Anyone can do them. If you do well, you get your fees paid for, free accommodation, and meals. A bit of money too. It's pretty sweet."

"Oh." I make a mental note to apply for Schols and get it at all costs.

Griffin looks like the teenage son of one of the Beatles. He has a generous mop of curls. A coin necklace dangles in his chest hair.

"Where are you from, Griffin?"

"Ardee, County Louth."

"You don't sound like you're from Ardee."

"Why, thank you."

"We've a hoof-parer from Ardee."

"Excuse me?"

"A hoof-parer. Don't know his name. His accent is hilarious though."

"You don't introduce yourself a lot to people, do you? You skip over the whole farming background thing, go straight for the hoof-parer." He seems like he's trying his best to embarrass me.

"So you have a plan then, after graduating?" I ask.

"I eventually want to specialize in oceanography."

"Wow, so like, climate change?"

"My PhD will examine the Ice Ages—how ice sheets formed and why they eventually began to retreat."

"Fancy."

"He's a tutor as well," says Xanthe, his official spokesperson.

"Sometimes. It doesn't pay well, but it keeps me fed and watered."

"We should go drinking," Xanthe says. "Debbie, come drinking with us."

"I can't. I've to go home. It's James's birthday."

"Oh, lovely! No worries, next time." She turns to Griffin. "Come drinking with me."

"I need to go home and change," Griffin says.

"Nonsense, you look great."

"I like your jeans," I say.

"Thank you." He strokes the exposed knees of his ripped black denims. "These are new actually. Tommy Hilfiger. The label said they are distressed."

"How very existential of them."

"You're my damsel in distressed," Xanthe says, ruffling his hair. "How much were they?"

"Can't remember. Two hundred quid?"

"You know you can get a pair of them in a secondhand shop for like, a tenner?" I say.

"Ohhh!" Xanthe pokes him in the stomach.

He smiles, but can't think of a comeback.

I say goodbye and walk away, feeling like I've won something.

Twenty-Five

My head is heavy from drink so I let it fall. I collapse onto the toilet seat until my belly touches the inside of my thighs. I have an upside-down view of the part of me that I shaved for the first time a few hours ago. I'd only trimmed it before—fingered the bristles and smoothed them out the way a mother cuts the curls of her baby's hair. I wonder if everyone's looks like a plucked chicken afterward—pink with red spots after the deforestation. The lips still have hairs from the bits I couldn't get at with the razor like the end of an elephant's trunk. A sideways tongue sticks out. I've never really noticed it before. It's hard to believe it was always there, poking out of the beard.

I wish there were other girls in the toilet with me, like when everyone piles into the same cubicle to down the naggins in our handbags and take it in turns to pee. It seems like a waste of a shave for nobody—not even drunk girls—to take a sneaky look to see how presentable I have made myself. I usually whip my knickers down at the last second and close my legs to hide the nest, or avoid the situation altogether by waiting outside and forging a fake friendship with the toilet attendant sitting on her stool who hands out squares of toilet roll and guards her collection of deodorants and mints.

I don't really have girlfriends anyway. Some of the girls in school would tolerate me the way you would a stray cat. I just about managed to make it into the group that sat around the back of the prefabs, but there were boys there too. That only lasted a few months. I only started going there because I was shifting a lad in that group and when he got a girlfriend we stayed friends in the way that you can be friends with lads. He still tried to throw Skittles into my mouth until the girlfriend told him to stop. Then they started going to the shop for lunch and I was too scared to follow them so I used to go around the prefabs on my own and read.

I inspect what I just squirted out of myself before I flush it away. Foam fizzes on top of the watery gold like froth on a pint. I wriggle about on the toilet seat and start flipping my hair, first to get volume into it and then a few more times for the thrill of it until I crack my head against the cubicle wall.

The bathroom in Cassidy's has all the charm of a cowshed in winter. A bird has installed a nest in the corner of the ceiling and splatted its shit down the tiles of the wall. Still, I see that Shirley has splashed out on a new bar of soap for James's birthday. The top has come off the tap in the sink so you have to twist a rusty nail to turn the cold water on. There's a knack to it, so everyone tends to scald themselves with hot water. A full-length mirror has been put beside the sink. I'm surprised by how pregnant I look when I stand in front of it. I keep forgetting to suck my stomach in. I'm wearing a black strapless bandage dress and heels that are already giving me blisters.

The bathroom light is unforgiving. My hair is flat and greasy. My eyes are black, my face is white, and I'm orange with streaky fake tan from the neck down. There's a spot on my knee. I try to pop it and that's when I notice the hairs on my legs that I missed while shaving. The most upsetting thing is that I really tried to look well for tonight. I actually made an effort. It took up so much space in my brain to decide what to wear. I've been mentally and physically preparing myself for days—even weeks.

I take a sip of my vodka and white and look in the mirror again. It helps. Narcissus must have been drunk when he fell in love with himself.

I go back out and consider finding Mam, but I don't want

to get caught up in her latest feud with Shirley. Mam wants to put the cake she made for James out on one of the tables but Shirley insists it should stay in the back as she already has a proper cake. Mam's cake is impressive. The 2 is made entirely out of boiled potatoes and the 5 is made up of eight loaves of brown bread, the great loves of James's life. In fairness, the potatoes were boiled today so they are fresh and Mam has kindly offered to attend the cake and peel a potato or cut a slice of bread on request. Shirley says it will start a food fight, disrupt the party, and destroy her pub.

Shirley and Mam never got on. Apart from Mam leading James up the garden path, there was always a strange sort of competition between them. Or jealousy. I don't know. They both crave male attention and Shirley gets plenty of it being behind the bar. The clucking hen in her doesn't take kindly to Mam sidling up to punters and distracting them until the night ends. There's a running joke that closing time comes quicker when Mam is in.

I scan the crowd, looking for Billy. I study the faces of women with the intensity of a palm reader as if I can tell by their expressions whether they just do their bikini line, or if they are more of a landing strip or Brazilian type. I get to Alannah Burke and imagine she is all silicone underneath those high-waisted jeans. She started waxing the hair off her arms in fourth class.

I wonder if anyone else can sense that I'm naked down there. There is a morning shadow that I couldn't get rid of, no matter how close I got with the razor. If any boy was to slip a hand under the cotton of my knickers, he may as well be stroking the stubble of a man's chin.

※

And oh God, there he is.

The boy who stands at the back of mass.

❊

I walk over to the old man section of the bar. I hope that he's watching me. Maybe if I pretend he doesn't exist, he'll notice me.

"Heyyyy Debbie." A drunken child stumbles toward me and puts his hand on my shoulder to steady himself. He's one of the Condrons, I think. He must be about thirteen.

"Hi," I say to his hand on my shoulder.

His ears are red with embarrassment but the drink has loosened his tongue. "Any chance of a shift?" he asks.

I remove his hand from my shoulder and say, "Come back to me when your balls have dropped."

His posse of friends laugh and I feel myself blushing, so I walk away. My heart is beating faster than it should after a confrontation with a thirteen-year-old. Word has obviously gotten around to the younger generation that I would shift anything with a pulse. They just have to ask, or get their friend to ask.

I kiss boys out of curiosity. I can tell if it's their first time. It usually is, even now that we're eighteen. You'd be surprised. Some of them use me as a crash test dummy. Others think that they can grab a boob or put their hands down my pants, until I set them straight. I'm strictly PG. I've had one request to replicate the upside-down Spiderman kiss. Another guy messaged me when it was raining one break-time to meet him behind the prefab and we kissed in the rain. He had awful chewing-gum breath and thanked me profusely after-ward. I was worried that he'd ask again and I wouldn't have the heart to say no. That's the thing. Once you start saying yes, it's very hard to say no. I've kissed so many boys that I don't fancy just because I feel sorry for them. I facilitate a moment where their fantasy drops into reality. It's sad though, because reality is so wet and disappointing. I'm not the fantasy girl they have in mind. I've only ever had one fantasy and he stands at the back of mass.

Some of the guys are really sweet. Tom Murphy took off his glasses before he kissed me—folded them and put them on the windowsill at an angle so that it felt like they were watching us. He held my hand and traced the side of my face before he went in. We were fourteen. That was probably my favorite kiss. I've never kissed a boy that I actually fancy. I don't know what that would feel like.

The music stops and the DJ calls James up for twenty-five kisses. James went on a holiday to America for his twenty-first birthday, and Mam always mourned the fact that he didn't have a proper twenty-first. He's probably the first person in history to have a twenty-first themed twenty-fifth birthday party. A line of girls forms and I consider joining but it would be weird to kiss James, even on the cheek. A couple of the lads from the hurling team are straddling him. We're getting to twenty-three, twenty-four. James stands up and calls Mam up for his twenty-fifth kiss.

Sweet Sensations

I log into Facebook and creep on Xanthe's page again. Xanthe Woods (2,345 Friends). I have 71. And I'm really pushing the boat out. I'm accepting requests from people I haven't spoken to since primary school. Hairdressers. Personal trainers. I even accepted an organization called God's Power the other day in an effort to bump up the numbers. It's stressful having it right there in brackets, next to my name.

Xanthe seems to have no trouble with the task of curating her online identity. Her profile picture is not a pixelated zoomed-in version of her happy head—no, no. Xanthe is not so basic. She has chosen a black-and-white portrait of a bird taking flight. I flick back through previous profile pictures. The back of her head against a blue sky. An overhead shot of her sitting cross-legged in the grass reading *Middlemarch* with a daisy tucked behind her ear.

She probably does this all the time. She meets someone a few times in real life, stalks them online, and virtually begs them to be her friend. I imagine her trying to casually wrangle surnames out of people as soon as she is introduced to them.

I get a message notification and my heart hops up my throat. I wish I could be cooler about this. It's from Xanthe:

Hey Debbie! A few of us are heading for drinks tonight if you want to join. You're welcome to stay at mine if it's a hassle for you to get home. No pressure! Speak soon X

Does she mean X as in a kiss or X as in look-at-this-iconic-way-I-can-abbreviate-my-name? I write back:

Sounds great! Where do you live?

※

Xanthe lives in an apartment on James Street above a sex shop called Sweet Sensations. The shop advertises itself as an Adult Store and Cinema. I try not to imagine what the cinema looks like. Before I get there she warns me about a homeless man who has set up camp in the doorway of the apartments. I'm relieved that he's not there when I arrive. I don't know how to work the buzzer so I message her: *Hey! I'm outside.* A few minutes later she pushes open the heavy green door. She's in a dressing gown, her hair still wet from the shower.

"Hey! So glad you could come!" She grins at me to fill the space where we're supposed to hug.

"Thanks for having me, are you sure it's OK for me to stay?"

"Of course! The couch is really comfy. I hope it's OK for you."

"Of course, thanks so much." I look around the dirty cream walls and scuffed brown carpet. "I don't know why I thought you lived in Halls."

"Oh, I wish. No, my dad bought this apartment when there wasn't a sex shop underneath it. He thought it would be an investment."

"Your dad's a landlord?"

"Haha, he'd love that. Makes him sound like a medieval villain. This is the only property he owns, apart from our family home. He's a doctor. Actually he's working in the A&E across the road tonight."

"Cool." I smile politely.

"Yeah. Sorry we have to take the stairs. The lift is broken."

"Not at all, I'm so unfit. Need the exercise."

We reach a corridor of doors. It's obvious from the noise which one is hers. The door is held open by a stiletto. I'm relieved at the sight of it. I was unsure whether we were wearing heels or flats.

There are four girls squeezed into a bedroom in various states of getting ready. I recognize Orla, the roommate. Griffin is in the corner curating the music playlist. They don't acknowledge my entrance. The space is small. You couldn't swing a cat in it, Billy would say. A tiny kitchenette, a couch that faces out toward the window, and a balcony that seems more suited to a prison.

Xanthe throws out both hands. "Mi casa es su casa."

"Can I guess which room belongs to you?"

"Go on."

I point to the one nearest the bathroom with a massive crocheted blanket covering the bed.

"Is it that obvious?" Xanthe asks.

"Yeah," I say. She follows me into the room. There are books piled up along the wall. Incense sticks, a ceramic elephant, and an old-fashioned camera lie on her bedside locker. "Is that a Rolleiflex?" I ask.

"Yeah, I got it for my twenty-first."

She picks it up and points it at me. I instinctively put my hand up to my face, feeling like a criminal coming out of court. "You're twenty-one?" I ask.

"Mmm-hmm, I did an art course in NCAD before settling down to do another arts course. I've the life of Reilly, me." For the first time since I've met her, she seems uncomfortable.

"That's class," I say. I'm a bit relieved. She's so good at starting college because she's done it before.

"What are you drinking? I can offer you warm Polish beer from Aldi?"

"Oh no it's grand, I have a three-euro bottle of Lidl wine which I imagine is going to go down like water."

"Well, we've run out of glasses, but there are mugs in the press there."

"Sounds ideal," I say.

❋

It's only when I take off my coat that the other girls clock me.

"Nice jumpsuit," the most intimidating one says, looking me up and down before returning to the mirror to finish the flick of her liquid eyeliner.

"Thanks, it's my mam's."

"Cute."

She looks at Xanthe in the mirror. "Are we going legs in or out?"

Xanthe shrugs. "I haven't decided yet."

This is the reason I wore a jumpsuit. It's balanced in the middle of the legs in and out spectrum. Going legs in means going casual, wearing a pair of jeans and a nice top. Legs out requires more effort, shaving your legs, tanning, and putting on a dress.

"Charlotte Rampling," says Griffin, his head cocked to one side. He's staring at me. I feel a splotchy red wave spread across my chest and neck. "With a touch of Belle Dingle from *Emmerdale*."

"Stop it, Griff, you ghoul," Xanthe says.

"You look a bit like Harry Styles," I tell him. Xanthe laughs.

"I'll take that as an insult."

"Where are we going tonight?" I ask.

"Workmans."

"Where's that?"

"It's along the quays."

"Sounds like it's in a quarry."

The intimidating girl sits down beside me and crosses her legs. "So are you from a *farm* farm?"

"As opposed to a *not a farm* farm?"

From her expression, I gather that she has decided to like me.

❄

I'm drinking wine out of a child's sippy cup that a previous tenant left behind. It's bright pink and has Little Miss Princess on it. Three sippy cups of wine in and I've gone full-blown culchie. I've made a drum out of the windowsill and taught everyone how to sing "Don't Forget Your Shovel" by Christy Moore.

Xanthe has changed into tight red leather trousers—the type that would look ridiculous on a normal person—and a plain white T-shirt. A silver elephant dangles from her neck. She's wearing a pair of Converse. The other girls have been drinking in their pajamas until now. They have their hair and makeup done, they were just waiting for Xanthe to dictate their outfit choice. Within half an hour the girls take turns to go into the bathroom to change into black leather trousers, T-shirts, and flats. I feel ridiculous wearing heels.

Xanthe appears not to notice the power she wields. She's sitting on Griffin's knee drinking her Polish beer.

"So, are you two together?" I ask. Everyone bursts out laughing. Griffin reaches out and grasps my hand. "You're so new, I love you."

"You've no gays out in the sticks?" one of the girls asks.

"What? But you're so handsome," I say.

"I know." Xanthe ruffles his curls. "The girls are always asking me how many drinks it would take to turn him straight."

"Vultures, the lot of ye," Griffin says.

I'm unreasonably angry with both of them—at Xanthe for setting the casual dress code and at Griffin because I thought he was flirting with me. I was sure he was flirting with me and now I feel duped.

"You know, I thought your name was Santy when we met," I say to Xanthe. "As in Santa Claus."

"Oh my God, that is the perfect name for you," Griffin says, jigging Xanthe on his knee. "Our very own Santy."

I get up to refill my sippy cup and Xanthe opens out her arms and pats her lap. "Come here and sit on Santy's knee." I oblige and she wraps her arms around my waist. I feel Griffin's arms on my back and I start the sing-song again.

Fellas

"Jesus Christ, please wake up."

My eyelashes are stuck together. I peel one open with a finger. I'm naked in a bed I don't recognize, being jostled awake by a stranger.

"Morning," I murmur.

"Thank Christ for that. Listen, I'm really sorry but I have to go."

"OK bye."

"I can't leave you here."

"Where's Santy?"

"Who?"

"Santy," I say, frowning.

He crouches down beside the bed and looks at me. "I have to meet my mother for lunch and I can't leave you in my bed."

"Oh."

"So I would appreciate if you got some clothes on."

"All right." I feel around the bed for my underwear.

"They're over here," he says, reaching down the side of the bed and flinging my knickers in my face.

"Do you have any flats I can borrow?" I ask.

"I don't."

"I can't wear heels at this hour."

"You're going to have to."

"You're a hurler," I remember.

"Yes," he says impatiently.

"You play county."

"I played for the minors, once upon a time."

"What size hurl do you use?"

"A 32."

"That's small."

"It is."

"Where do you play?"

"I won't play anywhere if I'm late to meet my mother. She'll break my legs."

"Are you giving her your dirty clothes to wash?"

He smiles at this. "I am, actually."

"I think it's too early in our relationship to meet the parents," I say.

"Definitely," he agrees.

＊

There is no awkward kiss goodbye. He gives me directions to the train station. My pride prevents me from asking why we're not taking the same form of transport. He produces car keys from his pocket, clicks open the doors of his TDI Golf, and drives off in the direction of town.

People look at me with amusement as I clip-clop toward the station. I feel the thrill of being bold. Dark. Edgy. A divil. Then I remember something Griffin said last night when I tripped and fell down the stairs of the pub. "The lower the self-esteem, the higher the heel." He must have thought I was too hammered to hear. The pang went right through the haze of my drunkenness.

＊

I rest my head against the vibrating window of the train back into town. I look at my phone. Eleven missed calls. A message from Xanthe.

You OK, Debs?

> *Santy. Woke up in Drumcondra with a*
> *county hurler. On the way to yours now.*

Haha you're some woman. I've the kettle on.

I feel the power of the story formulating in my head. Meeting the guy out—I think I used him as something to lean against more than anything else. Kissing him meant staying upright. Losing Xanthe and Griffin. Hot chip burning the roof of my mouth. Spending ages sitting on a curb and walking blue-black streets in the rain to find a taxi that would take us back to his. Playing an uncoordinated indoor hurling match with his housemates in their sitting room. Tumbling into bed and resting my head on his warm chest and not thinking about anything, not being afraid of going to sleep.

It's just Xanthe in the apartment when I get there. She's sitting up in bed with two pillows behind her back like a patient in a hospital.

"It smells like boy in here."

"Griff is hardly a boy."

"He slept here last night?"

"We passed out in bed together. We may have kissed. It doesn't matter. He's gay."

"How gay is he though? Honestly?"

"Very." She sighs. "I've always had a thing for him. And then he came out to me, and I felt kind of relieved. Like, it's not me, it's my gender. Is that stupid?"

"I think he's a bit of a prick to be honest."

"I know." She laughs. "You made that clear straightaway."

"Oh fuck, did I?"

"Yes, Debbie. He knows you think he's ridiculous in his expensively ripped jeans."

I shrug. "Well, he got me back last night."

"What did he say this time?"

"He made fun of me for wearing heels. Said something about how having low self-esteem means wearing higher heels."

Xanthe frowns. "I wouldn't mind that at all. Griff is a funny one. He gets jealous sometimes."

"Of what?"

"You're an attractive girl who guys fancy. Griff tends to fall for straight guys. It took a long time for him to accept his own sexuality. He's still in the process of trying to accept it."

"Oh."

The silence is filled by the sound of the kettle boiling. It trembles and shakes before it clicks off.

"Do you take milk in your tea?" Xanthe asks.

"I live on a dairy farm."

"Oh, is oat milk OK? It's all I have. It actually tastes really nice. It's sweet."

"Yeah that's fine. Are you lactose intolerant or something?"

"Haha, no." She blushes. "I'm actually vegan."

I gasp in pretend shock. "Really?"

"Yeah, I try to keep it on the down-low."

"An unusual trait in your kind."

"I know, we're like the new Jehovah's Witnesses. Anyway, was yer man nice? The county hurler?"

"Yeah. He asked for my number but I gave him a fake one," I lie.

"Why?"

I shrug. "We have nothing in common."

"How do you know?"

"I always fancy guys that I have nothing in common with."

"Maybe you just don't give yourself a chance to get to know them."

"Maybe. What about you?" I ask. "Any fellas?"

"There is one actually. Met him out last week and we're texting. Nothing serious at all, but he's nice. He's doing Physio in UCD. Another hurler actually, but there's no photos of his face on his page at all, which is a bit strange. There's just hurling ones." She taps her screen to bring up a profile picture and turns the phone around to show him to me. "You can't really see him. He has a helmet on."

"I know him," I say. It's the boy who stands at the back of mass. "We went to school together."

"Oh my God! This is gas. So, what's he like?"

I hope she can't hear my heart thumping in my ears. "I mean, I don't know him. I don't think we've ever said two words to each other."

"Well, do you like him?"

"How do you mean?"

"As a person like. Is he nice?"

"You've met him. You know him better than me."

"Does he play center-back? He told me he plays center-back."

"I'm sure he didn't lie to you. I haven't seen a hurling match in ages." I've been following his progress in the local paper. He scored 1–5 from wing-forward last Saturday.

"He seems to be good. He's always going on about it. It's a serious commitment."

"Yeah, it is."

"Have you ever seen him play?"

"I'm sure I have. A lot of the lads are good. They bring their hurls everywhere they go sure, even to mass. They leave them outside the church on their way in and collect them after communion."

"Oh my God, he goes to mass? That's lovely!"

"Yeah, well there's nothing much to do around us. It's more of a social occasion to have a gawk at the neighbors."

Xanthe smiles. "You actually live in the 1800s."

"Sometimes."

"This is so mad. OK, I like what I'm hearing. We're going to the cinema tomorrow. I'll ask him if he knows you."

"Oh God, don't. I mean we know of each other, but he doesn't *know* me."

"I'm sure he thinks you're great. Your village sounds really cute."

"Thanks. I just—" I say, pointing to the bathroom. "I'm just going to pee."

"You don't have to tell me," Xanthe says.

"Tell you what?" I ask.

"That you're going to pee?"

"Oh sorry. It's the hangover," I say, closing the bathroom door. My heart is pounding in my head. My hands are shaking. I'm not crying over a boy I hardly know. It's the hangover, I tell myself. It must be.

Train

I could have taken a train home at any time today, but I ended up in the station at rush hour. The carriage is packed. It's roasting. People are beginning to surrender their personal space. Hands reach for the yellow poles or railings and fingers, shoulders, hips, and bags squeeze together. I've had more physical intimacy with these strangers than any member of my family and the train hasn't even left Connolly.

I see a flash of a GAA gear bag swing onto the carriage and my heart jumps—but it's not him. I let myself imagine what would have happened if it was him. We'd have to acknowledge each other. Make small talk. Or maybe our eyes would meet for a dangerous second before we'd look away and the world would readjust itself. We'd just stand side by side without saying anything, and I'd wonder if he could hear my heart beat or feel the same giddy tingle in his brain.

A well-dressed woman rushes onto the carriage in a pair of knee-high boots and shoves her way through to the disabled seats.

"I'm pregnant," she announces.

I know that everyone is thinking the same thing. She can't be *that* pregnant. She's wearing heels, for God's sake. The people on this train carriage have probably heard the news before most of her family and friends.

I feel sorry for the three pensioners and the man with a pair of crutches beside him. A woman in her seventies gives up her seat. The self-professed pregnant lady sits down, crosses her legs, and takes out a magazine. I can see a bald man tutting and shaking his head. He catches my eye and I look away. I've learned the hard way not to engage with strangers who love to complain.

I've ended up being squashed next to a handsome man in a suit. He's slender but well built. He looks like Action Man if Action Man was born and bred outside of Galway, in one of the Gaeltacht areas, maybe. I can make out his pectoral muscles through the white shirt that is stuck to him—as tight as a corset—buttons straining to hold him in. He is one of the only people on the train who isn't wearing headphones or watching his phone. He's staring intently at the floor.

The train jerks as it slows down to stop at the next station. I bump into him and murmur my apologies but he hasn't noticed me. We're still rubbing shoulders. I'm tired. I lean my head against the yellow pole and begin to drift off.

❉

The train jolts forward and I wake up with my head on his shoulder.

"I'm so sorry!" I say, springing away from him.

"No worries." He coughs and smooths down his shirt. "I drifted off myself."

I feel myself blush. I haven't even looked him in the eye, but it feels like we've seen too much of each other. He moves toward the door. We're in Maynooth. The train announces that this is the final station. He presses the flashing green button to open the doors.

I'm looking at him differently now. I recognize him the way you'd struggle to place an actor playing a different character in another film. He slides into context and clicks into my frame of reference. I'm just after waking up from being inside his head. And I know how he's going to do it. He's been thinking about it every day on the train home from work. He's planning the best way to kill himself.

It will happen some time in the next month. He'll make his excuses to his pregnant wife who will be lying on the L-shaped couch with their dog watching *Game of Thrones*. She is used to him going for a solo drive in the evening. She encourages it. She thinks that it's good for him to get out of the house. He hasn't been himself since he had to pull out of training for an ultramarathon after injuring his cruciate. So he'll go on one of those drives where he turns the radio off and just starts shouting at himself. He'll make himself cry and the only thing that will bring him relief is to end it. Swerve off the road. Make sure of it. He'll make it look like an accident so that it won't be so hard on his family.

I ignore my first instinct, which is to tap him on the shoulder. What would I say? Give him some sort of cryptic message? Give him a hug? Every scenario I'm imagining is too dramatic for the everyday end of a commute. So I watch him disappear through the turnstile along with everyone else.

Incubus

We're being chased. There's a crowd of us—people I don't know but recognize the way you sometimes do in dreams. I figure that I must be in the lead because I'm not stopping to help the others. The dream chugs like a bit of sleep gets caught in its moving cogs and then it grabs hold of me.

I'm in a cave. We're shackled together, a human chain shuffling toward a tank of water. They shove us into it. It's hot—like liquid fire. I swim through it and wash up naked on a beach. A little girl puts a foil blanket around my shoulders like I have just finished a marathon and gestures for me to wait in a line of sunburned people.

The place has the atmosphere of a dentist's office in a spa resort. I wait to be called in front of a woman wearing a conical hat. She takes my blanket away and inspects me. Then she takes a scalpel and carefully cuts across the top of my hairline.

She starts to peel my screaming face away. A helmet of hair comes away from the back of my skull like the shell of a cracked coconut. Her scalpel works slowly and methodically, trying to keep the sheet of my skin intact from the top of my head to the soles of my feet.

I wake up screaming and touching my face. I'm in my mother's bed. She pulls me over to her side of the mattress and turns the pillow around to the cold side. She holds me tight and rocks me, shushing into my ear. I'm crying so much that she can't understand what I'm saying but I keep repeating it: "There was a man inside me, there was a man inside me, there was a man inside me . . ."

Conch

I wake up again holding something cold and hard against my ear. It's a seashell that usually sits on Mam's dresser—a conch bigger than my hand with white whorls and gaping pink lips that open into a mouth. I stick my fingers into it. The inside is smooth and nearly wet, the outside dry like an ancient ceramic bowl.

"Morning." My mother is sitting at the end of the bed.

"Why?" I ask, holding up the shell.

"I use it sometimes." She shrugs. "I didn't make you hold it. I just put it beside the pillow and you reached for it and it calmed you down. You were thrashing in your sleep." She puts the back of her hand against my forehead. "You have a temperature."

I feel hungover. "What time is it?" I ask.

"It doesn't matter."

"I'm supposed to be in college."

"Do you remember how you got here?"

"I had a bad dream," I say.

"You did," she says and reaches across the bed to grasp my hand. "You dreamed someone else's dream."

I sit up in the bed. "Hah?"

"You didn't think you made it up yourself, did you?"

"Oh Jesus, Mam, I'm fine."

She looks at me closely as though she has just caught me masturbating. "I know that you know that wasn't your nightmare."

I lie down in the bed and put the pillow over my head. "I need to go to college."

"It's two o'clock in the afternoon."

"What? Why didn't you wake me up?"

"You had a lot of sleep to catch up on."

"Mam, please leave me alone."

"You're in my bed."

"Right then, I'll go." I throw off the covers and swing my legs out of bed. "Did you drug me?"

"What? Why would I do that?"

"Never mind," I say.

"Why would you say that?"

"Mam, I'm sorry. Please. I had a bad dream and now I would like to forget about it and go about my day, or what's left of it."

"You didn't *have* a dream. It didn't belong to you. You *saw* a dream—witnessed it." She stares at me. "There was a man inside me?"

"Did you keep me dinner?" I ask, trying to change the subject.

She flops down onto the bed. "You haven't had a dream like that in a long time."

The queasiness at the pit of my stomach disappears the minute I walk out of the room. I imagine a corridor of doorways and glide through them before going outside to Billy's.

Rise

I knock on the caravan door but Billy isn't in. There's a laptop open on the countertop. It's a silver MacBook with a blue screen saver that floats definitions of words across the monitor, like fish on a modeling catwalk, gliding along the ocean floor. I tap the touchpad and the screen lights up showing the blue-bannered world of Facebook. The laptop is logged into an account I don't recognize. The thumbnail photo is of a man in 1940s gear, like a catfish from another era. I click on it. A sepia portrait of an auld lad in a tweed jacket pops up at me. The duvet tumbles out of the bottom bunk bed and Billy rises up from the covers.

"O brave new world that has such people in it!"

"Are you impersonating Patrick Kavanagh on Facebook?" I ask.

"I am merely keeping his contrary spirit alive."

"Why?"

"I asked myself who would be the most miserable fucker to rise up from the dead and transpose into cyberspace. It was between himself, Stalin, and Yahya Khan's eyebrows."

"Of course, that makes complete sense."

"Come here," he says, running outside. I follow him to the doorway. He throws out both of his arms and genuflects toward the satellite on the roof of the house. "Behold! I bring you a new dimension. Or the prisoner crawling back into the cave to worship some new, shinier shadows."

"How much did this set you back?"

"What was that? Was that a, 'Thank you, Billy, I will stop making ridiculous demands of you and I will accept my privilege to go to college?'"

I smile. "Is that my laptop?"

Billy shakes his head. "Women. We're going to share it. I have to update my miserable statuses."

"You absolute loser, why don't you go on it as yourself? Actually, forget I said that. Where are you getting all this money?"

"Working hard or hardly working." Billy grins. "Your mother told me you were in bed all day."

"I conked out last night just. Dead to the world. Didn't even realize how much I slept until I woke up there."

"You're only after waking up there now? That's some going."

"Yeah. I had a bad dream."

Billy looks at me. "You didn't tell your mother."

"Well . . ."

"For fuck's sake, Debbie. That's what she was so smug about. Don't fucking encourage her."

"I didn't tell her, she just found out."

"Did she now."

"I woke up in her bed. I must have sleepwalked. It's not like I came running to her with it."

"Eh well, clearly you did."

"I have no control over what I do in my sleep."

"Here we go. Listen, Debs, do yourself a favor and don't remember your dreams. Please. Do that one thing for me."

"How do I go about doing that?"

"Easy. Don't dream. It works for me."

"You mean you don't remember your dreams."

"No, I don't. And you shouldn't either, if you know what's good for you."

"That sounds like completely healthy advice. Ignore your dreams."

"Put it this way, Pocahontas. The river splits into two and you're in your little canoe. You can either take the easy smooth-sailing route, or the choppy one. Don't come crying to me if you end up clinging to a capsized mind like your mother. She's sick, Debs. Don't let her drag you down with her."

"I'm afraid to go to sleep again."

"When you were little, she put the fear of God into you telling you that you were this dream-witnessing prodigy. It took all my strength not to hit her."

"I can't really remember."

"Good. Don't mind her." He claps me on the back. "Now, get some food into you. Then come back out here and show me how to work the YouTube."

Milk Bath

I'm afraid to go to sleep. I want to go and knock on the caravan door, but I'm not a kid anymore. I need to stop searching for the full moon from my bedroom window. I try to disappear into my phone, but the Internet is slow. The cool side of the pillow makes me feel like my head is floating on water. Then I remember the time Mam gave me a milk bath.

I creep downstairs and put one of Billy's coats over my pajamas. I open the back door and feel the relief of the night's wind in my face. The torch on my phone lights up the calf shed and makes it look like a silver castle. I grab the can and an empty bucket.

The milk comes out in a twirl of silk and smacks the bottom of the bucket. I feel somebody grab my elbow and turn around to find a calf sucking on my arm. It retreats to the back of the pen. I stretch out my hand and wiggle my fingers at him. He comes forward again, head bowed, and smells me. Finally, he gives the tips of my fingers a lick and lets me slide them into his mouth.

The suckling gets rougher the more frustrated he becomes when my fingers don't squeeze out the milk he is looking for. It's warm in there. I can feel the ridges along the roof of his mouth. I pull my hand out. Saliva stretches across it, webbing my fingers together.

The bucket lags against my leg, weighing me down as I carry it toward the back door. In the field, one of the cows is bawling. I shine the torch over and see that she's down on her knees, calving. The calf is still in the amniotic sac. I know that's bad. Usually, the pink balloon bursts and dangles from the cow's tail for a few hours until it splats onto the ground

for Jacob to come along and eat it. I watch the cow push the
sac out of her like it's a giant squid. It slides out onto the grass
in a slimy bubble. All it needs is a prod or a poke and it would
pop. I know that I should call Billy but I wouldn't be able to
explain why I was out in the yard at this hour. I'm so tired
that I'm not even sure it's happening.

I take the stairs slowly, trying not to slosh any milk over the
sides. I fill the bath with hot water and tip the milk in. It
spreads like smoke underneath the water. A bunch of dried
lavender floats on its surface, their stalks overlapping. Mam
used to use the pretty white-headed weeds from the garden
that looked like sprigs of baby's breath, but they give me a
rash.

Once, when I had a really bad dream, Mam gave me a
milk bath. I woke her by climbing into her bed and brushing my cold feet against her sleeping legs. There was a moment when I held my breath as she opened her eyes, but she
didn't give out to me. She ushered me out of the bed and
led me to the bathroom where I was given orders to strip off
while she got milk from the calf shed. I stood in the quiet
of the early morning on the cold tiles of the bathroom floor
and watched the water gush out of the taps, my arms crossed
over my flat chest. Fresh ripples of goose-bumps rose in waves
over the back of my neck. The bruised light made everything
blue.

Mam came back in with a heavy bucket of milk and a fist-
ful of daisies from the garden. I turned them over in the bath
and watched as their white umbrellas bobbed upside down on
the water, the tips of their petals tinged with purple.

She tried to teach me how to hold my breath underwater. I lasted half a second before coming back up and thrashing water out of the bath. She shoved my head back under again but I bit her finger. Then she dragged me out by the hair and unplugged the bath. I watched the drain swallow the heads of my daisies.

"Are you happy now?" she shouted, her bark echoing off the bathroom walls. I was howling. "Keep your head under the water," she ordered. "It will help you with the dreams."

So I tried harder. I stayed underwater until hot colors flickered and scorched holes in my eyelids. When I emerged from the water, my throat was on fire but Mam was in a good mood again. She collected the daisies' spongy yellow centers and rubbed them in circles on my back. Then she toweled me dry in rough, swift movements. "You'll have a great night's sleep after this," she said, her breath tickling the hairs on the inside of my ear. "A great night's sleep." And she was right. The dreams went away after the milk bath.

✳

The milky water burns my toe and then my foot until it reaches my chin and makes a lake around my neck. The cream rises to the top of the bath and little white islands congeal on the surface. Shapes of steam rise out of the bathtub and I wrap the chain of the plug tighter and tighter around my big toe until it hurts just the right amount.

I stay in the water, bow-legged, until I have the shriveled fingertips of a wise old woman. My knees are chilly from being out of the water. I play at being a corpse in a coffin or a naked bride, clutching the bunch of lavender to my chest. I brush the bouquet up and down my body, twisting around to get at the backs of my legs, stroking all of my skin. The flowers tickle my face.

I am in the shower rinsing the milk out of my hair when I let myself cry. It is a relief, a comfort, like touching my body before I go to sleep to make sure I am still there, still me, still alive.

Wentletrap

I wake up to a letter under my pillow. Mam must have heard the bath running last night. I open the envelope and a tiny shell rolls into my hand. I recognize it immediately. It's one of my favorites. It's called a *wentletrap*, the Dutch word for winding stairs, after the staircase structure inside the shell.

Shells help. Collect them on beaches. Wash them in the bathroom sink. Pocket them to keep as talismans. A cochlea listens. Shells are fossils of thought—ossified dreams. They know what it is like to abandon yourself, leaving behind an echo chamber of cold bone, waiting for others to inhabit your skull.

I hold the tiny white shell in the palm of my hand. From the outside, it looks like a corkscrew tooth. Inside is a spiral staircase waiting for sleep to tumble down it.

Theories of Literature

The only thing I'm learning in college is how to hide. Mostly, I hide my family. It's not that I never talk about them. I bring them up in conversations all the time, disguising them as characters in a world that Pat McCabe could have imagined. That's why I get thick when Xanthe pulls a leaf of paper out of my notebook. She studies it and frowns. It's the letter Mam wrote me. The *wentletrap* one.

"Did you write this?"

"No, give it back."

She looks at it again before she hands it back. "If you wrote it you should send it out."

"It's not mine."

"Who wrote it then?"

"My mam."

"Is she a poet?"

I laugh. "She wishes."

"Well, that's a good piece of writing."

"It's awful tripe."

"It's not, it's good."

I don't know if she's trying to humor me or sabotage me. "No one would publish that."

"Of course they would. I'd like to meet her. Your mam."

"You'll get to meet her at Christmas."

Xanthe is meeting her new boyfriend's family over the holidays. Since he only lives up the way from me, we're planning to drink hot whiskeys down the pub on Stephen's night. I've already decided on the outfit I'm going to wear.

❄

I went to the gym this morning. My gym routine is limited to running on the treadmill because it's the only machine I know how to work. I don't have enough confidence to look like an idiot while trying to figure out the other ones. I'm not on enough steroids to get into the weights section anyway. I'm afraid I might get knocked over or shoved out of the way by the posh bicep boys.

I run ten kilometers. Sometimes, I get into a passive-aggressive competition to outpace the person beside me, especially if they're pretty. I sprint the last kilometer every time, no matter how empty I'm feeling, just to prove to myself that I still exist. My heart hammers the message home. I'm here. I'm alive.

✳

I met Xanthe and Orla in the arts block after the gym. We're having a picnic, eating a multipack of crisps and brown rolls. I bought some hummus to dip my roll into.

It would be better if Orla wasn't here. We have better conversations when Xanthe manages to shake her off, but we tolerate her when she's around, which is an awful thing to say, but it's the truth. Xanthe is trying to drag me to a yoga class.

"I'd love to do yoga," I say. "It's just . . . it's so . . . middle class."

"You are middle class," Xanthe says.

"No I'm not. I'm a farmer."

"Bullshit. You buy hummus in Tesco. Accept it. You're middle class."

"Well, so are you."

"I know I'm privileged. I've accepted it. I've learned to be grateful. I try not to hate myself."

"But my family is not, like, considered well-off in the village or anything," I point out.

"Ah now. You've enough money to be able to go to college and buy cheap wine on a night out and a bag of chips on the way home."

"That's true," I say.

"Being middle class doesn't make you a bad person."

"It just makes you spoiled."

"Well, I was going to join a yoga class, but now I'll just wallow in the guilt of my middle-class privilege," Xanthe moans.

"That's not what I'm saying."

"What are you saying so?"

"Nothing. Don't listen to me," I say.

"What do you have now?" Xanthe asks, as I pack up to leave.

"Theories of Literature."

"You mean, Vocabulary for Wankers?"

"I mean, you're not wrong."

❋

Tutorials are a painful affair. At the end of our last session, the teaching assistant asked us if we thought the French structuralists were right or wrong. This was followed by a long silence where we all concentrated on remaining invisible. Some brave heads moved in a vague way, not committing to the nod or the shake, like when you're not sure of the spelling of something so you scribble both letters over each other. The teaching assistant breathed out and said, "We're all controlled by language. Yay." People eyed each other, trying to spot an appropriate reaction. We couldn't be sure if she was being sarcastic or not but we laughed along anyway.

This week, we are learning how to apply psychoanalytic theory to a text. The others are becoming more confident about their readings. The class has transformed into a nerdy, giddy game of innuendo bingo.

"Holmes and Watson are clearly lovers."

"I agree, the text is just chock-full of phallic symbols. I mean, the pipe, the pen, the fact that they share a cigar."

"What do you think, Deborah Martha? It is Deborah Martha, right?" The teaching assistant has noticed my silence. I made the mistake of including my middle name on the registration form, so I sound even more like a country bumpkin.

"It's Debbie," I say.

"Where do you stand on the psychoanalytic reading of Arthur Conan Doyle, Debbie?"

"Well . . . if you set out to look for dicks everywhere you're going to find a lot of them." My face is burning. I get a laugh.

"That's a reasonable argument." The tutor grins.

"Well, it's certainly an opinion—an opinion that is not supported by the text or secondary criticism." This, coming from a guy who on Marxism week argued that we lived in a classless society.

"What do you think . . . Nicòlo?" The teaching assistant asks the guy who hasn't spoken yet—a handsome Italian who smokes rollies outside the arts block. He looks like he's wandered out of an Elena Ferrante novel.

"Excuse me, what's the question?" he asks.

"Do you think it's useful to see dicks everywhere?" I offer.

"No," he says, looking relieved. "No I don't."

Batman

Xanthe looks suspiciously cozy in her dressing gown.

"So . . . we're not going out?" I ask.

"I'm not feeling it," Xanthe says. "I want to go to the library in the morning."

"OK."

She's not feeling it because she has a boyfriend.

"Sorry," she says.

"No need to apologize. It's fine."

"You could ask Orla to go out with you?" she suggests.

I look over at Orla's bedroom. Her door is always closed.

"Orla? Is she even home?"

"I don't know."

"It's like you live with a ghost."

"Ssshhhh, she might be home."

"Is himself coming over?" I ask. "I can go home if ye want a bit of space?"

"No, don't be silly. I usually go to his. UCD is an absolute trek, but his place is nicer than this kip."

"I like this kip."

"Thanks."

❋

I'm taking the whole situation with Xanthe and the-guy-I've-fancied-since-forever reasonably well. She rarely brings him up so I ask how it's going. I tease her. I actually smile and giggle, but I can never bring myself to say his name.

I'm not able to sleep at night. I used to use the fantasy of him to feel safe enough to lull me to sleep. There were different scenarios that I directed in my imagination that always ended—not with kissing or anything—but with my head on his shoulder or his arm wrapped around me; those first tentative steps toward intimacy.

I seesaw between being furious with myself, full of self-loathing, to being indignant and angry with him. A really ugly part of me thinks that he's using Xanthe to make me jealous, but that's just my ego diving down endless rabbit holes to try and find a hint of the improbable: that he thinks about me too.

❄

I have settled into a routine, saving up good behavior like coupons that will get me a free night out. Nights out mean drinking and drinking is like taking a holiday from my head. I welcome the oblivion it brings. The buzz. When I black out, I don't dream. I wake up hungover, but a hangover is predictable. I know how I'll feel. Fragile, but also myself. A nice, easy, childlike version of myself who thinks a glass of water is the most miraculous thing on earth.

Griff christened my alter ego Taz because he says getting me home is like trying to get a Tasmanian devil into a taxi at the end of the night. The best way of dealing with Taz is to allow him out at least once a week. Xanthe says it's like taking a dog for a walk. All of the pent-up energy is released and eventually, he tires.

Nights out mostly happen on Wednesdays. Sometimes, we go out on Mondays or Tuesdays as well, but we always go out on Wednesdays. Except tonight. I just took it for granted that we were, so I was looking forward to it all day. All week, even.

"I think some of the girls from home are going to Cop-
pers," I say.

"Oh, you should go!"

"I don't know if I'm bothered, to be honest."

I haven't heard from any of the girls from home. I'm toying
with the possibility of going out by myself. Even if I went
out with Xanthe, we'd probably lose each other on the dance
floor anyway.

"You brought your going out gear up with you and all. Get
ready here, grab a taxi, and meet them there."

"They'll probably be hammered by the time I get there
though. They'll have been drinking on the bus," I say.

"So get a bottle of wine in the shop. Drink it here while
you get ready. I'll supervise."

"OK," I say.

"Yay! I'm excited for you."

※

It's not enough to look well on a night out. You need to smile
the right amount. Otherwise, a lad will come up to you and
tell you to cheer up. That's what happens in the smoking area.
He volunteers himself as my personal comedian and puts his
hand on the small of my back. I don't know why I laugh at
his terrible jokes. I think I'm just trying my best to be polite.
When he leans in for the shift, I tell him I have a boyfriend.

"No you don't," he says.

"Why would I make one up?" I ask.

"Because you don't fancy me."

"That's not true," I lie.

"Listen, love. You might as well be holding a neon sign
that says 'Open for business.' Don't worry about it. Just, take a

bit of advice from your uncle Mike. You shouldn't lead a man on. You should have told me to jog on a long time ago. I can handle rejection, I'm a big boy."

"So I can't talk to men without first announcing that I have a boyfriend."

"Ah but remember"—he raises a finger—"you don't have a boyfriend." He winks and pats me on the arm. "Have a good night."

The best-looking guy on the dance floor is wearing a Batman T-shirt. I've made it into a circle of nurses who I met in the queue to the bathroom. I thought he'd go for a tall blond whose legs go on forever. But he's eyeing me.

He waits for some backup from Westlife before he makes his move. His group of friends Venn diagram their way into us and he takes my hand, pretending to be Shane. Or Nicky, or Kian. He's not Mark anyway. He goes for the theatrical approach. He has a black straw behind his ear which he bends into a Britney Spears microphone. He's funny, and tall and charming and has probably shifted half of the girls in here already. But I go for it, and he's already acting like he's in love with me.

"You're a great kisser" is the first thing he says to me, when we both come up for air. "Do you want to get out of here?"

✳

I insist on getting chips from Babylon before we go home. I have the chats with the staff. I promise them a visit to the farm and a tutorial on how to milk cows. They give me a complimentary bottle of water with my bag of chips and a paper hat. He holds my hand and marvels over my conversational skills.

"You're proper sound like!"

"Don't act so shocked, Roy Keane," I say.

"I mean, at the end of the day, you're a sound girl. There's not many of them around."

He's from Cork, studying some obscure course in UCC. He's staying with a friend, so we can't go back there. I know that I'm going to bring him back to Xanthe's. I'm too sober to go to sleep.

✳

I'm aware that I'm walking a tightrope of expectation. I've never had sex before, but that's not something that he needs to know. I've told guys in the past and they stare at me like I'm a mythological creature. Some of them don't believe me because I kiss so easily. I don't mind tasting them. Kissing still feels clean and innocent. Romantic even. Kissing is playing pretend. It's comforting. Anything more than that is not acting anymore. It's dangerous. It means letting someone else in.

✳

"I'm just going to put it out there now. I'm not going to have sex with you," I warn him.

"Oh Jesus, I wasn't presuming—"

"Well, most lads presume."

"Oh God, no, like."

"And I'm staying at a friend's too, so if we go back there, it's a couch we'll be sharing. And all I want to do is sleep."

"That's grand. I'd love to sleep with you. I mean actually sleep like."

"I mean, at the end of the day, you're not going to get laid."

"You're a lady, Debbie. An absolute lady." He kisses my hand.

※

He sits in the front seat of the taxi and makes decent conversation with the taxi man. When we get out, he insists on paying. Jack is passed out in a sleeping bag outside the apartment. Xanthe knows him from volunteering with the Simon Community. We invite him up for lunch on Mondays and he is the most comfortable out of us all sitting at the table. He told us all about his gambling problem, but he never mentions the drink. When Xanthe started giving him money, I told her he'd piss it away on drink and drugs and she said, "So would I if I was sleeping on the street." Last week, he told me that I look like his daughter.

While I fumble in my bag trying to find Xanthe's key, Batman bends down and tucks a twenty-euro note into Jack's sleeping bag. So when we get inside, I kiss him like I really mean it. Because I do.

I shush him when he starts talking.

"Sorry!" he shout-whispers, tripping over Xanthe's bike on the way in.

Then I kiss him to stop him from talking. We lie on the couch and he unclips my bra with one hand. Still, it's nice until he goes to unzip my jeans.

"No, no, remember I said," I say, pushing his hand away.

"Sorry, sorry." He takes off his Batman T-shirt and jeans and tries the zip of my jeans again.

I start laughing. "No, I really mean, I can't like."

"Are you on the rag, like?"

"Yeah," I lie.

He considers this. "I don't mind."

"Well I do."

He gives puppy dog eyes. "Please?"

"No."

He sits back on the couch and sighs up at the ceiling. "You're killing me."

"Sorry," I say. "But I did say."

"I know, I know. It's just hard like. Literally." He points at his crotch. He's like a child but I find it endearing so I kiss him like I'm making up for something. He pulls me close to him. Then he shoves his boxers down and starts putting pressure on the back of my head.

"No, no," I say.

"Ah, come on, like!" he exclaims. "You can't fucking go around bringing men back to your place and not doing anything with them."

"I told you that all we would be doing is going to sleep."

"But then you kiss me like that? You're giving me blue balls so bad. You've no idea how painful that is."

The kitchen light goes on. Xanthe is half-asleep in the doorway. "Debs, are you OK?"

"Santy, I'm so sorry!" I give her a bleary-eyed smile. "I didn't mean to wake you."

"Hello there," he says, whipping his boxers back up.

She ignores him. "No bother, I just heard voices. Is everything OK?"

"Hello. What's your name?" he asks.

"Who wants to know?" She frowns.

"I apologize. I'm quite drunk. And your friend here brought me back to your house and," he cups his hands around his mouth and whispers, "it's not my fault but she won't have sex with me. Which is fine. It's fine, she's just a bit of a cock-tease."

"I feel your pain," Xanthe says, picking up his Batman T-shirt and jeans.

"You're very beautiful," he whispers.

Xanthe opens the window and flings his clothes out into the night.

"Hey!" he shouts, standing up. "The fuck you do that for? You fucking psycho bitch!"

He goes for her and I'm afraid he's going to hit her, but she stands her ground. They're nose to nose.

"Get out of my apartment," she says.

"You know what? You're not even worth it." He backs away and collects his wallet and shoes. "Jesus Christ. Pair of tight cunts, the both of ye."

He trips over her bike on the way out and slams the door.

※

"Thank you," I say as I sob into her shoulder.

"Sssshhh . . ." She kisses me on the top of my head and rocks me forward and back. "Come, sleep in my bed."

She leads me by the hand and gives me a packet of makeup wipes. I look in the mirror. There is mascara all over my face.

"Thanks," I say, my voice wobbling.

I spend a long time taking off my makeup, making myself feel clean.

"Are you OK?" Xanthe asks.

"Yep."

"Debbie, you can't be doing that."

"I know, it was stupid. I'm so sorry."

"It's fine. I don't mind you bringing guys back. That's grand. Just, mind yourself, you know?"

"I thought he was nice," I say.

"Nice guys don't act like that."

"You were such a badass."

"I know."

"You need to teach me your ways."

"I will."

She hands me a cup of tea.

"Oh my God, I love you," I say.

"I love you too."

Results

We're getting our essay results today and everyone is pretending not to care. We seem to have forgotten that the only reason we got into the course is because we're all overachievers who feed off external validation. A lot of people in our class got enough points to study medicine. We make jokes about our families mourning the fact that we haven't the heads for a more useful occupation. *Be a something,* Orla's mother told her. *Go to college to be a something.* I think of what my something could be and I hear Billy whisper professor into my ear. I cringe even thinking about it. It's like saying I want to be an old man in a tweed suit reading Shakespeare and smoking a pipe.

We're coming out of a lecture on *The Canterbury Tales* when a guy wearing a polo neck rushes up to Xanthe, places his hands on both her shoulders, and says, "They're out." He readjusts his glasses and skedaddles toward the School of English.

"I need to go to the bathroom," I say.

Xanthe squeezes my hand. "I'll wait for you."

There is graffiti on the back of the cubicle door, written under the advertisement for twenty percent off bikini waxing:

> *No matter how hard I work, I can't seem to get*
> *higher than a 2.1. What am I doing wrong?*

The anxious knot in my stomach tightens. I have been successfully hiding the fact that I haven't been able to read a word of fiction since the course began. I've discovered a hidden talent for tomfoolery. I go into tutorials armed with factoids from SparkNotes. I absorb plot development and character descriptions like scientific facts, happy to take on the role of sophisticated smatterer. It's easy to make people laugh with whatever scant material I have gleaned from webpages. I'm surprised at how much I can get away with speaking fluently about words I haven't read.

I'm used to being told I'm smart. It was easy to study in secondary school because I didn't question any of the information I was given. If the history book told me Hitler won the war, I would have believed it. Facts are incomprehensible to me until I turn them into aspects of a story. Photosynthesis and genetics make no sense outside of the realm of fiction. I ignored every practical application of what I was taught because I didn't remember any of the stuff anyway.

The truth is that I'm an idiot, but I can play the part of an intellectual for an exam. The night before a test, I'd cram the details of the story I needed to tell into my head. I'd pace my bedroom floor and feel like an actor reciting lines. The next day, I'd projectile-vomit the information onto paper and walk out of the room, my memory completely wiped clean of everything I'd supposedly learned. When I got an A in an exam, I felt validated. It made teachers like me. It made me like myself.

I don't know how to study in college. They don't hand out answers the way they did in the Leaving Cert. This first essay we had to hand in was on American literature. In the introduction, I spoke about watching *Pocahontas* as a kid. I even reference the film in my bibliography. I blush, imagining the lecturer laughing as they read it. But I suppose it could be refreshing? They told us that getting a first means that you've made a contribution to academic thought. Maybe all the stuffy world of academia is missing is some Disney sparkle?

❄

Xanthe and I walk arm in arm down to the School of English. We are managing our expectations. We have discussed the likelihood of getting a 2.1. We will be happy with 2.1s. Firsts are elusive. A 2.1 is achievable. We make our way through the crowd and scan the results. There are only a couple of 2.2s. The vast majority are 2.1s as predicted. There's one first near the top of the board and a PASS, which everyone knows belongs to the mature student who is the only one brave enough to ask stupid questions in the middle of lectures.

I find my student number. My instinct is to trace my finger across to make sure I've the right line but there are too many people around and my result swims in the middle of a sea of 2.1s. There's a 2.2 hovering near my student number. I look away quickly. I tell myself not to stare. It will surely go away, like a stray dog. Don't look at it. It doesn't belong to me.

"You happy?" I ask Xanthe.

"Yeah," she says. "You?"

"Yeah. Going to find that nerd who got the first and shove their head down a toilet."

Xanthe has the same embarrassed look she had on her face when she told me she was vegan.

"You dickhead, it's you!" I say, loud enough for everyone else to hear and realize that it's her. She's the one to beat.

"Stop it," she says, elbowing me.

"Here, if anyone deserves to be annoyed, it's me," I say.

"A 2.1 is a great result."

"It's not a first," I say. "Fair fucks to you."

❋

The therapist introduces herself but I'm not listening. I'm still thinking about the security man downstairs and the way he looked at me. I flatter myself into thinking he tried to guess what was wrong with me. I locked myself into a toilet cubicle for a quick cry before I presented myself to reception. They gave me a registration form.

I realized as I was scoring myself from 1 (not at all) to 10 (all the time) that I wasn't even impressively depressed. I averaged a five or six out of ten. As it turns out, life and primary school spelling tests are both marked out of ten, although spelling tests are easier to gauge—you're either right or wrong. How much I identify with platitudes like *I feel like I'm a failure* is harder to judge. To score myself a ten would be melodramatic and attention-seeking, but zero would make me cocky. I scored myself a modest 4/10. I gave myself a 2/10 for the statement: *I have trouble falling asleep or staying asleep.* I don't have trouble falling asleep or staying asleep. I have a problem with sleep itself. *I don't recognize my own dreams* isn't an option, nor is, *I think my mother has brainwashed me and is slowly turning me into her own brand of crazy.*

The therapist asks about my family. I don't mention my mother's long-term relationship with mental illness because I don't think it's relevant to me getting a 2.2, which is the reason I've booked myself into therapy. Now, she's going on about mood disorders. When she hones in on anxiety I stop biting my nails. I'm repulsed by the accusation. Anxiety is a fancy word for worry, and worrying is not a medical condition. Depression is a fancy word for being sad, but it's a stronger synonym. I could forgive myself for getting a 2.2 because of depression. I can't forgive myself for getting a 2.2 because I'm a bit of a worrier. There has been no mention of depression at all yet. There's an epidemic of depression among students. Depression is like the 2.1 of mental illnesses and she's not even giving that to me.

I try again. "I just . . . I feel like I'm not enjoying life as much as I used to. I'm not coping with my workload. I'm tired all the time."

She gives me a sympathetic nod and opens her arms like she's about to give a TED talk. "College is hard, isn't it? Everyone talks about the parties and freedom. Finding yourself. Discovering your own identity. Nobody tells you about the assignments, the feeling that you're in way over your head."

"I know that," I cut across her but she continues to talk past me.

"Let's just imagine that we're walking down Grafton Street."

I can't imagine any situation that would require me to walk down Grafton Street with this woman.

"And you spot a friend. Give me a name of one of your friends."

"Orla," I say, upgrading her from irritating acquaintance.

"Great, so you say, 'Hi Orla,' but Orla doesn't say anything back. She keeps on walking." The therapist is looking at me like she has masterminded the most dramatic scene in the hypothetical universe. "How would you feel in that situation?"

"Em, relieved?"

"What thoughts would be running through your mind?"

"That I didn't have to talk to her."

"Any other thoughts or feelings?"

"Em, confused maybe."

She nods. "And why might you be confused?" She makes a circle with her hand that suggests that I'm getting warmer.

"Because she didn't seem to recognize me?"

"Oh interesting, so see there that we jumped straight to that conclusion. You wouldn't think she was angry with you or deliberately ignoring you?"

"I don't think so?"

"Well that's good. This is just one of the examples where Cognitive Behavioral Therapy or CBT might come in useful. In CBT, we learn to recognize that our thoughts are directly linked to our feelings. We can acknowledge the thought and how that makes us feel. We can catch that thought," she grasps a fist full of air, "and analyze it before we rush straight to our feelings."

She takes out a leaflet and opens it onto a page that looks like a diagram of the water cycle. "So seeing Orla on the street," she says and circles TRIGGERING EVENT with her blue pen. "Leads to THOUGHTS like why did she not say hello? Is she angry at me? Does she not like me? which lead to FEELINGS of confusion." She points at me. "Or anger, or sadness. Whereas, if we change that thought to something more positive, like, she probably didn't recognize me or she could have a lot on her mind, then we change the *feelings* we have surrounding that thought and that interaction."

"But the opposite could be true as well," I tell her, frowning. "She could hate me."

"Yes, but the likelihood of that is slim. The more rational thought is that she didn't see you."

"Which is what I thought in the first place."

"Exactly." She closes the leaflet. On the cover, there's a black-and-white drawing of a girl behind prison bars. There's a cloud over her head. It's raining. SOCIAL ANXIETY is written in bubble writing in the cloud. "This is just some information to take home with you. There are some exercises in there that you might find useful."

At this stage, I'm expecting a warning not to put crayons up my nose.

"Generalized anxiety affects one in ten college students," she says, sliding the leaflet across the desk.

Great, I think. It's not just anxiety, it's generalized too.

"It's very common," she says. "You're definitely not the first person that has come in my door today affected by it." She smiles at me. "Now, before you go I just need you to complete a quick online survey for me."

She lets me sit in the chair at her desk. It's another test from one to ten, this time with statements about how much I feel the session has met my expectations. I feel her hovering over my shoulder, so I give her all ten out of tens and thank her profusely on the way out.

"That's great to hear," she says. "Best of luck to you now, and remember to take one day at a time. It's all about the journey."

I ask at reception if I should book a follow-up appointment. The receptionist looks at her computer screen to check what the therapist said about me and says, "No, she says you're fine."

I stop in the bathroom on the way out for a quick break and another cry.

The Cure

A woman with a pram trundles across the driveway to our back door with a sheepish look on her face. I send her around to the caravan. Billy hasn't had a visitor in a while. I imagine her walking in on him in his boxers sipping whiskey and perusing one of the old newspapers that he stockpiles out there. I hope he's not drunk.

Billy is a reluctant practitioner of the cure. It's been in the family for generations. If you happen to know a man who knows a man who knows a man who has the cure—well, Billy is one of the men they send you to. It's potluck. Most of the others take it seriously. Billy says that he hardly believes in it himself, but it's harmless enough. Most people leave feeling better. Sometimes, he completely takes the piss, but he has a good track record despite himself. People come to him to get the cure for all sorts of things—babies with colic, burn victims, farmers with ringworm, teenagers with warts or eczema, to middle-aged men with gout or back problems.

I hear the woman drive out of our gate and head over to the caravan. I spy Billy putting away his grandfather's wedding ring and the handwritten prayer that he uses in his practice. He looks embarrassed when he notices I'm there.

"Well," he says.

"Colic?" I ask.

"No, she had bad eczema. It was all scaly around her ears."

Billy doesn't take appointments and he doesn't accept money, but some people are so grateful that they send him gifts. Most of them are women who have been charmed by the caravan and by him. They see the trinkets that he collects and want to add to his collection. A woman called Julie gave him an expensive vinyl record player. I've lost track of the things in the caravan that are gifts or things Billy has sourced himself—candlestick holders, a garden gnome, a tiny brass rocking-chair. He keeps most of the postcards he collects in a box, but he blu-tacks his favorite ones to the wall by his bed.

"I went to see Deirdre today," Billy says, sitting down in his armchair.

"Oh," I say.

I know not to ask how she is. I've only been to visit my great-grandmother with Billy once, when I was very young. I remember sitting in the conservatory of the convent nursing home, eating stale Kimberley Mikado biscuits and drinking milky tea from a china cup and saucer. Deirdre had been wheeled in by a nun not much younger than her who placed her in front of the television, gave us a tight smile, and let us be. The cast of *Home and Away* looked out at her but she stared off into the middle distance. There was a string of drool hanging down from her mouth. Billy wiped it away with a tissue, but a fresh string of spit soon replaced it. Deirdre didn't realize that she had visitors. I don't think she knew there was anyone else in her world.

"If I ever go like that," Billy says now, "get the shotgun."

"I think you have a few years to go," I say.

"It can get you young too. Early onset. Look at your mother."

"Billy!"

"What?"

"Mam doesn't have Alzheimer's!"

"She's getting there."

I fill up the kettle.

Billy tries to change the subject. "Have you got Christmas exams?"

"No, just essays."

"And they mark you on them?"

"They do."

"You'd be looking for an A so."

"Well, it's a different marking scheme from school," I say, feeling my face getting hotter. "There are no As and Bs. There are firsts and seconds."

"Right, so we don't do sloppy seconds."

"If we could avoid them, that would be great," I say, trying not to blush.

"I have every faith in you. What constitutes a first?"

"Over seventy percent."

"Sure you're laughing so. You've been getting nineties in school," he says.

"Yeah but that was kids' stuff," I say.

"It's all kids' stuff."

"Yeah right."

"I'm dead serious. If you can't explain what you're thinking about to a kid it's not worth thinking about at all," he says.

The kettle comes to the boil and spurts hot water out the top of its spout. I get a hot water bottle out of the press.

"What are you doing?" Billy asks.

I point at the roof of the caravan. "There's a full moon tonight."

"Oh." He sighs. "I don't feel like stargazing tonight."

"OK," I say, putting the hot water bottle back in.

"What are you doing now?" Billy asks.

"You said you didn't feel like it."

"Sure you can go up yourself," he says. "You don't need me to hold your hand."

"Am I annoying you?" I ask.

"You've annoyed me every day of your life."

"Thanks." I flop down on his bed.

"Are you not making tea?" he asks.

"No, I wasn't going to."

I stare up at the ceiling.

"Do you want a cup of tea?" I ask.

"I'd love one."

"Grand." I drag myself off the bed and over to the kettle again.

"James pulled an inside-out calf today," Billy says.

"How do you mean inside-out?"

"Well," Billy puts his hands together, "everything that should have been on the inside"—he opens the palms of his hands like an open book—"was on the outside. It was like someone took a knife, cut open his stomach, and just hooshed all of his organs out of him. His four legs were stuck together like he was hanging up at an abattoir. When Jim-bob put his hand inside the mother's hole to feel around for it, he could put his fingers between every one of its ribs. He was able to grab a hold of its heart and everything."

"And the heart was beating?"

"Yeah. It was still alive inside the womb all right. Poor bastard. James called the vet. It was a C-section in the end."

"And did it survive?"

"Have you ever seen an inside-out calf knocking around the place?"

I take the teabags out of the mugs and slingshot them into the bin. Billy takes even more milk than I do, in case it's too hot. He blows his tea before taking a sip. He hates burning his tongue.

"That's mad," I say.

"Yeah, the vet said it's the second case he has come across

in twenty-five years. It's not the strangest case of a cow calving I've ever come across though."

"What was?"

"It was a cow that was pregnant with twins. I didn't see the birth now." He holds up his hands. "But I went in to check on her and she was after doing the business. Job done. There was one perfectly healthy calf beside her, which she was completely ignoring. Instead, she was licking this ball of gray-blue hair. It was like a burst football—no ears, no eyes, no head, no limbs, no defining features at all. And here was the cow, licking away at it."

"Was it alive?"

Billy stares at me. "Have you ever seen a ball of fluff knocking around the place?"

"Sorry," I say.

"It wasn't alive but it *had been* alive inside the womb."

"The same as the inside-out calf?"

"Yeah."

"And the other twin calf was fine?" I ask.

"He was grand! Perfectly normal. Bob's your uncle and Fanny's your aunt. But this other yoke scared the shite clean out of me."

"It had no head at all?"

"None."

"It must have had a heart though."

"Yeah. It must have had, in order to develop and grow hair. But it made me think, what classifies something as a living thing? Like, was that ball of fur alive because it was able to live in the womb?"

"Did it dream?" I wonder aloud.

Billy leans back in his chair, crosses his legs, and exhales. "That's a good one actually," he says. "I wonder if it dreamed."

Power Take-Off

I'm bopping along on the tractor spreading slurry. The seat is squeaking up and down on its springs and the arse of the tanker is shitting out the back. Then everything slows down and the dream chugs, like a bit of sleep gets stuck in the moving clogs. My head is still going ninety but the tractor isn't sucking properly. And it's like moving underwater trying to get out of the tractor to check on the vacuum pump.

As soon as I see the PTO shaft rotating, it speeds up again until everything is in fast-forward. I have always been terrified of PTO shafts. They scare the shite clean out of me. I've lost count of how many fellas I see at the mart, missing arms and legs after getting caught up in them. The pipe looks as innocent as a plastic yoke you get out of a Kinder egg whirring about, but if it sees so much as a loose thread of a shirt hanging out, it has you. The closest thing you will ever get to a black hole.

I'm checking the vacuum pump because the tractor isn't sucking right. I'm bending down, when one of my earphones comes loose in my ear and as it's falling, I stick my arm out to catch it and it has me—the machine judders, laughing, making a joke out of my skin and bones, swallowing more of me down its throat until—

❋

Mam is calling me for dinner. I wake up in bed kicking my leg out as if to stop myself from falling. I take my head off my pillow and sleep slips out of my ear. She's thick because the lads aren't in from the yard. We presume Billy is still in bed, but it isn't like James to be late for dinner. Mam peels his potatoes to have them ready for when he comes in, fussing over the way the food looks on the plate. She places it in the low-heat oven to keep it warm for him. Then she throws two unpeeled spuds onto Billy's plate and covers it with cling-film for him to eat later.

"James milked on his own this morning," Mam informs me, sitting down to her dinner. "He didn't want to wake you."

I take a sip of milk. "It isn't my fault that Billy sleeps in."

She shrugs and continues to mash carrots into her potatoes. "I'm just saying."

I look down at the food that she has laid out for me—it's not as pretty as James's plate but not as slapdash as Billy's.

The way it's arranged seems familiar, perfect even, like there are just the right amount of peas and carrots gathered in congregation beside the potato. I'm sure I have seen that exact piece of salmon before. I've slipped into an uncomfortable déjà vu.

It's like looking at a rerun of something on the telly except that I am in the telly—I *am* the telly and I'm watching the screen through my own eyes.

As if on cue, there is a bang at the back door and I watch from inside myself as I get up from the chair to meet a winded Billy in the hall, gasping, shouting that James is after having an accident. His arm got caught in a PTO shaft. He tells us to ring an ambulance and Mam rushes to the phone shouting, "Oh God, oh God, oh God." Billy runs back out to the field clutching a bunch of tea towels.

I don't move anywhere. I know what happened. I'm just after waking up from it.

❋

Billy says that sometimes, if you look at a star directly it can disappear. Peripheral vision is best for looking into the far distance. If I try to look at the dream directly it disappears. It's only when I'm not threatening it that it comes nearer, flirting at the edges of my mind. I think in circles to lure it in.

I circle around the dream looking for the missing pieces, but I don't know where I end and James begins. James shouted for help, but the only person who was close enough to hear him was Billy, who was asleep in the caravan. By the time Billy woke up, James had lost too much blood.

Maybe I could have saved him, if I had paid attention to that dream.

The Wake

We don't know if we're welcome at the wake but we decide to go anyway, for James. I get ready too quickly and wander around the house looking for jobs to do. I clean the kitchen and the sitting room—bring out the bins, sweep, hoover, polish the mantelpiece and inside and outside the glass cabinets. It's only when Mam emerges from the steam of the bathroom with her hair wrapped in a towel that I decide to wash my hair too.

I turn the handle as hot as it can go and scrub my skin clean. I grab a razor and shave under my arms and my legs. I hesitate before bringing it between my legs and shaving there too.

After the shower, I change into my outfit and go check on Mam. She is genuflecting in front of the mirror on the low windowsill beside her bed. She leans into her reflection with a pair of tweezers and tries to get at a stray hair at the tail of her left eyebrow. She keeps misjudging the root so she prunes around it, shedding the bulk of the thick hedge that frames the left side of her face. The tweezers plow up the hairs and nip at her flesh, leaving a trail of pink furrows on her new patch of forehead. Her eyes water and pinpricks of blood appear.

"Mam?"

She jumps. "I didn't know you were there."

"I can do your makeup if you like?"

"Only if you want to."

"Yeah, I got ready too early," I say, even though we are already late. "It will give me something to do."

She surrenders the tweezers. I kneel down beside her and

survey the damage. Her eyebrows look like mistakes a child has drawn and is beginning to rub out. I spit on a ball of cotton wool and get her to hold it above her eye to stop the bleeding.

Mam has emptied her wardrobe onto her bed. I survey the different outfits she has. A white cotton T-shirt and a pair of blue jeans, a man's white shirt and gray cardigan, or her red knitted jumper, James's favorite. He calls it the red *geansaí*.

I dollop moisturizer onto her forehead, cheeks, and the tip of her nose—it's cold, like yogurt on my fingers.

"Plenty of concealer under my eyes, please," Mam says.

"Yep." I dab the creamy paste onto the shadows. "Do you want to chance mascara?"

"Do I want to look human? Yes please."

"I'm just saying, you've no waterproof—"

"Debbie, put the mascara on. I'll be fine. I have tissues."

Mam's eyes are mostly brown, but there is a crack in her left eye and half of it is light blue, as though she has another person inside her trying to break through.

"Look up for me." The mascara wand latches onto her lashes and works its magic.

"Lipstick?"

"There's a boring pink one in here, that'll do."

"Nearly there," I say, taking a pencil and drawing back on the rest of her left eyebrow.

"Can we have a drink before we go?" Mam asks in a small voice.

"Of course."

"It doesn't feel like he's gone yet," she says.

"I know."

Our eyes lock. Now is the time to tell her about the dream. But I don't.

❋

James's wake takes place in his mother's pub exactly a month after his twenty-fifth birthday. We dodge the women going around trying to alleviate the mood with their offers of tea and paper plates of biscuits. The place is filling up. I spot Billy on his stool at the bar and drag Mam over to him.

"Where is he?" I ask.

Billy nods toward the fish tank that separates the pool table from the rest of the place. "Whatever bright spark agreed to put the coffin on the pool table needs to be shot."

"Are you for real?"

"Shirley wanted him there apparently."

"Shirley doesn't know what she wants. She's still in shock."

"How's?" He tilts his head toward Mam, who is still holding my hand. The fingers of her free hand are tangled in a mesh of hair that she is pulling across her face.

"We had a bit to drink in the house," I explain.

"That probably wasn't the best idea."

"Don't start."

"I'm just saying, it probably isn't the smartest—"

"You're one to talk."

That shuts him up.

"How is Shirley?" I ask.

"Well you can imagine . . ."

"I mean, what's she like? To you, like?"

"Grand, I've already gone up and sympathized."

"Do you think—" I stop and start again. "Do you think Shirley will go after you? For, you know."

"That it happened on our farm? I wouldn't think so. Although, I didn't think she'd lay out her dead son on a pool table either. But it's not me she has the problem with."

"Do you think it's all right for us to go up to him?"

Billy takes a moment. "Yeah, just. Look after her."

"I'm trying."

❄

I walk toward the fish tank and feel Mam's fingers tighten around mine. The water in the tank is inky blue and filled with a metropolis of plastic that looks like it was built from Lego. There used to be fish in it—a black and white angelfish called Guinness and a pair of goldfish called Gin and Tonic— but it was only a matter of time before people started pouring sups of their namesakes into the tank. The little bit of light that comes from the halogen fixtures at the corners of the tank makes electric veins in the water and pushes the blue beyond the glass so that it sometimes feels like drinking in an aquarium.

We join the line of people shuffling toward the casket. The pool table is covered with a white tablecloth. A little girl with a chocolate-smeared face emerges from underneath it and makes a cape out of it before tottering into the crowd waiting to pay their respects.

Shirley is standing beside the pool table at the top of the open casket, stroking her son's hair. When people shake her hand, she looks pained as though they are bothering her. Her ex-husband isn't at the coffin. I imagine that she has barred him from getting past the fish tank and he's somewhere in the pub, demoted to the lower echelons of mourners along with the rest of us.

James's coffin takes up most of the pool table. He is covered with a shroud from the chest down. They have dressed him in a suit with a white shirt and a black tie. One sleeve is empty from the accident. A lonely hand lies on his chest, a bunch of rosary beads tangled around the fingers. The club jersey is draped over the bottom of the coffin, along with a county medal and a Player of the Year trophy that he won at the dinner dance at Christmas.

I am at the top of the queue to say goodbye and I'm aware of how little time I have with him. I stroke his index finger with my own, from the tip of his nail to the knuckle. His skin feels cold and greasy, like the top of a mushroom. I want to lift up his eyelids to see the dead moons lying in their sockets. I wish that I could take off his clothes to examine the stump where his arm used to be. His neck is swollen and folded into rolls that remind me of the breadmen that I used to maul into existence with the leftover dough from Mam's mixing bowl. It's strange to think that James used to live inside this wax-work we are left with that nobody knows how to act around.

I go to shake Shirley's hand and she pulls me into a hug. "Oh, honey bun." That's what she calls me—honey bun or chicken because she never remembers my name. "It's OK, chick, I don't blame you. I would never blame you," she whispers into my ear.

"I'm sorry, Shirley." I pull away and turn around to let Mam know that I'm still on her side, but she's gone.

※

A shriek of feedback comes from the sound system that is set up in the corner of the bar. Father John bangs the microphone with the heel of his hand. He's in no fit state to be leading the rosary. He loosens his collar with one finger and puts his fist to his mouth to silence a burp.

A confused silence descends on the crowd as though we

can't decide if we are still afraid of the devil or just blessed with a polite, Irish tolerance for people talking shite. Father John closes his eyes and steadies the waves inside his head. "In the name of the Father and of the Son and of the Holy Spirit."

"Amen."

"We are gathered here to give comfort and support to the Cassidy family during this difficult time . . ."

The drone of Father John's voice makes me scan the crowd, and sure enough, he comes into view like God has summoned him there in his GAA tracksuit. It's nice to see him again. It's nice to be seen by him.

I spot James's younger brother, Mark, slipping out the side door and decide to follow him. I tell myself that I need the fresh air.

The cars are not so much parked as abandoned outside the pub. Compared to the streets of Dublin, our village is little more than an intersection of lost roads bumping into each other. Mark is sitting down on the gravel with his back against the wall, his shoulders hunched over, hugging his knees into his chest. I sit down beside him.

He takes a breath as if he has just come up from water. "Jaysis Debbie, I didn't see you there. How's the form?"

"Not so bad. Listen, I'm sorry—"

"Thanks."

"There's a good crowd here."

"I wish they'd all fuck off to be honest," he says. "Not you, I mean. Just—"

"I know."

We sit in each other's silences for a while.

I snap back into myself. Mark stubs out a cigarette on the gravel. I start to get up, but he puts his hand on my arm and I sit back down again. I let him kiss me. I focus on the mechanics of his mouth on mine. His tongue slides around and his chin tightens. Our lips smack together and he makes little slurping noises like a calf. I push myself into his mouth, wanting to suck the emptiness out of him, but he pulls away.

"Sorry," I say. I can tell that he is disgusted with himself—disgusted with me. I pick myself up and try to brush the guilt off my jeans.

I bump into his girlfriend outside the toilets on my way back inside. "Sorry," I say again.

※

The noise level inside the pub has lowered to the grumbling of a congregation waiting for mass to start, except for the screaming coming from behind the fish tank. The murmurs get louder and people turn around to look at me. A man I don't recognize comes over and says, "She won't get out of the coffin."

They're all staring at me, expecting a reaction. I walk toward the fish tank until I see Shirley standing at the bottom of the coffin in tears, screaming at Mam who is lying on top of James. Mam has splayed herself over James's body and put the stiff fingers of his remaining hand in her hair. Her arms are wrapped around his waist and her head is on his chest. A thick stream of mascara is running down her face, staining his white shirt. The undertaker is holding onto her leg, the only bit of her that he can pry away from the body. He has a blank look on his face as though he is waiting for someone to tell him what to do.

I rush over and put my hand on the small of Mam's back. I climb up onto the pool table and bend down. Mam's muscles are flexed, keeping a firm grip on James. Her eyelids are closed but fluttering.

I lean into her ear and whisper, "Mam." I feel her eyes

open. Her body stiffens and I try again. "Come on now, we'll get out of here and go home." I put my arms around her waist and help her to sit up. Her legs are now spread either side of James's crotch. She picks up the dead weight of James's hand and brushes her lips against his knuckles. Billy gives me a hand to lift her out and down onto the floor. We each take an arm across the backs of our necks and shoulder her weight, making our way slowly through the pathway that has opened up in front of us.

Caterpillar

The morning after the wake, I find Mam curled up in an armchair in the sitting room with the pop-up edition of *Alice's Adventures in Wonderland* on her lap. She doesn't register the existence of anyone or anything beyond the pages of the book. She stays in that chair for weeks. She begins by quietly flicking through the world between her fingers, but as the days go on she settles on one page—the page with the caterpillar.

The food in the fridge starts to go off. I throw out tomatoes and blueberries with full-grown beards. The spuds in the back hall grow tentacles. Billy knows not to come in for dinner. He fucks off down to the pub and Shirley makes him sandwiches. He offers for me to join him. I eat the head off him. I'm milking more than ever. I pretend to be thick about it but it's a relief to get out of the house.

It's reading week in college. I feel guilty for not reading until I see photos of ski trips and people dining alfresco in Italian villas on Facebook. Xanthe is on a yoga retreat in Nepal. She keeps sending me photos of herself doing headstands and meditating on top of a mountain. I wonder who is taking the photos. She's posting self-care and motivational quotes on her Instagram stories. I don't tell her about James. It still doesn't feel real. I don't want to use his death as some sort of personal drama either.

She texts me:

Debs! Meditation has been such a game-changer for me. You should try doing it on the farm x

I message back:

I've been meditating on the farm for years. We call it milking cows.

I frighten Mam whenever I walk into the room. I try to establish my presence without making her jump. I exaggerate my movements and stomp around the place like I'm onstage. When that doesn't work, I start to hum the theme tune to *The Great Escape*. I think it's working until I realize she has stopped registering me altogether.

I make cups of tea and bring her cigarettes. I pour her a glass of white wine, hoping to coax her out of her trance, but she doesn't touch it. People are still too awkward to ask after her, but I have my answer prepared for when enough time has passed. She's managing, I'll say, and it'll be true. She's managing to smoke cigarettes and tear strips of cardboard off a children's pop-up book. She ripped the whole caterpillar off the page and shredded it into pieces that she still plays with in her lap, but at least she's managing to do something.

I kneel down beside her to give her dinner, hoping to catch her eye, willing her to say something. She takes a drag of a cigarette and looks straight through me.

She exhales a cloud of smoke in my face. "Who are you?"

"Debbie, Mam. It's Debbie."

She shakes her head. "Who?"

I tell myself that I'll call the doctor when she stops eating the carrot and potato I mash up with butter and milk for her. When she stops feeding herself, I tell myself that I'll call when she stops swallowing the food. After she pisses herself, I go as far as dialing the number but I hang up before they answer. I have no words to tell them what's wrong with her.

Stairs

I mistake the throbbing in my eardrums for my own pulse until I get out of bed. The steady rhythm is getting louder. It's coming from the landing. My head goes numb. All I want to do is to get back under my duvet to muffle it out, but the beats are already inside me. The stretches of silence between them are getting longer. Every time I think they have stopped, another one comes.

I open my bedroom door and creep out onto the landing. Mam is lying in a heap at the end of the stairs. Her hair is splayed across the bottom step. She lifts up her head, her eyes lost in the rhythm of what she is doing, her gritted teeth looking like broken headstones, chipped and yellow, sinking in a marsh of blood. She lowers her eyes to make sure that her teeth are in line with the ridge of the second step. The ruins of her mouth brace themselves for the collision and she sends them crashing down.

I make it down the stairs in time to stop her from doing it again. I wrap my arms around her head and lift her chin toward me. Her lips are pushed inside out, tender, blue-veined and bloody like raw fish, one front tooth chipped, the other dislodged completely, leaving an angry hole in her gum. Tears leak from bare eyelids. She has run out of lashes and brows to pull out, but she jerks a hand up and rips strands of hair from her scalp. I wrestle her arm away and stroke her hand. There is a bald patch at the crown of her head—soft and vulnerable like the fontanelle of a baby. The pinholes of her scalp look up at me. I don't know what to do.

The stench of sweat hits the back of my throat. I drag her off the floor and bring her up the stairs. I'm trying to carry her weight on my back, but she won't hold on to me. I keep losing my balance. She slumps against the wall and I push her up the side of the wall to keep her there, but I'm not strong enough. She keeps falling.

※

Eventually, we reach the bathroom. I sit her down and prop her up against the side of the bath. Her head lolls to one side and rolls down to her chest. I peel her trousers off to find crusts of menstrual blood in her crotch, hanging in clumps of her pubic hair, baked dry and flaking off in cinders. I cut the tufts of hair off with a nail scissors and gather them up to put in the bin. She keeps spitting out the tissue that's stanching the blood in her mouth. More blood is coming from her nose now. She flinches when I try to touch it.

When the ambulance comes, the polite men start asking questions. I tell them that she fell down the stairs. I don't care that they don't believe me, or that they speak to Mam directly as if she cares about what is happening to her.

"She can't hear you," I tell them.

They shine a light in her eyes like they do in films. "How long has she been like this?" they ask.

"Bleeding?"

"Unresponsive," they say.

"I don't know . . . a while?"

"A few hours?" they ask.

I shake my head. "Around two weeks?"

※

"She fell down the stairs," I say.

"You saw her falling down the stairs?"

"Yes," I lie.

"And nobody else was at home."

"No."

"Your dad?"

"He isn't around."

"It's just you and your mother at home?"

"Yes. My uncle lives near us."

"OK, and where was he—"

"He was out milking the cows. Look, she's had a tough time recently. A close friend passed away. She's grieving."

"I'm sorry for your loss."

"Thanks."

"Who?" Mam says.

It feels like we've been found out. They want to assign me a social worker but their hands are tied when I tell them I'm eighteen. It's OK, I reassure them. My uncle is at home. I won't be on my own. They tell me it's not my job to look after my mother.

I clutch the foil blanket one of the ambulance men put around my shoulders. When he first gave it to me I thought it was laughably unnecessary. I hadn't escaped a burning building or run a marathon. I'm grateful for it, now.

I don't know what time it is. I'm confused when it appears to be sunny outside. I feel jet-lagged, like we've been traveling for a long time.

Billy rushes into the hospital foyer as I am getting chocolate out of the vending machine.

"Are you OK?"

"Yeah."

"Where is she?"

"This way," I say, walking back to the ward. "You might get a shock when you see her. She knocked out two teeth and chipped two more. She's broken her nose and has something called an orbital fracture."

"A broken eye socket?" he asks.

"I think so."

"What happened?"

"She walloped her head against the stairs. Repeatedly."

"What? Why?"

"How would I know? Mam hasn't talked to me in weeks, Billy. She won't talk to the doctors. I doubt she even knows what's going on."

I let that piece of information sink in, feeling a mixture of superiority and guilt. We reach the ward and walk around the curtain that has been pulled around Mam's bed. It's hard to tell if she is awake. A cast covers her nose. There are prune crinkles underneath her eyes. The left one is swollen shut.

"They're letting her out," I say.

"Like this?"

"They say she can recover at home."

"She's a fucking vegetable."

"Apparently she's showing all the vital signs."

Billy is sitting in a chair with his head in his hands. He sits up and sighs. "OK," he says, as though trying to convince himself. "OK."

✳

I spend two days at home dressing Mam, feeding her and putting her to bed. Billy bursts in the back door while I'm putting her on the toilet. He sees me holding her by the waist, struggling with the zip of her jeans. He grabs the keys of the car.

"Come on," he says. "We can't go on like this."

❋

We spend thirteen hours back in A&E waiting to see a doctor. The triage nurse is initially concerned, until we tell her we've already been to the hospital and they discharged her.

❋

Mam stares into space while the doctor reels off a list of options, most of which are unsuitable for the state she is in. A mindfulness class is his most bizarre suggestion. Billy and I exchange glances.

"Unfortunately, the waiting list for inpatient treatment without private health insurance is insane." He says the word with no irony.

"And with insurance? If I insure her straightaway?"

"Well, there's no guarantee, but she would certainly have a better chance."

"Leave it with me." Billy shakes the doctor's hand like he sold him a herd of cattle.

Hotel World

They call Billy saying they have a bed for Mam. He accepts the news as though he has landed a last-minute hotel reservation.

"Great, OK. Thanks a million. Thank you." He gives me a thumbs up.

I have her bags packed, ready to go. We've been waiting for this call for days. Every time Billy came near the back door, I had to stop myself from running out and begging him to ring them again.

Billy gets off the phone. "Debs, I'll drop her up. There's no need for you to come. I'll manage on my own."

"I want to see the place."

He sighs. "OK."

On the way up in the car, I keep opening and closing my eyes to make sure I'm not dreaming. My belly has wound itself into a tight fist, like it's trying to hold on to reality. When I close my eyes I'm at home in the smell of cow-shite and shite-talk on the radio. I open them and rain warps the city outside the window. Heuston station flies past and I'm proud of myself for recognizing it, clinging to it as a landmark of sanity.

Everyone knows St. Pats. It's the place where alcoholics and anorexics go to surrender. I was expecting it to be out in the suburbs but it's a red-bricked building, smack-bang in the middle of Dublin.

"It was Jonathan Swift's idea," I say to Billy as he's pulling in.

"What?"

"This place. When he died he left money to build it."

"The fella who wrote *Gulliver's Travels*?"

"Yeah and *A Modest Proposal*—the one about eating children."

"Your grandfather had a great expression for when he was hungry. He'd say, 'I'd eat a child's arse through a steel chair.'"

"Lovely," I say.

※

The rain hits Mam's face as we're getting her out of the car. For a moment I think the tiny splashes of water will instigate a miracle. She shivers with the cold, but isn't able to stand on her feet. Billy and I go on either side of her and walk her to the front door.

They get Mam a wheelchair, but we get the impression they think she doesn't need it. As a nurse settles her into the seat she turns and winks at Billy. "I'll have her walking by the end of the week."

We drop Mam's stuff in her room and the nurse gives us a tour of the place. We walk into bright rooms. A chair seems to assert its purpleness. The tables are undeniably blue. Everywhere I look, I see circles rather than ovals. Squares triumph over rectangles. The whole place reminds me of being encouraged to color in between the lines in primary school.

We're shown the music room and the art room. There's a library. The nurse seems optimistic about the chances of Mam using the gym.

"These are just some of the things that we will be getting up to," she says.

I like how she uses the royal we when referring to Mam. It suits her.

※

Before we know it, we're leaving Mam to settle in, abandoning her to this simplistic space. I wait until Billy leaves before I root around in her suitcase for the queen conch. I'm not sure if I remembered to pack it but now it seems crucial. I grope around the clothes until I feel the coldness of it—the odd, twisted bowl of bone.

I hold the conch up to Mam's ear. There's no change in her eyes. I put the shell in one palm and put her other hand over it. I feel like I'm trying to coax a bird to protect an egg that is not her own, silently pleading with her to adopt this delicate, alien hope.

Technical Love

I'm on Xanthe's couch, watching the credits to *Lost in Translation* roll down her laptop screen. She said it was her favorite film and I'd never seen it so we stuck it on. And it was just yer man from *Ghostbusters* and Scarlett Johansson hanging around Tokyo, trying not to be bored. And now it's over. I feel stupid for expecting something to happen. Xanthe is explaining why she thinks the director is a genius. I don't think I know the name of any film director apart from Steven Spielberg.

"You didn't like it," she says.

"I did!" I protest, but she knows I'm lying. She kept on looking at me during what she thought were the best parts, monitoring my reactions.

She cleans under her fingernails, collecting the grime under the corner of her index nail and flicking it away. "It's the kind of film you need to watch on your own."

I'm stung. She's supposed to be making me feel better. I have been scheduled into her week as the grieving friend in need. I finally told her about James and her desire to be a good friend immediately kicked up a few gears. I notice the time allotted to me on the planner above her desk—she's crossed out volunteering with Vincent de Paul and yoga to spend time watching movies and making me tea. She sprayed lavender mist on the couch to help me relax. She's even given me something called a care package. It's a shoebox filled with bath stuff, tissues, scented candles, and chocolate that I know she won't help me eat. She never eats. She pretends that her stomach is dodgy or blames food allergies but I've figured her out. I flicked through a tiny yellow Moleskine on her desk while she was in the bathroom and saw the list of foods with all the calories she had eaten that day.

40g porridge with water	*149*
Half a grapefruit	*52*
Rice cake	*35*
100g soy yogurt with honey	*81*
Superfood salad	*203*
Tea with oat milk	*22*
WASHED TEETH.	
TOTAL:	*542*

I thanked her awkwardly for the care package. I haven't even told her about Mam. I'm supposed to be grieving James, but it still hasn't sunk in that he's gone. If I force myself to think about him, I don't feel anything at all.

Xanthe has done more with the apartment since I saw it last. During her latest shopping rampage, she bought the entire contents of an indoor plant shop.

"It's embarrassing how many there are, really," she says. "I saw a post on Instagram about the easiest indoor plants to keep and clicked into it and it spiraled from there. I spent so much I got free delivery."

She introduces them to me like they are members of a newly acquired family.

Her eyelids are painted yellow and bold strokes of black liner frame her lashes. She's wearing a yellow silk kimono that matches the fresh sunflowers in her bathroom.

I saw a bank statement on her kitchen table. She has five thousand euro in her bank account. I can't remember the last time my bank account was out of overdraft. Billy pays me three hundred euro a month by direct debit. Before I started college, I thought it was loads.

❄

We decide to watch an episode of *Gilmore Girls*. A pop-up ad comes on, the type you have to watch for five seconds before you're allowed to skip to your show.

> There's one four-word question you must absolutely NEVER ask a man if you want him to be your boyfriend or husband or anything beyond just a "hookup" who you never hear from again.

Xanthe goes to skip it.

"Leave it," I say.

"Seriously?"

"Don't you want to know what this sociopath thinks is the question women should never ask men?"

She sits back.

"This gobshite has over 60 million views," I say.

"I bet my left eyebrow we have to subscribe to something to reveal what the secret question is."

> The question is "_____ you _____ me?"

"Well, that's more than I thought we'd get."

> I've asked a LOT of women if they know what this question is
>
> and only one out of every hundred get it RIGHT.
>
> That's only one percent.
>
> SO
>
> Do you know what the QUESTION is?

A photo comes up on screen of a guy with his arms folded and one eyebrow raised. His list of credentials includes best-selling author, relationship expert, and television personality. The website is called Technical Love. It advertises courses on how to tap into the male psyche and make them want to adore you.

"People actually subscribe," Xanthe says.

"I think I know the question."

"What is it again?"

"Blank you blank me?"

"And what do you think it is?"

"Will you fuck me?"

"Jesus, Debbie."

"What?"

"Wow."

I wonder if Xanthe ever talks like that with him. Does she buy nice underwear for him or tease him? Is sex a kind of confidence game? Does she perform for him? Or is it more real than that? Is it vulnerable? Has he told her he loves her yet? I shove the thoughts back down my throat. I feel sick. Maybe I can go to the bathroom and vomit out the jealousy.

"Do you like me?" Xanthe asks.

"Of course I like you," I say too quickly.

"No, I'm trying to fill in the blanks." She laughs.

I look at her.

"The blanks in the sentence?"

"Oh."

"Thanks for the reassurance though." She narrows her eyes. "Sometimes, I think you don't like me."

"What? Of course I like you!"

"Hmmm . . ."

"I'm just jealous of you," I admit.

"Well, I'm jealous of you too."

"What? Why?"

She shrugs. "You seem more real than other people. It's the farm, I think. You're not stuck in the college bubble. I'm envious of you living at home and being close to your family. I couldn't stand to live with my parents. Not anymore."

"I want to get away from home," I say.

"Are you OK?"

She noticed the crack in my voice and she's going for the jugular. It feels like she's won. She has achieved her goal for the day. She gets to be there for me.

Fuck it, I think. "My mam's not well," I tell her.

"Of course she's not, after all she's been through."

"No, like, really not well. She's in the hospital."

"Oh God. What's wrong?"

"She's in St. Pats," I say, and let out a nervous laugh. "Just across the road like. She's not well in the head. She's never been well. In the head, like. But I've never seen her this bad."

"It's been so hard on all of you," Xanthe says, rubbing my shoulder.

"I killed James," I whisper.

"Oh Debs, that's not true. It was an accident."

"It's my fault that he's dead."

"It's normal for people to blame themselves after a traumatic event."

"No," I insist, trying to break out of the cliché. "I saw it happening. I dreamed it while it was happening. I was there, in my sleep. I know I sound mental. I know it doesn't make any sense but I was there when it happened and I could have stopped it."

"You just had a bad dream, Debs."

"The bad dream was *real*. It happened in real time. I was there as it was happening. I *was* James in the dream. I felt him dying."

"That sounds really horrible. Really, really horrible."

"I sound like my mother," I mumble into her duvet.

"It's OK, Debs," she says, stroking my back. "It's all going to be OK. I promise."

❉

Xanthe is still rubbing my back. I've cried so much I feel hungover.

"I'm really sorry," I say.

"Don't apologize. You needed that."

"I'm embarrassed now."

"Why would you be embarrassed?"

"Because you think I'm mental."

"No I don't."

I look at her.

"Seriously, I don't," she says. "You're my best friend, you know that?"

"I haven't had a best friend since primary school."

"Well, you've no choice. You've a best friend again. Can't get rid of me."

"OK," I tell her, sniffling.

"Now, will we watch *Gilmore Girls*? The early Jess and Dean years?"

"Team Jess," I say.

"Jess is a dick."

"But he reads!"

"And he's a dick!"

"They're all dicks. Self-absorbed dicks the lot of them. Apart from Kirk . . . and Lane." She opens her laptop. The Technical Love ad is still on the screen.

"Blank you blank me," she says. "How about 'Do you love me?' That would definitely send them packing early doors."

"Maybe."

"Definitely."

She presses play and we bop along to the familiarity of the *Gilmore Girls* theme song.

Drinking Lessons

The morning after a night out, Billy finds me passed out in the calf shed in my trusted bandage dress and heels. He carries me into the house and puts me to bed, placing a pint of water on my bedside locker and a bucket on the floor. Later, after I drink the water and puke into the bucket, he knocks on my bedroom door.

"Debs?"

"Yeah?"

He pokes his head around the door and grins at me. "The dead arose and appeared to many."

"Mmmm."

"I thought you were staying in Santy's?" he asks.

"I was," I croak.

"How did you make it home from Dublin?"

"I can't remember," I say.

"How'd you get that bruise on your leg?"

I lift the duvet up and see an impressive purple bruise flowering on my thigh.

"No idea," I say.

"What was your poison of choice?" Billy asks.

"Blue WKD."

"Oh, the Lord Lantern. We need to get you some drinking lessons."

"Hmmm."

"I'm serious. No relation of mine is to be seen getting pissed off alco-pops—they're only sugary shite. How many did you have?"

"Dunno."

"Was there vodka involved?"

"Maybe."

"There's only one thing for it." He sits down on the edge of the bed and takes my pulse. "I'm putting you on a prescription of pints."

"I don't like pints, they taste like piss."

"You'll have to get used to them. They're the only way to go."

"Go away, Billy."

"This Sunday. Eight o'clock. I'm bringing you down the pub and teaching you how to drink properly."

＊

We milk the cows together on Sunday.

"What are you wearing down the pub?" Billy shouts over the milking machine.

"Are you afraid our outfits will clash?" I shout back.

"You're not planning on wearing those stilts you had on the other night?"

"Hardly."

"That's a relief."

"I'd look well now, wouldn't I? Tottering into Shirley's in stilettos on a Sunday evening."

"I was just asking."

"You think I've no cop on at all."

＊

I steal a blue jumper from Mam's wardrobe. I have been wearing a lot of Mam's clothes lately. I wear the jumper with black jeans. I consider wearing knee-high hooker boots to piss Billy off but settle for Docs. He's waiting for me at the gate.

"Well, do I pass the test?"

"Those seem fine. They look like you should be able to walk in them."

"What do you have against heels?"

"I have nothing against heels themselves. It's only when they're on the feet of young ones that they seem to transform ye all into newborn calves taking your first steps."

I can't think of anything smart to say so I let him think he's won.

"The lads are probably there already," Billy says.

"What lads?"

"The lads. You didn't think we'd be drinking on our own?"

"Ah Billy, who do I've to talk to?"

"You don't have to talk to anyone you don't want to. All you have to do is cough up when it's your round."

"Sure I'll just get my own."

Billy stops in the middle of the road. "You will not. You'll be civilized. There is a right way of doing things and a wrong way. Vodka, I can assure you, is the wrong way. You'd know that if you ever witnessed your grandmother on the tear."

The old man's bar is a tiny section through the door to the right at the entrance to Cassidy's. It's a pokey spot reserved for regulars on wooden stools. On a busy night, anyone sitting there has a view of the whole pub except for the pool tables around the back of the fish tank. It's a VIP area, like having a box at the theater—the ideal vantage point for nosy old fuckers.

"Debbie is here for her first legal pint," Billy announces. "Shirley. What do you recommend?"

Shirley comes out from behind the bar and gives me a hug, squashing her boobs into my face. "Come here to me, chick. Billy, what do you reckon?"

They both look at me like proud parents. Billy points down at a beer mat and spins it over to me to inspect. There's a smiling red-headed girl holding a pint of piss. "Want to try that?"

I shrug.

"Two Heinekens please, Shirl."

"How's Jacob holding up?" Shirley asks as she pours the pints.

"Ah, the poor craythur doesn't know which way is up," Billy says.

"Like the rest of us," Shirley says.

Shirley wanted to keep Jacob as a house dog after James died but Jacob was having none of it. When he went missing on her, she called Billy to keep an eye out for him. Billy found him in his old spot in the tractor with his head slumped against the window, waiting for James to come. He whimpered when Billy tried to move him, so he left him there, thinking he'd eventually move. He hasn't left the tractor since, not even for food. We still have to feed him in there. A weird feeling comes over me when I climb the steps of the tractor to shovel a tin of dog food into Jacob's bowl on the tractor seat. I feel James there. It's like I'm visiting his grave.

✳

There's a snug in the corner of the old man's bar where Billy is known to hold court. Two men are sitting there, nursing the dregs of their pints.

"Men, Debbie, Debbie, men," Billy introduces us. I know

better than to expect Billy to name them. I'm supposed to know who they are.

There's Dooley, who divides his time between eating breakfast rolls, looking after his elderly mother, and supping pints with Billy. The other man is younger, in his thirties. He's a Mooney. I recognize him from being Minister of the Eucharist at mass.

Billy ushers me into a seat and lays out the game plan for me. "So the lads here are finished theirs, which means they will probably be in rounds together. We don't have to worry about them—they'll look after each other. The only person you have to worry about is me. I bought this round so I expect you to get the next ones."

Mooney smiles. "What's this, Billy giving a lecture on drinking?"

"To be fair, it is his area of expertise," I say.

The men laugh.

"What's your poison, Debbie?" Dooley asks.

I've established that it's frowned upon to say vodka so I say, "Wine."

"Oh Jesus," Billy rubs his temple. "Right, OK. A glass of wine is the way to go with dinner or a good book for company, but you can't be drinking wine all night. You'd be a basket case."

"Billy, do you ever take your own advice?" Dooley asks.

"Shut up you," Billy says. "What else? Listen, there's one golden rule when it comes to drinking in a pub: If someone buys you a drink, by God you get them back."

"My glass has been empty this half hour waiting on this prick to get me another," Mooney says.

"Don't listen to him, Debbie, he's a liar," Dooley says, but he stands up and takes his wallet out of his back pocket.

Billy continues as though he hasn't been interrupted. "If

you're going to go cheap and swig naggins, swap the vodka for whiskey and learn to drink it neat. If you feel like you're losing it order a sparkling water with ice and lime and pretend it's gin. Never actually buy gin though. It's a rip-off and makes you cry. Pace yourself. You're looking for the sweet spot where you can act the maggot, not lose control altogether. There's no freedom in that. Do not expect anyone to look after you when you get so hammered you can't stand and if someone does look after you, make sure to thank them the next time you see them sober, no matter how embarrassed you are."

He pauses, watching my face for a sign that I'm taking it in. "There are unspoken rules of social drinking. Just because someone offers you a drink doesn't mean you should take it. The other night was not the last time you will end up bollocks drunk," Billy says. "You're entitled to one of those every now and again, as long as you don't go making a habit out of it."

"Not end up like you, you mean?" I ask.

Mooney has dimples when he laughs.

"Less of that," Billy says.

Billy's attention is snapped away by Shirley calling him over to the bar. "Back in a minute," he says.

❋

I manage the silence between me and Mooney by tearing up the beer mat into tiny bits and piecing them back together, staring at them intently and pretending not to notice him looking at me. "You know," he pauses and I look up at him, "you're the ringer of your mother."

"So I hear," I say, looking back down at the jigsawed beer mat.

"I was in her class at school. Maeve White. Smartest girl I've ever known."

I nod awkwardly. He's talking about her like she's dead.

"How is she?" he asks.

"Not great," I say.

"Tell her Murt Mooney was asking for her next time you see her."

"I will."

*

I'm relieved when I see Billy and Dooley coming back over with Shirley.

"Myself and Billy were just talking, hun," Shirley puts her hand on my shoulder. "About what to do with James's car. We thought you might like it, for traveling back and forth to college."

"But I can't drive," I point out.

"You're not the first who can't drive to take to the roads around here," Billy says. "I'll teach you."

"I don't have my theory though."

"Well you better get it." Shirley seems annoyed.

"Sorry, I don't mean to . . . Are you sure?"

"Of course, hun," she says.

"Thanks, Shirley."

"You're welcome," she says, clearing the empty glasses off the table. She seems to have forgotten that Violet originally belonged to Billy in the first place.

"Billy," I say, once Shirley is out of earshot, "Violet hasn't seen a motorway in ten years."

"You don't have to drive all the way into the city. You can start by driving to the train station."

"But it doesn't even have seat belts."

"We'll sort that." Billy downs his pint and turns to me. "It's your round."

I stand up, relieved that the conversation is over. I can feel Mooney's eyes following me up to the bar.

✳

By my sixth pint, me and Murt Mooney are the best of friends. Dooley and Billy have gone over to the other side of the bar to play pool. I decide to tell him, "I like your dimples."

"You've got some too," he says, poking his finger in my cheek.

"Dimple comes from *tümpel*, which means pond. I like that, like you've a pond in your cheek." I poke him back.

"You're smart, like your mammy," he says.

"Or a pothole. A pothole in your face. A big crater of a yoke." I poke his face more.

He looks at me. "Come on," he says, getting up from his seat. "Let's get a bit of fresh air."

I get my coat, grab my pint, and follow him out the door onto the road. I already know where we are going.

✳

The gate is open at Fourknocks. Murt is talking but I'm not listening. I'd be afraid of this place if we hadn't been drinking. I run up the steps of the hill and judder back down again. I spin around in circles faster and faster until I know I'm going to fall.

I let him catch me.

Then I hear Billy's voice coming from inside my head.

"The fuck are you at?"

Murt rolls away from me and stands up. Billy is looking down at us.

"I swear, Billy, she came on to me," Murt says. "I would never . . . I mean she's a child, I was only . . ."

"Yes, Murt, you're correct. She is a child."

"Billy . . ." I try.

"Don't," he says.

＊

We walk in silence the whole way home. When we get to the gate Billy turns to me and says, "You know that phrase, it takes a village to raise a child. Well in your case, it took a village to conceive a child. Any man you meet around here could be your father. So be awful careful whose mouth you go sticking your tongue into—I mean, good God, Debs. Murt Mooney has no more interest in you than the man in the moon. He's still mad for Maeve and you know that you have to be mad to be mad for her. You can't go around throwing yourself at men—"

"I didn't throw myself at him."

"What do you call that then?"

"It was only a kiss."

"My arse. Debbie, I'm only trying to help you."

"Help me with what? I'm not a kid anymore."

"But you are! You fucking are, you have your whole life ahead of you."

"So I'm meant to bow to your every command then? I'm meant to say at the end of every life lesson, 'Thank you, Uncle Billy, I want to be just like you when I grow up.'"

"You won't be like me, Debs," Billy says, turning away and walking back toward the pub. "You're your mother all over."

Driving Lessons

I arrive back at the house from a run, trampling over the cattle grid. Before I set off, I could already feel the burn of a blister on the back of my right heel. I enjoyed making it angrier the faster I ran. I wipe the sweat from my forehead. The tips of my fingers scrape crusts of salt away from my skin. I can hardly walk with the blister now. I hobble into the house for a glass of water. I open the door, checking my phone to see what distance I ran. Thirteen kilometers is pretty good, I think. I'm happy with that.

"Well Debbie!"

"Jesus Christ!"

Mark Cassidy is standing in my kitchen in his boxers.

"How's the form?" he asks, pulling a T-shirt over his head.

"What are you doing here?"

"I was giving Billy a hand out in the parlor there. How's the form?" he repeats.

"Grand," I say. "How are you? How's Deirbhle?"

"Grand, yeah," he says. The girlfriend. We're both surprised I brought her up.

"Is Billy still out in the parlor?"

"Yeah he should be on the last row there. I had to leave early. We've a match."

"Right," I say. "Best of luck."

I descend the steps of the milking parlor to the sound of Billy beating a cow with a length of Wavin pipe. "Get—the fuck—up—you dirty—lookin'—bastard."

The cow has refused to move up to the first feeder. She's scared shitless, paralyzed by fear. Billy keeps whipping her and she kicks her back leg out at him either as an act of rebellion or a last resort. I can't tell. She's a fresh heifer who's just after calving, placenta still dangling from her tail swaying back and forth with all the kicking she's doing. Her whole body shudders and finally, when Billy has to take a breather from whipping her, she daintily steps forward to assume the correct position.

"Why is Mark Cassidy in our kitchen?" I ask.

"He was giving me a dig out."

"Why didn't you ring me?"

"Because you're never home when I need you. I look around for you to give me a hand and you're out the gap, running the roads out of it. And he offered. What was I supposed to say, no?"

He puts the milking machine on the first in the row of docile cows. The familiar clip-clop rhythm of the four tentacle-hoovers sucks milk out of each teat. Their rivers flow together. I wonder if they know how much is being taken away from them.

❋

I stick on the kettle when Billy comes in from the yard.

"It's a bit on the nose replacing James with Mark," I say. "We've already killed one Cassidy."

"Shirley will be fine about it."

"I couldn't give a fuck about Shirley."

"Are you ready for your first driving lesson?" Billy asks.

"When is it?"

"Now."

"Thanks for the notice," I say, knowing the thought just popped into his head.

"You're welcome. Free lessons, and she wants notice."

"I'm going to have to take actual lessons before my test, you know."

"Ah, that's bullshit."

"It's not. I have to log my lessons."

"Sure we'll get Murt Mooney to sign them off. He's an instructor."

"That won't be awkward at all."

"It's you that made it awkward, not me."

He opens up the fridge door and frowns. "The fuck is this?" He's spotted the carton already.

"Oat milk."

"Oats have tits now, do they?"

"I'm trying something new."

"You're paying for fake milk as opposed to getting the real deal for free. I thought college was supposed to make you smarter."

"I'm expanding my horizons."

He sighs. "You get away with blue murder around here. Come on. Get those car keys."

❋

Violet splutters into action. "I think she has the flu," I half-joke, hoping for the lesson to be postponed due to carsickness.

"She'll be grand. We'll stop en route to get her petrol."

"En route to where?"

"Don't know yet. Depends on how good you are on your lefts and rights."

"We're going on the road?" I ask.

"Where did you think we were going?"

"I don't think I can go on the road, Billy."

"Of course you can. Come on. Get her into gear there."

I blink at him.

"First gear. Up here. Go on. Clutch and move the stick."

"Which is the clutch again?"

"Don't give me this shite. Same place as it is in the tractor."

"I'm not going as far as town, Billy."

"Why not?"

I see myself cutting out on the humpbacked bridge on the way to the garage, rolling back into another car because I can't pull up the handbrake properly. "I need to know where I'm going before we go anywhere. Baby steps. It's my first time."

Billy sighs. "OK. We'll take her around the block first. Does that sound reasonable, my ladyship?"

"OK."

"Go left," Billy says.

"I'm not going up the hill."

"Fine, go right. Indicate there."

I go to indicate but I turn on the windscreen wipers instead. Billy pretends not to notice. I pull out of the entrance. Everything's going too fast already.

"Up to second," Billy says, but I've lost control of my body. Violet is revving in protest.

"Clutch!" Billy orders and I do. He jams the gear stick into second and third for me.

The world outside bleeds past my windows and I'm going so fast I feel like we're disappearing into the road.

"Keep her going," Billy says. I look at the gauge. I'm not even doing thirty yet.

The only way I can do this is to think of everything outside the car as not real—outlawing it all to fantasy. And I'm coping better. I move into fourth gear on my own, thinking, surely this is a video game because we shouldn't be able to move through reality so fast. A car is coming toward me. The road isn't wide enough for both of us and we're playing chicken.

"Pull in, pull in, PULL IN TO FUCK," Billy says, but I'm already forcing the other car off the road. "Fuck's sake, are you trying to kill me? Next time we see a car, you pull in. Stop sulking."

We're on the home stretch, coming down Clock's Hill when another car comes into view. "Slow down, slow down," Billy says. I take my foot off the accelerator but we're free-wheeling down the hill and I've forgotten how to brake. I try to pull in anyway.

"That's a ditch, that's a ditch, THAT'S A DITCH!"

Violet bounces on the bank of the road *Dukes of Hazzard* style and I begin to melt into the road . . .

"Mother of divine Jesus!" Billy looks shook.

We're—somehow, miraculously—in our driveway. I don't remember how we got there.

"Sorry," I say. I grip the steering wheel so that he doesn't see my hands shaking. "I completely zoned out."

This is one of the very few times Billy seems to be stuck for words.

"Next lesson in the field?" I suggest.

"No." He gets out and slams the door. "Next time we're going into town. You'd want to cop onto yourself. You don't appreciate what I'm trying to do for you. College handed to you. Car handed to you. Lessons handed to you. Wake the fuck up, will you?"

8th December

Mam is being discharged from Pats next Friday. She is coming to the end of her three-week educational program and the hospital feels like she is ready for the next stage of recovery. She rings Billy to tell him she wants to go shopping.

"I'd like to tip into town to pick up a few bits before we head home."

"On Friday?"

"When you collect me, yeah."

"Are you sure now, Maeve?" Billy asks. "Does the doctor know about this?"

"It was his idea. It's a step in my recovery plan."

Next Friday is the eighth of December—the day that me and Billy make our annual trip to town to see the Christmas lights. Mam has never come with us before.

"It'll be very busy on the eighth now," Billy warns her.

"I know. That's why I want to go. It's an important step to prove to myself that I can cope with spending an afternoon in a city."

"Right. You know what they say about baby steps though?"

"Billy, will you take me out or not?"

"Of course I will. Is there any way I can speak to this doctor though?"

"No."

"Right so. The eighth then?"

"The eighth."

"See you then."

❈

We're sitting outside the psychiatrist's office. He wants to talk to Billy before he discharges Mam.

"I feel like I'm being called to the principal's office," Billy mutters to me.

"Dr. Allen will see you now," the receptionist says.

"Good luck," I say.

"You're coming in with me."

"I don't think I'm invited."

"I just invited you. Come on."

A tall, handsome man stands up as we walk in. "Mr. White," he says, extending his hand.

"Call me Billy."

"And this must be Debbie," the doctor says, and smiles. "Nice to meet you."

I force myself to meet his brown eyes and feel myself blush.

"Please, take a seat. My name is Dr. Patrick Allen. I am a senior consultant and have been overseeing Maeve's treatment. I think you'll find a significant change in her. She has improved under our care."

"Well, that's a relief."

"Yes. So we have diagnosed Maeve with bipolar disorder, sometimes known as manic depression. Have you ever come across it before?"

"Is it the yo-yo one?" Billy asks.

"Well, yes. Alternating moods of abnormal highs, known as manic states, and lows of depressive periods. It is called bipolar disorder because of the swings between these opposing poles of mood. Sometimes, severe episodes of mania or depression can trigger symptoms of psychosis. When we were able to get Maeve to talk, she told us about the recent death of a good friend and neighbor, James. It is our opinion that it was James's death that produced this psychotic episode."

"Well, I could have told you that, Doc," Billy says.

"Yes. Well, we have discussed treatment plans. I have started Maeve on a course of medication, which you will have to monitor. It is important to make sure she takes the proper dose at regular times. And of course, she will continue to have weekly talk therapy with me."

"I've to arrange to bring her up here once a week?" Billy asks.

"Yes."

"And that's it?" Billy asks.

"Well, yes. I mean, you have my secretary's phone number. If you ever want to contact me, don't hesitate—"

"—to call your secretary."

"Yes."

"And how is she supposed to help if my sister starts bashing her teeth out on the stairs again?"

"Well, she will relay any messages you give her to me."

"Right, along with the hundreds of others you can't afford to keep in beds in here," Billy says.

"I can assure you, Mr. White, we see to it that all of our patients get the care they need."

"Call me Billy. I know it's not your fault, Paddy. It's the system that frustrates me."

Billy stands up and shakes the doctor's hand again. He tells us that Maeve will be waiting for us in the lobby.

"I think you'll see a great improvement in her," Dr. Allen says.

❋

Mam gives us a sheepish smile when she sees us.

"We have to do something about those teeth," Billy says.

Mam closes her mouth.

"The teeth are grand," I say. I call her Mammy and give her a long, tight hug.

The cast has been removed from her nose and the swelling in her face has gone down. The purple bruising across the bridge of her nose has faded to yellow.

Billy rubs his hands together and winks at us. "Are we ready for the annual culchies' day out?"

✳

The whole thing feels surreal. Mam has been returned to us walking, talking, and evangelical about the power of therapy. She seems to have gotten a kick out of her diagnosis. She says the word, "bipolar," with a kind of bemusement, like she found a fifty-euro note in the pocket of her jeans. "Can you believe it?" she asks us, wide-eyed. "Dr. Allen is thinking of using me as a case study for his next paper."

Mam's attachment to her therapist comes as no surprise. She has always craved external validation. She needs to be admired. Worshipped even. Whatever she lost in James, she seems to have found in this guy.

She shakes her pillbox at us. It rattles like a box of tic-tacs. It's a plastic, multicolored wheel divided into triangular boxes marked with the first letters of the days of the week. It looks like it should be part of a trivia board game. "He made me promise to take them," she says, leaning her chin on her hand. "Even though they freeze my brain. You know when you hit a bump in the road and your brain kind of jumps up in your head? Well, it's like that, only constantly"—she throws her hands up—"up, up, up in the air."

"Well, if it works?" Billy says.

"We'll see," she says. "He's especially interested in my dream research."

"Really?"

"I lent him some of my journals."

"You gave him your diaries?"

"They're not diaries, Billy. It's research."

"Still, Maeve. Surely that's violating some code of ethics?"

"Studying my dreams has been an integral part of my treatment actually."

"Right," Billy says.

We park the car in Jervis. Mam wants to go to Bewley's, so I try to tell Billy it makes more sense to park in Drury Street.

"I know where Jervis is," he says. "We're going to Jervis."

We make our way across the bridge to the other side of the Liffey. They both trust me to navigate our way through the crowds. I usher them on at traffic lights. They're scared to cross as soon as the green man turns orange.

"Ye're like a couple of tourists," I say.

"We *are* a couple of tourists," Billy says, clasping Mam's hand and leading her across the road. It's nice to see him being so good to her.

They stop to look up at the lights on Grafton Street.

"*Nollaig Shona*," Mam says and puts her arm around my shoulder. "I wanted to call you Nollaig when you were born."

"Really?"

"Yeah. Your grandad wouldn't have any of it. He said you'd be bullied."

"I wasn't born around Christmas anyway."

"Why does that matter? It's a nice name."

"Dublin's fierce racist these days," Billy roars over the noise of the busker playing an electric guitar. "There's a shop called Brown Thomas. But then again it'd be worse if it were Black or White Thomas. Or Yellow Thomas."

"You can't call black people black anymore, Billy. They're colored," Mam says.

"Oh God," I moan.

"*Daoine gorma* is the Irish term. Blue people. I forget the origins. Something to do with the devil."

"You know, sometimes, I forget why I'm so worried about the stuff that comes out of your mouth, Billy. And then you come out with a cracker like that," Mam says.

"You're worried about what comes out of *my* mouth?"

✳

There's a queue to get into Bewley's. Mam's eyes light up as soon as we see the stained glass windows, polished floors, and the gigantic Christmas tree.

"I once saw Sinéad O'Connor in here," Mam says, beaming. "She knew I recognized her and winked at me, like she was asking to keep it our little secret."

"Then she stole a Bible in Eason's and the rest is history," Billy says.

"Me or Sinéad?"

"These days, I find it difficult to tell ye apart."

"I'll take that as a compliment," Mam says. "The woman's a genius."

I try and change the subject. "You know Lisa O'Neill used to work here?"

"In Bewley's?"

"Yeah."

"Now, there's a talent," Billy says.

"Who's she?" Mam asks.

"You'd love Lisa O'Neill, Mam."

"Maeve is suspicious of music she's never heard before," Billy says. "She prefers the music of the dead."

"That's not true."

"It is too. Mozart, Bach, Luke Kelly—"

"Sinéad O'Connor is alive and I found her on my own."

"Because she was such an obscure artist like. 'Nothing Compares 2 U' was played to death on the radio in the nineties. Her little, bothered, bald head crying on the telly in every pub."

On our way to Henry Street, Billy starts hurling abuse at a billboard. It's an anti-dairy campaign. There's a poster of a cow licking her calf. The caption reads: *Dairy takes babies from their mothers* and is followed by a call to arms to #GoVegan.

"What are we fucking meant to do?" Billy bellows. "Leave the calf there for it to grow up enough so Mammy and son can start riding each other? Is that what we should do? Fucking inbred, deformed cattle is what we're aiming for? Herds of bovine, royal families and exploding udders and mastitis to beat the band? Ha?"

"Just ignore it, Billy," I say.

Mam nudges me. "We're going past the GPO in a minute. That will calm him down."

Mam is unimpressed with the Spire. "And Joyce like a dwarf beside it," she tuts, drifting toward the frozen Joyce with his walking stick, hand on hip, hat cocked, and nose in the air. Mam gazes up at him. "My love, my love, my love. Why have you left me alone?"

Billy and I look at each other.

"We'll get a decent bit of grub in there," Billy says, nodding at the revolving door of the Kylemore.

"What did you say you wanted to buy, Mam?" I ask.

"I need a new pair of shoes for Midnight Mass."

"Great, sure there's loads of places to look," I say, cajoling her away from the statue.

※

After spending an hour and a half hemming and hawing in Arnotts shoe department, Mam buys a pair of boots. They are black patent leather ankle boots with a modest-size heel and a gold buckle. She wears them out of the shop and walks halfway down the street in them. Then she winces, takes them off, and announces that she wants to return them.

The sales assistant is furious.

As soon as we enter the next shop, Mam takes off her shoes and traipses around in her bare feet looking at the stock. We're all starting to flag now. Billy is sulking. He refuses to go into shops and stands with his arms folded outside them, striking up conversations with security men.

I spot a pair of silver lace-up boots Xanthe said she got in a charity shop for a tenner. These cost 145 euro. They look like the kind of footwear you'd need for a rave on the moon.

I turn around and Mam isn't there. Her shoes are though. She can't have gone far. I spend another ten minutes browsing, waiting for her to reappear.

✳

I go out to Billy, carrying Mam's empty shoes. He's talking to a painfully gregarious man who works for Amnesty International, one of the people in yellow coats whom I have learned to avoid.

"Debbie! You'll never guess who this man is. We're related to him."

"She isn't with you either," I say, beginning to feel dizzy. "Billy, I think I've lost her."

Billy's face drops. "Maeve?"

"Oh sugar, is that your daughter?" the yellow-coated man says. "If you go to the customer service desk in Debenhams they'll call her name out over the intercom."

✳

Five customer service desks and two hours later, we find Mam lying in a doorway on Moore Street, spooning a homeless teenage boy. Billy grabs her by the scruff of the neck and tries to drag her up but she's zipped into the sleeping bag with the boy. The boy moans. His eyes roll around in his head.

"Sorry, sorry," Mam apologizes like she's slept in or forgotten to get up for mass.

I offer to put on her shoes but Billy tells me to leave it. "She's gotten this far without them."

✳

No one speaks the whole way home. I check my phone. There's a message from Xanthe:

Hope you're having the cutest day in the city with your mam and Billy. You all deserve it x

Billy pulls into the yard. We're getting out of the car when he says, "Do you reckon Pats will give me my money back?"

I think he's joking but then Mam starts to cry.

"This is FUCKING BULLSHIT," he shouts at her. "You are FUCKING BATSHIT." He's spitting in her face. "And I'm fucking tired of all of it."

"We're all tired," I say. "It's too late to do this. Can we please just all go to bed?"

✳

I put Mam to bed and leave a glass of water beside her.

"Do you want me to stay with you?" I ask.

Her lip trembles. "Could you?"

I climb into the bed with her.

"Leave the lamp on," she says, wrapping her arms around my waist and putting her head on my chest.

"Why did you do it, Mam?"

She sighs. "When you came to collect me from the hospital, I wanted a normal, nice day out in town with my family. I was looking forward to it. I was ready for it. I imagined coffee in Bewley's and shopping . . ."

"Mam, we did all that."

"It was those *fucking* boots. I was never going to find the right pair. It sent me into a spiral. I thought it was one of those anxiety dreams. And so I just, tried to break away from it, change the direction of the dream. So I did. I just, drifted away."

"And do you remember what happened?"

"Oh yeah. But I remember nearly all of my dreams. Sometimes, I feel like I'm only alive when I'm asleep. So this didn't seem so different. The boy asked for money and I just sat down beside him. We got talking . . ."

"Mam, did you let him . . . did you sleep with him?"

"The boy?" Mam smiles. "He surprised me. When we fell asleep, he had the most beautiful dreams."

Alice in the Arcade

"So, it was a cute day?" Xanthe asks.

"Really cute," I say. "We went to Bewley's, saw the lights, did a bit of shopping . . ."

"Did you go to the Long Room?"

"Where's that?"

"Ah Debbie, the Long Room? The Book of Kells? The thing that all the tourists queue in the rain for?"

"Oh, well Mam doesn't really have the attention span for queues."

"You don't have to queue! We get in free because we're students and you're allowed to bring two guests in with you."

"Oh, I've never been."

"One of the most beautiful places in the world at your feet, and you've never been?"

"I'll bring them next time."

"Promise me you'll go there soon. I feel like dragging you along right now."

"I will, I will."

❋

We're in George's Street Arcade waiting for Orla to get her septum pierced. Orla wanted Xanthe to come along for moral support, and Xanthe has dragged me along with her.

"I swear to God, she goes to Workmans once and thinks she's alternative," Xanthe mutters to me. We just left Orla with the woman at the stall to help her pick out a ring.

"If Billy caught me with a bull ring in my nose, it would be the end of me."

"How's your mam finding being back at home?"

"Good, yeah."

Xanthe stops by another stall to flick through some posters. I look at the badges stuck to a corkboard—the faces of Coco Chanel, Frida Kahlo, Charlie Chaplin, and Che Guevara stare back at me. I can't decide which one I should start worshipping enough to wear.

Xanthe is smoothing her hand over a poster for *Pocahontas*.

"My first crush was on John Smith from *Pocahontas*," she says. "I liked the way he gave Miko the raccoon biscuits and I liked his yellow hair. I used to fantasize about our wedding. I was a cartoon too, of course. I converted over, for his sake. Then I got older and found out he was a pathological liar."

"And voiced by Mel Gibson of all people."

"Yeah. Not a great choice."

She flicks past the *Pocahontas* poster and lands on *The Witches* by Roald Dahl.

"What a book," she says.

"It's amazing."

"The film ruined it by turning him back into a boy at the end," she says.

"It really did. Mouse and grandmother contemplate their looming death. The happily ever after we all deserve."

"What's your favorite book?" Xanthe asks.

"*Alice's Adventures in Wonderland*. No wait . . . actually no, I'll sound like a dick."

"No, go on," she says.

"My favorite book is a specific *Alice's Adventures in Wonderland* pop-up book that Mam used to read to me. I've never actually read Lewis Carroll's *Alice's Adventures in Wonderland*. I've tried like, I just . . . I don't like the way he narrates her story. I know it sounds wanky but it's like she's trapped in his narration."

"Well, Alice owes her existence to an oddball mathematician who had a penchant for befriending little girls," Xanthe points out.

"Exactly," I say. "But really, she shouldn't belong to anyone, least of all Lewis Carroll. She exists independently of him."

"Except that he made her up," she argues.

"He didn't though."

"He actually did though, if you think about it," Xanthe says. "Anyway, I think you're complicating your relationship with Alice."

"Maybe. It was Billy who got me thinking this way. It started with the Greek myths. He said that they didn't belong to anyone."

"Myths are different though. They famously don't belong to anyone."

"They must have at some point though. Anyway, he'd tell me the stories of the Greeks all the time, only they were his own stories. And then he got me to retell his stories. And he said that's what stories were. They didn't belong to anyone."

"Billy sounds like a legend."

"He has his moments."

Xanthe grabs a top hat from one of the stands, a pocket watch from another, and places a pipe to her mouth. "Mad Hatter," she says, pointing at the hat, "the White Rabbit's pocket watch and the Caterpillar's hookah, or close enough. Pick one."

"Why?"

"I'm getting you one for Christmas."

"No you're not. We're not doing Christmas presents."

"Don't be a Grinch," she scolds.

"I have a feeling the Grinch was just broke."

"Fine," she says and sighs, putting the hat back on the stand.

I wonder what she's getting her boyfriend for Christmas. A new hurl? Socks and jocks? No, Xanthe is better than that. What would he get her? I can't imagine he would be any good at buying gifts.

"What are you thinking about?" Xanthe asks.

"What's your favorite book?" I ask her.

"That's an impossible question."

"You just asked me!"

"I didn't expect you to answer."

"Look at it this way. If you only had one book to read for the rest of your life, what would it be?"

"*Just Kids*, by Patti Smith."

"Who's Patti Smith?"

"Oh, Debbie . . ."

❊

We've nearly done the full loop of the arcade when we see the photography stall. There are the standard tourist photos of Dublin—a view from the Ha'penny Bridge, the Georgian doors, the Oscar Wilde statue. Then the display branches into photos of the sea. A clatter of cockles and mussels washed up on a gray, seaweed-strewn beach. In the corner of the photo—grinning—is a set of false teeth.

"Most people don't notice them at all," the man at the stall says when Xanthe points them out to me.

She grins at him.

"Have you ever heard of the Glass Beach?" he asks.

He points out another bigger, more expensive panoramic photo of a beach surrounded by snow, only instead of pebbles, there are glistening jewels shining in the bay.

"Holy crap," Xanthe says.

"Ussuri Bay in Russia. In the Soviet era, it was a dumping ground for broken bottles and cracked porcelain."

"Wait, this is all just glass?"

The guy nods.

The photo of the beach transforms into a kaleidoscope of time—a collage of years of erosion. I imagine the sea cradling the empty glasses—polishing and buffing them like the hair and makeup team around an actor getting ready for their red carpet appearance. Finally, they are ready to be presented as jewels—beauty frozen in time.

"You took the photo?"

"Yeah, on my way back from Japan. I spend a lot of time there. I specialize in photographing snow, actually." He points to a selection of other photos of snowflakes.

"These are glass too?"

"No, these are snowflakes."

"No way!"

"It's macrophotography."

"Wow."

Xanthe buys the framed photo of the Glass Beach and a couple of the snowflake ones.

"They make great Christmas presents," the guy tells her. He acts like he's giving her a bargain while he wraps them up for her. "I'll throw in my business card if you have any questions," he says with a wink.

The framed photo is so big I have to help her carry it. "That guy was undressing you with his eyes," I say.

"Ew, no he wasn't!"

"Xanthe, he couldn't have been more obvious."

"He just wanted to sell his work. They're so cool. I never knew snowflakes really looked like that," she says.

"What do you mean?"

"I thought they only looked like that in cartoons."

"Wait, what?"

"Yeah, like the way they put smiley faces on animals, or dress them in human clothes. I thought snow was just a dot."

I burst out laughing.

"What?" Xanthe asks.

"You're being serious?"

"Yes!"

"I can't believe the only person who got a first in our year doesn't know what a snowflake looks like."

Xanthe laughs. "I just thought it was a cartoon."

"It would be a fairly elaborate design for a cartoon."

"That's true."

"I can't imagine someone going through life without grasping the concept of the iconic six-armed snow crystal," I say.

"OK, I'm an idiot, sorry."

We browse a rail of T-shirts in silence for a while.

"My mam used to read me a story about a snowflake who didn't believe in snow," I say.

"I can't wait to meet your mam."

"Well, you will. Billy is already making the joke that Santy's coming for Christmas."

"Haha brilliant. I can't wait."

A woman comes out of the piercing stall with Orla traipsing after her.

"Your friend, she fainted," the woman says.

"Oh God, are you OK?" Xanthe asks.

Orla winces. "I fainted before the needle went in."

✳

We stop in the shop on the way back for Orla to get Lucozade.

"Do you want to go to the Long Room now?" Xanthe asks.

"No, I've that doctor's appointment," I say.

"What's wrong with you?" Orla asks.

"Ah it's just for the pill," I say, hoping she doesn't see me blush.

＊

Xanthe had a bit of a meltdown the last night we went out. She drank too much at pre-drinks and got sick in the taxi on the way in, so we went straight home. She was crying a lot—she kept saying how much she hated herself. I got her out of her new playsuit and into her pajamas. Griff made her drink a pint of water. We tucked her up in bed and we were both trying to cheer her up—telling her she had no reason to hate herself. She was gorgeous and talented and smart and funny.

Then Griffin went a little too far. "I mean, don't get me wrong. Debbie, you're attractive in a culchie, girl-next-door kind of way but Xanthe, you could be a Victoria's Secret model. There is no contest."

"I appreciate your honesty and agree wholeheartedly," I said.

Xanthe made a face.

"Why are you getting thick? We're complimenting you." I said.

"I mean, you've a lot to thank her for, Debs," Griffin said, continuing to dig. "Lads come over to get with Xanthe and end up sleeping with you."

"Except I don't sleep with them," I said, flicking my hair over my shoulder. "I'm a lady."

"Yeah, you keep telling yourself that."

"What? I'm not joking. I don't sleep with them. I've never had sex before."

There was an odd, confused silence and then Griff laughed. "Ah here. Xanthe you hear that? This one's trying to tell me she's a virgin when she's slept with a different guy every time we've gone out."

"I go home with them," I corrected him. "I don't sleep with them though."

"Debbie," Xanthe said, hiccupping. "You kiss very . . . passionately. There's nothing wrong with it, it's just the guy gets very excited and that generally leads to action in the bedroom . . . and you drag him toward the bedroom so . . ."

"But I always warn him before we go that it's not going to happen."

"Wow." All of a sudden, Xanthe was sober. "OK, Debbie, you have had sex before. I've witnessed it. You had sex on that couch."

"Lads, I haven't. I swear. We do things but it never goes in."

"I've seen it go in," Xanthe said.

"What? Do you've night goggles and a pair of binoculars?"

"I didn't need them! Jesus Christ, Debbie. I thought you were using protection. You should get yourself checked."

"I don't need to!"

It strikes me then how rude it is to bring lads back to Xanthe's place. I do it because I'm terrified that her boyfriend is going to be there when we get back. I imagine the scenario often, me trying to sleep on the couch with them in the next room.

"I don't know why I bring them back here. I'm really sorry," I mumbled.

"Oh God, I'm not giving out to you for bringing them back."

"It's out of order," I said.

"No, it's grand. It's just—it's worrying you don't remember what happens."

"I do though. Nothing happens."

"Debbie, go to the doctor. Make an appointment. Get yourself checked for STIs."

"I'm not a prostitute."

"I think you should see a doctor too, Debbie. Just to make sure," Griff said. He seemed both amused and embarrassed for me.

"No one's calling you a prostitute," Xanthe said. "But you need to know what happens when you're drunk. You're blocking things out. I'm only saying this because I love you. Please book the appointment. For me."

I'm flicking through magazines trying not to get sucked into *The Jeremy Kyle Show* on the telly in the waiting room. I lied to the receptionist and told her I had an earache. I'm considering going along with the earache charade because I'm not sure how I'm going to approach the subject. The handsome male doctor who I hoped I wasn't going to get eventually calls my name.

"What can I do for you today?" he says as he welcomes me into his office.

I wait until he closes the door. The rehearsed lines have disappeared from my head. "Em, well, first of all, I should apologize. I lied to the receptionist saying I had an earache because I was a bit embarrassed to tell her."

"OK, that's no problem."

"I'm wondering if there's a test you can do to find out if I've had sex or not. I realize that it's a strange request. I just, I'm not sure." The words come out quickly, tripping over each other. I'm staring at his shoes.

"Has there been an incident?" he says gently.

"Em, a few."

"An assault, I mean."

"Oh God no. Just sometimes when I drink, I can't remember."

He taps his pen on the desk. "Right, well. It is virtually impossible to know if someone is sexually active through a physical examination."

"Of course. I'm sorry, this is stupid. I shouldn't be wasting your time."

"No, no. It was definitely the right decision to come in and talk to me. There are a number of things we can do. You can book an appointment for the clinic to get you checked out for STIs. The likelihood is, there will be nothing to worry about. It's probably a good idea to go on some sort of contraception. I will discuss those options with you. But most importantly," he scribbles a phone number on his prescription pad. "I really think you would benefit from talking to a counselor. It's a free service and they are doing really great work over there."

I take the piece of paper. He goes through the contraceptive brand that he thinks is best suited for students like me. Then he gives me the prescription and reminds me to book an appointment for the clinic. I thank him. I don't book in for the clinic or fill out my prescription. I have no intention of ringing that phone number either.

Hedgehog

There's a hedgehog stuck at the bottom of our cattle grid. I bend down to look at the mound of prickles down in the corner of the pit. I imagine it moseying around in the dark the night before, snout first, carrying its cape of spikes and stroking the grass with its little feet before falling down the gap between two metal bars.

"Stupid fucker," I say, getting down on my hunkers to get a closer look at it. It doesn't give much away. Beside it, two recently deceased hedgehogs lie on their sides. Their unfurled bodies expose vulnerable bellies. They seem far more relaxed than their friend who is still alive.

I'm lying flat on my stomach now, looking down at him through the bars of his prison. There's a swish of feet in the grass and the bars creak under the weight of a boot. Billy is crouching down next to me.

"What are we looking at?"

"There," I say, pointing to the corner.

"Stupid fucker."

"I know."

"They really should be hibernating by now. It's a mild December but there's going to be snow in the next week or two."

"Thanks Met Éireann."

"I'll get the long shovel from the shed and try to lift him out. Sometimes they puff up so big you can't get them out through the bars."

"No don't," I say, grabbing his arm before he has the chance to move. "We're best leaving it there. We can't be lifting them all out."

"It's a big lump of a yoke. It'll take at least a couple days before it starts to starve to death."

"That's what happened to the other poor devils and where were you when they needed a dig-out?"

"I never had you down for a sadist, Deb."

"I'm not, but shit like this happens all the time. You can't come rushing over pretending to fix it all."

Billy stands up and starts pacing the length of the cattle grid. "So I'm not allowed to lift poor hedgie here from his death?"

"No you're not, and you're not allowed to turn this into a joke either. It's not funny."

"I gathered that," he says. "You just seem a bit . . ."

"A bit what?"

"Nothing. I'll leave the hedgehog alone so. Should I apologize to it?"

"Go away."

He leaves and I stay lying on the tarmac, thinking about the fist that is curled up in my belly. I watch the spikes inflating underneath the cattle grid until I'm able to feel the sharp prick of its needles inside me.

Wizard's Sleeve

I wake up thirsty. My sweaty face is stuck to Xanthe's leather couch. It makes a noise like Velcro when I peel myself off it. My head is still giddy with drink. I'm getting used to the sound the city makes in the morning. The whirr of the Luas going by. Its warning bells seem to ding against my head.

Xanthe's bedroom door creaks open. I turn around to see a sheepish Griff in the doorway of the kitchen.

"Good morning," I say.

"Morning," he mumbles, pulling his hair over his face. "I'm supposed to be teaching a class in fifteen minutes."

"Good luck with that."

"It's too late to send an email to say it's canceled, isn't it?"

"I think so."

"Right." He sniffs under his arms. "Do you have any deodorant?"

"Not with me, no."

"Xanthe!" he shouts and heads back into the bedroom.

❄

When he's gone, Xanthe creeps into the kitchen, ready for the confrontation.

"What the fuck?" I say.

"Nothing happened, obviously."

"You have a boyfriend."

"He's gay."

"Did you kiss?"

She says nothing.

"You have a boyfriend!"

"Stop. I know."

I sigh. "He's using you, Xanthe. He knows he can crawl into your bed anytime he likes and that's not healthy for either of you."

"It was just a cuddle though," she insists.

"Was it?"

"I don't know."

I hand her a cup of tea.

"You didn't bring anyone back?" she says.

"Why the tone of surprise?"

"Just . . . it's good? Progress?"

I'm about to be offended until I realize this is one of the only times I have gone out with Xanthe and not brought a stranger back to her apartment.

"How was the doctor the other day?" she asks.

"Good, yeah."

"What did you talk about?"

"My sexual health." I can't say it without being sarcastic.

"Did you figure out whether you . . . you know, actually had sex?"

"The memories are coming back. Like, one time, it was really sore. Afterward. In the morning. And I was bleeding. But I don't know if that was from, like, his fingers or—"

"You really can't remember?"

"No. Like, some of it has to do with the alcohol. But I disconnected from my body as well. Sort of like when you go for a run but you completely forget that you're running. And even afterward, you're sweaty but you can't remember the run itself."

"I can imagine sex can become automatic when you've done it for a while, but the first time? You can't remember your first time?"

"I don't even know if it was my first time." I look up at her. "You don't believe me."

"It's not that I don't believe you, it's just—it makes no sense."

I imagine Xanthe's first time was in the morning, in soft sunlight. He definitely asked her if she was all right, and she was as adorable as Reese Witherspoon in that *Cruel Intentions* scene. Was it recently? With him? "When was your first time?" I ask.

"Haven't had it yet."

"Oh."

"I tell people I have, if they ask. I almost believe myself. I came close with Griff before, but I couldn't go through with it. He still teases me about it."

"Dick."

"In hindsight, I'm glad I didn't lose it to him."

"It's not a gift, you know. Virginity."

"I know, but it is something he could hold over me."

"Only if you let him," I say. "I used to hump the armrest of the couch in the sitting room. Mam used to hit me when she saw me doing it, like I was a dog. Can you remember the first time you—you know—touched yourself?"

"I think I do it wrong."

"There's no way of doing it wrong."

"No, I googled it and I'm definitely doing it wrong. It doesn't help that I hate my vagina."

"What did you google?" I ask.

"How to masturbate," Xanthe mutters.

I whip my laptop out of my bag.

"What are you doing?" she asks.

"Googling masturbation. I want to see where the word comes from."

"Nerd."

"Were you never into etymology as a kid?" I ask. "It was my favorite pastime. Huh. Nineteenth-century Latin. Origin unknown. Wow. Do you know what the synonyms of masturbation are? To abuse oneself. To practice self-abuse."

"Jesus."

"So, what are you doing wrong?" I ask.

"I can't touch it directly. I have the world's most disgusting genitals."

"Ah don't be getting full of yourself now. Everyone has disgusting genitals."

"Mine are the worst," she says.

"How do you know?"

"I have a wizard's sleeve."

"A what?"

"Google it."

"Is it a *Harry Potter* thing?" I ask.

"No, it's not a *Harry Potter* thing."

It's only coming up on Urban Dictionary. " 'When a lady's lower region has been hammered that much it has expanded and seems to have no end.' There is so much wrong with that sentence."

"I know."

"Ah lads," I snort. "A baggy fanny? Are they serious?"

"It's not funny. The flaps, they, like, dangle down. It's so embarrassing."

"So how do you—manage?"

"I do it through my knickers. I have to. I can't touch it. Some people get their teeth straightened, but if I could change one thing about myself I'd have normal labia. I'd like a coin slot."

"What do you think you are, a vending machine?"

"I'm serious. I can't imagine letting anyone else see it."

I'm surprised and a bit relieved that her boyfriend hasn't seen her naked.

"People don't tend to inspect," I tell her.

"I only really noticed how deformed it was after a sex education class in secondary school. Mine wasn't like the diagram at all. I wanted to cut the protruding lip shorter. I got as far as stealing my dad's surgical scissors and placing the cold blade against the excess. Anyway, I couldn't do it. I wasn't brave enough."

"Jesus Christ, Xanthe. You know in some cultures they do that to girls."

She nods. "FGM? Yeah. In our culture, they let us do it to ourselves."

Mad Cow

I catch Mam sitting in the dark in the kitchen. The open laptop makes her face glow blue. It's a bit of a shock, like finding Jacob on the phone trying to dial the number for a takeaway with his paws.

She shuts the laptop as soon as she sees me.

"I didn't know you knew how to work it," I said.

"I was researching," she sniffs, looking away from me.

I sit down beside her and open the laptop expecting to see something about dreams, but it's the Wikipedia page for mad cow disease.

"I think I must have contracted it."

"Hah?"

"The BSE virus. It can infect humans too, you know. The symptoms make a lot of sense."

I reach out and take her hand. "Mam, you don't have mad cow disease."

"No one fucking believes anything I say."

"I'm not saying I don't believe you."

"I'm the best judge of what's happening in my body."

"OK, but is it fair to say that you might not have mad cow disease?" I ask.

She crosses her arms. "But I might!"

"Yes, but there is a very, very slim possibility."

"All I have to do is eat infected meat, which is very possible. I know it's irrational, but every time I see meat I want to vomit."

"Well, how about we just don't eat meat for a while. How does that sound?"

"Can we?"

"Yeah, of course we can," I say.

"That sounds good, yeah. What about Billy though?"

"What about him?"

"What about dinners?"

"Fuck him, he'll eat what we give him."

I look at the other tabs that Mam has open. She is reading academic articles on JSTOR about cows.

"OK. So no ham even?" Mam says, and looks doubtful about her vegetarian future.

"Does ham make you feel uncomfortable?" I ask.

"Not really."

"OK so, ham's all right."

"OK, thanks. What'll we eat so?"

"My friend's a vegan. I'll ask her for some recipes."

"That's a lot of effort though. What about stew?"

"Well, there's meat in that too."

"I don't mind that sort of meat. Just maybe not steak, like."

I've never seen Mam eat a steak. "Yeah, sounds good," I say.

"Thanks, Debbie."

"No bother."

❋

There are underwater cows—three of them—white, red, and black. They have shackles on their hind legs and they are on a mountain that is rising up from the sea. Their eyes bulge when they emerge from the water.

❋

I wake up and try to reach back to remember more of the dream. The bit before the underwater cows . . . There were just flashes of webpages. It was like I had been studying for a test and I was processing information. Still, there was a tug of familiarity to them. There were facts about cows.

I open the laptop and check the Internet history. I feel like I've seen flashes of the webpages before. *It's good for calving cows to eat seaweed*—that was one fact. *The dewlap of a cow is the fold of loose skin hanging from the neck or throat*—that was another. *The word cumhall originally meant female slave.* It made me think of Fionn MacCumhall, whom I knew from school. Fionn (meaning "fair" or "white"), Mac (meaning "son of"), and Cumhall. I thought of my own name, White. But I didn't know any of this before I went to sleep. It was Mam who had read these facts, not me.

The logic creeps toward me and I back away from it. There is no way I could have fallen down the rabbit hole of my mother's mind in my sleep.

Coffee

My phone vibrates.

It's Xanthe:

Are you around for coffee?

I message back:

Always. Meet you in Starbucks?

I'm in the hipster café on South William St.

She sends me the location. I really want to ask her to go to Starbucks because that's our usual. I know the people who work there so our interactions aren't awkward. I've only gotten used to calling a normal coffee a *grande Americano* without blushing like a twat.

I work on psyching myself up to entering new territory. I head toward the place, following my blue dot on Google Maps.

＊

It's only four o' clock but it's getting dark already. The city descends into a deep blue fog. The hipster café is next to a sushi place. There are fairy lights outside.

＊

It takes a while for someone to notice me. I order an Americano from a girl with an asymmetrical haircut and loads of ear piercings. She takes my money and gives me a laminated sheet of paper. I look at it. It's a map of Central America. The only country labeled is Guatemala. I sit down at our table and show it to Xanthe.

"What should I do with this?"

"When your order is ready, they'll shout Guatemala."

"Is my order from Guatemala?"

"No."

"But what does Guatemala have to do with it?"

"Nothing. It's just a way of sorting out whose coffee is whose."

"Why don't they ask your name, like Starbucks?"

She laughs. "You love Starbucks."

"It just makes more sense."

"Starbucks coffee tastes like shit, Debbie."

"Why do you drink it then?"

"Because you always want to go there!"

"Guatemala!" someone shouts.

I raise my laminated map and my coffee is placed in front of me. The mug is a little bigger than an eggcup. The handle is so tiny that it is redundant. I feel like I'm at a hipster doll's tea party. Xanthe is staring straight past me. She is wiping tears away from her cheeks as though they have nothing to do with her.

"What's wrong?"

She shakes her head. "Nothing."

"What happened?"

"Nothing."

"Something must have happened," I say, handing her the serviette that came with my coffee. I can't believe that she has the balls to cry in a public place.

"No, nothing happened," she says, wiping her cheeks. "Just, having a bad day."

"But"—I say, and stare at all of her carrier bags—"you went shopping."

"Yeah." She laughs. "I always go shopping when I'm having a bad day."

"But, you're always shopping."

"Exactly." She sighs. "I just feel like shit and I don't know why."

"But you're not shit. You're the opposite of shit."

"Thanks."

"I mean it."

She starts taking stuff out of the shopping bags and puts them on the table. A mindfulness coloring book, a mood diary, a bullet journal, a briefcase of art supplies, candles, incense sticks, bath bombs, essential oils, pajamas, face masks, a foot spa, fluffy slipper socks. The last thing she takes out is a self-help book. She turns the title toward me. It's called *Overcoming Depression*.

"I have depression." She sniffs. "Why is that so hard to say?"

I'm expecting the whole café to have turned into an expectant audience wondering what I'm going to say, but I look around and see everyone is busy going about their own day.

"Oh Santy." I reach out and clasp the tips of her fingers.

I let her tell me about her problems. The therapist that costs eighty euro an hour who she thinks is flirting with her. Her beef with CBT workbooks and meditation. The yoga retreat she went to over reading week where she cried all of the time but didn't tell anyone because they might have suspected her secret—her terrible secret that she's a little bit sad sometimes.

I want to shake her. I want to slap some sense into her

beautiful face. I want to tell her that she can't be depressed. The diagnosis the doctor gave her must have been a mistake. If I haven't earned the title of depression, then neither has she. Because she is a lot less miserable than I am. Or she certainly ought to be.

Snow

We have been snowed in for two weeks now. I'm glad of the excuse not to go to college. There's a video on Griff's Facebook of an epic snowball fight in Front Square. I watch rosy-cheeked people prancing around campus in the latest skiing fashion. The elation on their faces gives me anxiety. I don't think I'll ever feel like a student. If I were there, I would hide in the library until it was over.

Billy keeps trying to get me out of the house but I tell him I've loads of college work to do. I'm supposed to be writing an essay on *Jude the Obscure*. Every so often he asks how Jude is getting on and I try to impress him with an answer. He hasn't read the book but he knows the gist of it. It gives me license to convince him of whatever nonsense I'm trying to sort out in my head.

I want to do well on the essay because I like the tutor. She has short pink hair and brings in pastries to class. And she's not condescending like the others. She talks to us like we can teach her things too.

In our introduction class to Thomas Hardy, she said she was tired of teaching him.

"But I like him," I said in a small, petulant voice.

She looked at me and said, "I liked him too, when I was sixteen." Then she clasped her hand to her mouth as if she had said something horrible. "I have no idea why I said that. I'm so sorry."

I had no idea why she felt the need to apologize. At the beginning of the next class, she called me by name. "Debbie. I had a think about what I said to you last week and why I said it. I'm really sorry for patronizing you."

"That's OK," I said.

"When I was your age, I loved Hardy as well. But then, as I grew up, I realized that he treated his characters unfairly. All of Hardy's characters—their desires are beyond their remit. So I'm angry with him really, because they all have unachievable dreams."

"His dreams were as gigantic as his surroundings were small," I replied. It was a line that struck me when I was googling *Jude the Obscure* quotes.

"Exactly." She smiled.

"Read *Tess*," she said to me later, as she passed me on the way out of class. "You'll love it."

When I couldn't get to class, I sent her an email saying why I couldn't make it, playing up to my poor culchie persona. She sent me an email back offering to meet for a coffee after the snow to go over some material I had missed. But then the whole country went into shutdown. The university has been closed for a week now so she's probably forgotten. I tell myself that it doesn't matter. If I speak to her one-on-one, she'll only find out that I'm a dope.

Milking has been a nightmare. I spent this morning outside in the dark, early hours, trying to unfreeze the pipes with a blowtorch. We wouldn't be able to cope without Mark Cassidy. He has been a godsend cleaning out sheds and feeding calves. Billy has been out in the digger trying to clear the roads so that people can get to the shop. He went to the shop in the tractor yesterday to get provisions for Shirley and brought Mam back a crate of mini bottles of wine from the pub. The tinkling of the bottles Billy shoved under her bed woke her up. She whispered a surprised thank-you.

Mam is struggling with cabin fever. A lot of her recovery has focused on being outdoors and reconnecting with nature. Usually, she goes outside in her pajamas as soon as she wakes up. Then she puts her bare feet in the grass, closes her eyes, and breathes. It's called grounding. Billy and I have agreed that it's better than letting her sting herself in a bunch of nettles. When the snow started, she was stubborn about sticking to her morning ritual. She shoveled the snow off her patch of grass. Then she got the flu and gave up.

❋

Mam can't get to her appointments in town. The psychiatrist must have gotten sick of her endless phone calls so he recommended a local therapist. Very local. She lives across the road from us.

"Audrey Keane?" Billy frowns. "Is a shrink?"

"A psychotherapist, yes," Mam says.

"Audrey Keane, my old piano teacher?" I ask.

"Yes," Mam insists. "And she's supposed to be good."

"Ah Jesus. You can't go to Audrey Keane, Maeve." Billy sighs. "That's just . . . it's too close to home."

"Billy, I'm not well. I need to talk to someone."

"Well, talk to your daughter over there."

I shoot Billy a look.

"She's been very good about the fee. It's only fifty," Mam says.

"Fifty euro!" Billy shouts. "How many mini bottles of wine would that get ya?"

"It's a reduced rate."

"So I'm supposed to give you fifty quid of my money for you to go and spill your guts to our neighbor. What am I supposed to be getting out of this?"

"Please, Billy."

He makes her sweat for a bit before leaving a fifty note on the kitchen table and going out to milk.

Mam has a shower and blow-dries her hair. It's the first time I've seen her wear makeup since the wake.

"You look nice," I say.

"Thanks." She smiles and then shuts her mouth, conscious of her teeth. "See you later."

"Good luck."

✳

Three hours later, I'm sitting in an armchair waiting for her to come home. She opens the door and jumps when she sees me.

"Jesus."

"Sorry," I say.

"It's OK, I just wasn't expecting you," she says.

"How did it go?" I ask.

"Great, yeah," she says flopping down on the sofa. "It was really nice just to talk to someone outside my head, if you get me."

"I do," I say. "Did she make you play the piano?"

"Haha, no."

"You know what my favorite part of going to piano lessons was?"

"What?"

"Going to the bathroom. Audrey Keane had the most glorious bathroom I've ever seen. It was so magical. I went at least twice a session. Candles lighting. Relaxing music. Matching towel set. Pure heaven."

"I didn't get to see it."

"You don't know what you're missing."

"I can't remember you doing piano lessons," Mam says.

"I begged Billy to let me go because the girls in school were doing it. I didn't last long. Audrey Keane is an absolute lady though."

"She is," Mam says. "She actually offered to see you for a session, if you were up for it. I think it might be good for you."

"I'll think about it."

Smooth Artemis

I'm trying to remember what Audrey Keane's garden looks like underneath all of the snow. There's a neat laurel hedge under there, and an arch that leads to the pond. Her Christmas lights are up. The rose bush is still hanging in there, pink petals frozen in the snow. I had to wait until Billy went to the pub to sneak out. He left the fifty on the kitchen table for Mam and she gave it to me reluctantly, like I was cheating her out of a session.

Audrey opens the door. I smell pine needles, cinnamon, and baking.

"Come in out of the cold." Audrey pulls me in by the hand and shuts the door. "Debbie," she says looking at me as though double-checking who I am. "It's good to see you again."

"Your hair is amazing," I say.

Audrey's hair has turned a gorgeous shade of silver.

"You haven't changed a bit." I smile.

"You have!"

"Thanks." I grin. I desperately want Audrey to like me. She takes my jacket, hat, scarf, and gloves and drapes them over the radiator.

"Come on through," she says and opens the door to her left.

Nostalgia pulls me toward the piano room down the hall. I don't know why I imagined the session would take place in the same room as I learned my major and minor scales, but Audrey shows me into the sitting-room conservatory. Two armchairs sit opposite each other by the fire, waiting for us to take our seats. A blanket of blue snow covers the glass ceiling. It feels like we're underground.

Audrey puts the fireguard to the side, opens the brass box, and uses the tongs to throw a bit of turf in the fire. The brass glints like gold.

"Would you like tea, coffee, or hot chocolate?"

"Tea would be great."

"Weak or strong?"

"Strong. And a drop of milk please. A big drop."

"Help yourself to the biscuits. The bathroom is up the corridor. It's the second door on the right."

She closes the door behind her. I delay sitting down because I don't know which armchair is mine. I have a proper gawk at her bookshelf. I like that she has the *Harry Potter* series next to her therapy books.

A terra-cotta bowl of shells sits on the small table by the fire, along with a plate of shortbread biscuits that smell like they are just out of the oven, two glasses of water, and a box of tissues. I take a pair of smooth artemis shells from the bowl—two white shells with their mouths and tails clasped together. I turn them over in my hand and examine the pattern. Blue semicircles run across their ridges.

I pry their mouths open. The two halves break in my hands, spilling sand on the table. I'm still cleaning it up when Audrey comes back in.

"Don't worry, there's a lot of sand in those shells," she says, putting my cup of tea on a coaster. "Your mother actually did the same thing."

She takes her seat and I follow her lead, as though we're on a chat show.

"Is this where the psychoanalysis starts?"

"Touché," she says. "Have you seen someone like me before?"

"No." I lie because I think it's more important to be polite than honest.

"Well, I've been to a lot of different kinds of therapy," she says. "Some were more helpful than others. Sometimes, I knew from the first session that I wasn't going to go back for round two." She gives me a conspiratorial look. "You can use all the techniques in the handbook, but when it boils down to it, therapy is just two people talking in a room. Me trying to understand you. So I always treat the first session with a new client as a trial run. If you feel at the end of this session that I'm not the therapist for you, there will be no fee. It has happened many, many times. I can't expect to be everyone's cup of tea. I will still shake your hand during the Sign of Peace at mass."

I laugh too loud. "OK."

"Everything you say to me stays inside this room. I will never stop you in the shop to talk to you about a session. When I meet you outside this room, I am your old piano teacher. Not a lot of people around here know what I do now."

"Billy was surprised."

Audrey seems amused. "Myself and Billy were in the same class at school."

"Really? You seem older."

She raises her eyebrows. "Is it the gray hair?"

I put my hand over my mouth. "Oh God. I mean wiser. Definitely wiser."

Audrey doesn't say anything. I sip my tea to have something to do. Recross my legs. Look down at my hands in my lap. Inspect my fingernails.

"So," she says. "It's difficult for us to start from scratch because we already know each other. Or rather, we think we know each other. I thought it might be a good idea to start by telling you two things that you probably know about me and one thing that you don't know. Then I'll ask you to do the same. Does that sound reasonable?"

I nod.

"OK, so two things that I think you know about me are rather obvious. I am a piano teacher and my father used to be the local chemist."

"I remember him," I say. Mr. Keane retired a long time ago but I can still picture him behind the counter in his white coat. He looked miserable and spoke through his nose.

"Something you might not know about me is that I trained as a doctor. I studied medicine in college, but I didn't practice for long once I qualified. I was diagnosed with depression in my early twenties and spent some time in the hospital. I became interested in psychiatry and well, that's how I ended up in this line of work."

"Oh." I'm struggling to find an appropriate response.

"Is there anything you think I left out that you know about me?"

"Yes. You have a magnificent bathroom."

"Ha!"

"The most magical in all the land," I say.

"Thank you," she says. "Now, it's your turn."

"OK. Well, you know my mother. And if you have ever spoken to my mother for any prolonged length of time, you know about the dreams."

I try to gauge her reaction, but her expression remains neutral.

"Something that you might not know about me is that I'm afraid of going the same way as my mother. I'm afraid of being stuck at home my whole life and not being able to deal with reality. And if I don't talk to someone about it soon, I feel like it will kill me," I say, looking at my hands. "I mean, I'm not suicidal. I don't have suicidal thoughts at all."

"I understand," Audrey says. "There are some things that you left out that I know about you. You were close to James

Cassidy, who died recently. I know how that has affected your mam. It must also have had a massive impact on you. I can only imagine how difficult it has been for you all. And you jog on the road sometimes. You have a very determined stride when you run. You also seem to have a very close relationship with your uncle."

"Mmmm," I say.

"What does Billy make of you coming here?"

"Billy doesn't know I'm here."

"Who gave you money to come here?"

"Billy thinks Mam is seeing you. Not me."

"So if you decide to see me on a regular basis, would money be an issue?"

"Well, Billy has already been so good to me putting me through college this year . . ."

I don't tell her how thick Billy would be if he knew I was talking to her, but somehow, I think she knows.

"OK. Well, for now, if you decide to come back to see me, there will be no charge. That would certainly make me feel more comfortable about working with you."

"Oh God no, I couldn't do that."

"That doesn't sit well with you."

"No. I mean, thanks a million, but you're providing a service."

"How about in return you clean my bathroom for me?"

"That would hardly cover the cost."

"You underestimate how much I loathe housework."

I laugh. "Are you offering to be my Mr. Miyagi?"

"A younger version, with better hair." She puts out her hand. "Do we have a deal?"

"Deal," I say.

Even though the fire is blazing right in front of us, her hands are cold.

First Impressions

We weren't sure if Xanthe would make it down with the weather. The trains and buses are still out of service. Her boyfriend picked her up on St. Stephen's morning in his dad's Range Rover. She went to meet his parents.

She texts me to say that she is walking over to see the farm.

I'm not expecting her over so early. The sink is full of dishes and we've run out of toilet paper.

"Shit, shit, shit, shit, shit." I grab some dirty dishes and put them in the sink. I text her back: *I'll meet you at the Church! X*

It's bright outside. The cold goes right down into my chest, burning my lungs. The snow has made everything seem celestial. It's like a sheet has been thrown over the village, disguising everything boring and playing up to the fairy-tale narrative of home that I've constructed in college. It almost feels like cheating.

I see her waiting by the entrance to the graveyard. She spots me and we both wave too soon. She's wearing a black faux-fur hat and a burgundy overcoat. She is carrying a basket that, as I get closer, turns out to be a hamper.

We do that thing that girls do when they haven't seen each other in a long time: we stare at each other in disbelief, then hug and squeal as hard as we can for as long as we can.

"How are you?"

"How are *you*?!"

"You look great!"

"You look gorgeous!"

We both know it's ridiculous but the script has to be followed.

"Where did you get the coat?" I ask.

"Oxfam."

"Who donated a coat like that—Anna Karenina?"

I'm looking at the image she has chosen to present to her boyfriend's family. Xanthe has managed to find a hair salon that was open in the snow. Her fringe is cut and her hair is blow-dried to perfection. She has black velvet earmuffs on underneath the hat. She's beautiful. I'm still wearing pajamas underneath my tracksuit and a ski jacket from Aldi that I grabbed from the hot press.

"Where are you going with the basket?" I ask.

"It's just something small."

"Ah Santy, it's huge!"

"Well, there's a reason they call me Santy."

"Thanks. You shouldn't have," I say.

"It's great to be here."

"Have you got the grand tour of the village yet?" I ask.

"No."

"So here we have the church, the school, and the pub." I point them out all clustered together. "Tour complete, all tips welcome."

"That's the pub we're going to tonight?"

"Yeah, that's Cassidy's."

"It looks like somebody's house."

"It is."

"And your house is this way?"

"Yeah, just around the corner, toward the screaming children on the hill. Billy opened up one of the fields as a kind of temporary ski slope for the kids."

"Oh my God, amazing."

"How was your Christmas?" I ask.

"Grand, yeah. I volunteered at the homeless shelter in the morning."

"Of course you did."

"I think my mother was angry at me for not being at home when she was there. She had to go into work in the afternoon so it was just me and Kevin from *Home Alone* keeping each other company."

"Was your dad working too?"

"I don't know actually. Dad doesn't live with us."

"Oh God. I'm sorry."

"Oh, it's completely fine, like. Where's your mam and Billy?" she asks before I can squeeze in another question.

"Mam is asleep but Billy should be around."

We cross the cattle grid and Jacob immediately runs nose-first into Xanthe's crotch.

"Jacob get off her."

"He is the best doggie." Xanthe is trying to look at his face but he insists on burying himself between her legs.

"He's not the worst," I say. When the snow came, Jacob finally left the tractor cab to sleep in the shed. He has put on the weight he lost when James died and he is looking more like himself.

I take the hamper from Xanthe and put it in the kitchen. I try to assess the house through her eyes. Our kitchen is a dark and dank room, almost as small as the one in her apartment in town. The seashells on the windowsill look like dirty crockery. Some of the handles have fallen off the wooden presses and the linoleum floor is warped and bubbling under her feet.

"Your house is so cute!"

"It's a tip at the minute," I say. "Do you want to visit the caravan before or after tea?" I ask.

"Oh before, please. Do you mind if I use your bathroom?"

"Yeah, it's just . . . I'm really sorry but we've run out of toilet roll." I fling presses open looking for kitchen roll or something I can offer her.

"It's totally fine," she says, producing a packet of tissues from her coat pocket. "I can use one of these. Where's the loo?"

"It's upstairs. The first door on the left."

❉

I hear the toilet flush and breathe a sigh of relief that at least the cistern is working. I drum my fingers on the table, waiting for her to reappear. Then I hear a murmur of voices. I leg it upstairs but it's too late. Mam is already showing Xanthe into the Tabernacle and she's walking around, looking at the walls like she's in the Louvre.

I aim for damage control. "Xanthe, this is my—"

"This room is just incredible." Xanthe turns around from inspecting a page of *Finnegan's Wake* plastered on the wardrobe. "It's *so* lovely to meet you, Maeve."

She's acting like she is meeting the Pope. Mam clutches the sleeves of her red knitted *geansaí* and pulls them down over her hands. She seems suspicious of Xanthe as she watches her touch the sacred items of the Tabernacle. It's an impressive room, especially compared to the rest of our house.

"Gorgeous," Xanthe whispers, placing Sebastian the skull back in his rightful place.

"Your coat is beautiful." Mam is looking at Xanthe with a mixture of admiration and envy.

"Thank you very much." Xanthe smiles. "Debbie tells me that you're a writer?"

Mam frowns. "Did she?"

"What kind of stuff do you write?" Xanthe tucks a loose strand of hair behind her ear.

Mam blinks.

"Sorry, that's probably an impossible question."

"I write down the dreams." Mam rushes to get the stacks of copybooks under her desk.

"Xanthe, I think we better go out to Billy," I say, but Mam has already given her an Aisling copy to flick through.

"I write down the dreams that come to me," Mam explains. "Most of them resist narrative form, so sometimes I attempt to record the audio or try to sketch the dimensions or certain images that stand out."

"You do this every morning?" Xanthe pulls out the chair and sits down at the desk. "Debbie, do you mind if I have that cup of tea?"

I sigh. "Mam, do you want tea?"

Mam bites her lip.

"There's some earl gray in the hamper I brought," Xanthe says.

"I might have one of those," Mam mumbles.

"Great! Me too," Xanthe says, flicking through the pages of Mam's journal. "Thanks, Debs."

＊

When I come back, Mam has lit some incense and they are talking about tai chi and chakra healing.

"Honestly, Maeve, it will change your life." Xanthe takes the cup of earl gray from me. "Did you put milk in this?" she asks.

"Are you supposed to?"

"It's OK, I'll drink it."

"No, I have oat milk in the fridge," I say. "Mam, do you want milk in yours?"

"Yes, please."

I stomp out of the room and down the stairs to play waitress again.

✳

An hour later, Mam and Xanthe are still going on about the dreams. Mam has loosened up and is talking freely, sometimes laughing and allowing Xanthe to see the gaps where her teeth should be.

"Honestly, Maeve, I think you're an inspiration," Xanthe says, clutching Mam's hand. "People have such a narrow view of what they consider to be reality. We only ever catch a glimpse of our shared imagination in art or music."

"Well, people are afraid to be ignorant," Mam says. "And they are uncomfortable with the thought that when we enter the deepest levels of a dream, we break free of ourselves. Our society is so fettered to the idea of the individual. Real inspiration comes from outside of ourselves, the communal, that which we don't know, that which can exist only in dreams. Mozart composed directly from dream states. Kafka wrote exclusively at night. Even the molecular structure of DNA was discovered in a dream." She throws her hands up in the air as if to say, "What more proof do you need?"

"And on that note, I think it's time to go outside," I say. "Xanthe hasn't seen the farm yet."

"Do you want to come with us?" Xanthe asks Mam.

I shoot Mam a look.

"No, I'm going to do a bit of writing," Mam says, letting go of Xanthe's hand. "You've inspired me."

I resist the urge to roll my eyes. Before we leave, Xanthe scribbles down a list of book recommendations, the name of a yoga class, and her phone number on the cover of an Aisling copy.

✳

"Is Maeve coming to the pub tonight?" she asks, as I show her the way to the caravan.

"Probably not."

"I could have talked to her for hours."

"She likes you."

"Well, I wasn't expecting her to be so . . ." Xanthe stops walking. "You know that your mother is amazing, right?"

"She is fluent in bullshit."

"I think she makes a lot of sense."

"You don't have to live with her," I say.

※

We open the caravan door to the sight of Billy adding an empty Heineken can to his Christmas tree tower.

"Billy—"

"Ssssshhhh," he says, raising a hand and placing the can on top of the tower.

He turns around to us. "This must be Santy."

"Billy." Xanthe shakes his hand. "Nice to meet you."

Billy looks at me. "She has a solid handshake."

"Not too much of a squeeze, but firm. And definitely not watery," Xanthe says.

"Oh, watery is the Judas of handshakes. Never trust one."

Xanthe's smile is trembling. I realize she's nervous. She puts her hands behind her back and walks around, surveying the interior of Billy's home and pretending not to notice him looking at her.

"Xanthe. I was expecting a blond," he says.

"I was a fair-haired baby."

"You share your name with an extraterrestrial mountain range."

"The Xanthe mountains on Mars, I believe," she says.

"A woman on Mars. Blessed is she among men."

"Oh my God," she squeals, and kneels down, peering into a cardboard box on Billy's bed. I go over to see what it is. It's the hedgehog.

"That's Edward," Billy says.

"He's so cute!"

"I'm glad someone thinks so. Debbie wanted to kill him."

"I did not."

"He's breathing quite heavily," Xanthe says.

"I know." Billy crouches down beside her. "You'd swear he was smoking forty a day. He got a bash on the snout, so that might have something to do with it."

"Look at his little feet!"

"Yeah, his feet are a lot longer than you'd expect." Billy points to the line that separates its spines from its stomach. "These are very strong muscles. Carrying an army of prickles on your back is like wearing a really expensive evening dress. When Edward here needs to move fast, these muscles are able to lift up the dress and he's able to make a quick escape."

"David Attenborough over here," I say.

"How did ye get a piano to fit in here?" Xanthe asks.

"Don't even get me started." I sigh. "Half the keys don't work, it's out of tune, and no one can play it."

Xanthe runs her fingers along the keys. Webs of dust collect in her fingers and she brushes them away.

"This girl can play," Billy says.

"Oh God, no," she says.

"You can tell by her posture." Billy nudges me. It's like he's taking about the hedgehog again. "When she sits down now her back will be poker straight."

"No pressure now, Xanthe," I say.

"I don't know what to play."

"Play whatever you like."

"Don't play anything sad," Billy says.

I punch him on the arm. "Play whatever you like."

The keys of the piano are a dirty cream—the color of cigarette-stained fingernails. Xanthe puts her fingers into position and lets her fingers spell out a melody, bowing her head toward them.

"What's the name of that?" Billy asks.

"It's called 'Dawn.' It's from the *Pride and Prejudice* soundtrack."

"The Keira Knightley one?" Billy asks.

Xanthe stops playing. "Are you a fan of Keira?"

"Well, she could do with eating a ham sandwich or two."

Xanthe laughs.

"Billy, you can't comment about women's weight like that," I argue.

He throws his eyes up to heaven, playing a charade for Xanthe. "Keep going there," he tells her. "You're a regular Marianne Dashwood."

"Xanthe is more of a Jane Fairfax," I say.

"You do *not* read Austen," Xanthe stops playing again and stares at Billy.

"It's his new guilty pleasure," I say.

"There's nothing guilty about it," Billy says. "The woman is a genius." There's something about the way Billy is looking at Xanthe, like there's a light behind his eyes that hasn't been switched on in a long time.

Twelve Pubs

Xanthe arrives down to the pub wearing a novelty jumper with a Rudolf bobble nose, a tight black leather skirt with sheer tights, and knee-high boots. I'm relieved and disappointed when I see that she is alone. I had psyched myself up to see them together.

"Where's your fella?" I ask.

"He's coming down later," she says, sliding into the snug beside me.

"What are you having?" Billy asks.

"I think I'll go on the Heineken."

"My kind of woman," says Billy. "Shirley! Another pint over here when you're ready."

We're gearing up for a long night ahead. Stephen's night is the village Christmas jumper party—a fundraiser for the local GAA club. Everyone calls it the Twelve Pubs.

"Are you doing the Twelve Pubs?" Xanthe asks.

"Oh God, no," Billy says. "Too much exercise."

Shirley's pub is on a little island of land that forms a Y-junction. Some people started a tradition of doing a lap of the pub after every pint, treating every lap as if it's a new pub. Only the hard-core ones do twelve laps but they take it very seriously.

"I might do a lap or two for the craic," I say. "It's actually great to do when the kids are still around. They get really into it."

"Off their heads on fizzy drinks," Billy says.

"What time does it start?"

Billy turns around and roars across to Shirley. "What time is kickoff, Shirl?"

Shirley comes over and puts down Xanthe's pint beside Billy. "Seven o'clock."

"Shirley, this is Xanthe, Debbie's friend from college."

"Nice to meet you," Xanthe says.

"Hi, pet." Shirley pats her on the head and takes the empties off the table.

Xanthe takes out her phone. I'm guessing she's making sure he's down before seven. My heart is thumping already.

✳

Xanthe is quizzing Billy about milking.

"Do they have names?"

"No, they have numbers though."

"Can you tell them apart?"

"You get to know them by their tits."

Xanthe bursts out laughing.

"I'm not trying to be funny," Billy says. "It's true."

"Xanthe's a vegan," I inform him.

Billy raises his eyebrows and inhales sharply.

"I'm not against all dairy farming," she clarifies.

"You have a T-shirt that says, 'My oat milk frees all the cows from the yard.'"

"I'm not against rural farmers making a living. And your cows seem to have it good," she says to Billy.

"Bitches have a better life than we do," Billy grumbles.

✳

Billy starts playing the generous uncle card, refusing to let us pay for drinks.

"What happened to rounds?" I ask when he tells me to put my money away.

"It's Christmas," he says, as though I'm the one who's been sulking all winter, bitching about how much work has to be done on the farm.

Xanthe and I watch him as he goes on a tour of the pub to shower season's greetings on everyone.

"He's like a politician," I say.

"He's class."

"It's embarrassing."

"Debbie, I don't know how to break this to you, but your uncle is a babe."

"What? Ew. Stop it. He's an old man."

"He's not that old. And he reads Austen."

"I made him watch some period-drama movies with me. And he's old."

"He's not that old."

"La-la-la-la-la, going to block this conversation from my memory."

"I'm just saying."

"You have a boyfriend," I remind her.

She laughs. "I'm allowed to have a boyfriend and fancy other people."

"Not Billy," I say. "Seriously, please stop."

"So . . ." Xanthe searches for a change of subject. "Maeve didn't make it down?"

"It's hard for her to be down the pub this year, with James gone," I say. "Shirley is James's mother and well . . . Mam and Shirley don't really get on."

"So she's home alone?"

"Yeah, she likes her own company though."

Xanthe looks like she's going to say something, but decides against it.

"How was Christmas?" she asks instead.

"We all survived anyway."

❋

Xanthe wants to go over and play pool with Billy, but Murt Mooney is over there and I'm afraid Billy would slag me about him in front of Xanthe.

We go to the bar. I say hello to Mark as he passes with a tray of drinks.

"Who's that?" Xanthe asks.

"James's brother. He milks with Billy now."

"You never mentioned him," she says, raising her eyebrows. "He seems nice."

"Mark is like a brother. I wouldn't go near him with a barge pole," I say.

"I didn't say anything."

"Anyway, he has a girlfriend."

She puts her hands up. "I didn't say anything."

It's past seven o'clock. The Twelve Pubbers are already on their third lap, sweating in their woolly jumpers. A few rule-enforcers are getting angry with the group beside us who keep forgetting to pull their invisible elves off their pints before taking a drink.

Xanthe checks her phone again.

"Himself?" I ask.

"Yeah he gets a bit anxious about going out. It's because he doesn't drink. He's afraid everyone thinks he's boring. I tried saying to him that having one beer wouldn't be the worst thing, you know, to be sociable. He's a bit off with me."

"As in thick?"

"No, he never really gets angry. Just, I don't know, distracted. I don't know if he'd give me the time of day if he didn't fancy me."

I laugh. "Oh boo-hoo, poor Santy. You can't complain about being too good-looking."

"I'm not saying that. And it goes both ways as well. Like, would I be with him if I didn't like the look of him? We don't exactly have mind-blowing conversations."

This piece of information makes me happier than it should. I take a sip of my drink and try to hide my delight. I want to get Xanthe drunk tonight, I decide. Very drunk.

❋

I clock him the moment he walks in. The girls from school perk up as soon as they see him. They talk in a more animated way, laughing louder, taking pictures, and looking scarily happy. He has a nervous energy about him, slapping the lads he meets on the back. He seems too skinny to be a hurler. The other lads on the team have potato faces and look like early versions of their fathers. He is all cheekbones and long fingers. He'd make a beautiful woman. He seems to be conscious of this femininity because he's all bravado when he knows people are watching. Some girl stops him to take a photo with her and he puts his arm around her shoulder, tilts his head sideways, and points to her.

He creeps up behind Xanthe and puts his hands over her eyes. I try to meet his eyes without blushing.

"Oh, I wonder who it is," Xanthe says drily.

He releases his hands and kisses her on the cheek.

"Debbie." He holds out his hand. "Thanks for putting in a good word for me."

"Ah, I can't take any credit for this," I say, and feel my face flush. I shake his hand.

"What are you drinking?" he asks Xanthe.

"Can you get me a glass of white wine actually?"

"Debbie?" He looks at me.

"Ah no, I'm grand for a drink," I say, holding up my glass.

"Two glasses of white," Xanthe says.

"No honestly, I'm grand." I kick her when he leaves. "Don't let him buy me another drink."

"He can do what he likes." She sighs. "I feel bad about bitching about him."

"You weren't bitching, you were telling the truth. That's allowed."

✳

He comes back from the bar with two bottles of white wine and two fresh wine glasses.

"I said two glasses!" Xanthe slaps his wrist.

"Sure bottles are cheaper in the long run."

"Ah Jesus, where are you going?" I say. "Thanks very much."

He holds his hands up. "I will not be held responsible for the carnage that comes after this."

He stands up and pours Xanthe a glass with one hand behind his back. "How was your day?" he asks.

"I prefer Debbie's house to yours," Xanthe says.

"Let me guess, more books?"

"More books, more cows, more craic."

"Debbie, she gives out to me because I don't read," he says.

"Not even *Harry Potter*?" I ask.

"I've seen the movies."

We both shake our heads. "It's not the same."

"It's not my fault. I have a condition. I get narcolepsy when I try to read. I just conk out. It's not something I have any control over. Anyway, I'm not book-smart like ye."

I smile over at Xanthe. I'm glad that he has at least put us in the same category.

✳

After our second bottle of wine, Xanthe musters up the confidence to play pool with the auld lads. She is trying and failing to use the cue as a baton twirler. Billy calls her and she swings around, nearly taking the head off Dooley.

I thought he would go off with the hurlers, but he takes Xanthe's seat beside me.

"How are you finding Trinity?" he asks.

"Oh good, yeah." My mouth is too dry to talk so I swallow and try again. "A bit overwhelming for a country bumpkin. How's UCD?"

"Much the same, really. It's massive. There are roundabouts on campus and everything."

"You didn't say that out loud did you?" I ask.

"I made headlines: Culchie Amazed by Roundabouts."

I laugh.

He nods over to the bar. "Father John is some man."

The priest is standing behind the bar giving out Tayto crisps to people like it's Holy Communion. The Twelve Pubbers have formed an orderly queue, shuffling toward him with hands clasped in front of them.

"Oh Jesus," I say.

"Mad for the session."

"Mad for Jesus and mad for pints."

A looming silence lingers around the edges of our conversation. We're already running out of things to say.

"Xanthe is a legend," I say, watching her take a shot.

"She's great. I feel really lucky to have met her."

"Good." I nod. "Good."

"Ye're good mates?"

I'm not sure if that's a statement or a question so I just nod again.

"It's packed in here," he says.

"It always is on Twelve Pubs."

I look over at the girls from school. They are eyeing us. Any one of them would give a fake tanned leg to be talking to him. I don't know why I'm getting upset. I'm disappointed that the moment is so ordinary. It takes a few seconds of silence to make me realize that I'm bored.

"I've to go to the bathroom," I announce.

He seems relieved. He stands up for me to pass him. There is no brushing of shoulders or spark of electricity.

I turn around to face him again. "You know, this is the first time we've ever actually spoken?"

His eyes widen. "I suppose it is, yeah!"

"Yeah." I go to walk away but I turn back again. "You know, for someone I've never spoken to, I have the most complicated relationship with you in my head. It's like a grudge that I can't let go of? Like I'm angry with you, but I don't know why?"

"OK." He nods, but his eyes dart away for a second. He has no idea what I mean.

I run away from what I've just said. I push past people queuing up for a pint, past the girls from school perched together in their stilettos, past Billy who is taking a photo of Xanthe pointing to the sign above the stove that says ARSE-WARMER.

❋

There's a girl vomiting in the cubicle beside me. I take deep breaths on the toilet seat. I'm not sure what I expected to happen. I'm annoyed with myself. I'm angry with someone I don't know because he is not fitting into my fantasy. He's not going out with Xanthe to make me jealous. He's a genuine, nice, boring guy who just doesn't fancy me.

I message Xanthe: *Why are you flirting with my uncle?*

My phone vibrates on the floor and flashes up a message from Xanthe.

What?

The phone rings. I don't answer.

Another message: *????????*

＊

A few minutes later there's a bang on the cubicle door. "Debbie, let me in."

If I don't move or make a sound this whole situation might go away.

Xanthe's head pops over the bathroom stall. "Are we going to talk like this?"

I unlock the door. She barrels into the cubicle and shuts the door behind her. "So, what was that about?"

I shrug like a spoiled child.

"What's wrong?"

"Your boyfriend thinks I'm a psycho."

"No he doesn't. I need to pee."

We swap places and Xanthe pulls down her tights.

"Oh my God," I say.

"What?"

"You have a full bush!" I exclaim.

"Excuse me?"

"You don't shave your fanny! This makes me so happy. Does he like a full bush?"

"What? No! He hasn't seen it yet."

"Oh, right."

She flushes the toilet, pulls up her tights, and shimmies her skirt down again.

"Billy fancies you," I tell her.

"Where are you getting all this from?"

"Don't tell me that you weren't flirting with him."

"I wasn't flirting with him. I'm trying to have a good night. Where is all this coming from?"

"It's coming from you flirting with my uncle."

"It's my first time meeting your family and I want to make a good impression."

"You could try not flirting with him."

"So fucking *what* if I *am* flirting with him?"

"You have a boyfriend!"

"I fucking know! You don't own people, Debbie. You can't control how other people feel. I swear to God, sometimes I feel like I'm in a relationship with you."

"Oh fuck off, Xanthe." I open the cubicle door to a queue of my neighbors waiting for the toilet.

❋

I try to lift up the hatch to go behind the bar. I knock a few glasses and everyone cheers when they smash on the floor. Mark is cleaning up the mess with a dustpan and brush.

I'm leaning against him when he says, "Debbie, I think it's time to go home."

"Are you coming home with me?" I murmur.

"No, Debs."

"Are you kicking me out?"

"I just said I think it's time to go home."

"For me to go home," I say, pointing to myself.

"Yes."

"Nobody else."

He sighs.

"I'll have a double vodka and tonic please," I say.

"I can't serve you any more drinks, Debbie. You've had enough."

"Everyone in the pub has had enough, Mark. Why are you picking on me? Is it because you fancy me?"

"No, Debs."

"So you won't go home with me?"

"I have a girlfriend, Debbie."

"Didn't stop you the last time."

"The last time, my head was all over the place. My brother was lying dead in a coffin and your mam was lying on top of him and you were all over me like a fucking rash."

"Wow." I feel those words rush around my head. They sober me up. "Thanks for that."

"I'm sorry. Listen, Debs, I want to be your friend. I think you're a mentaller—mad craic like, but I don't fancy you."

"You think I'm mad," I say slowly.

"Mad craic like. You're great craic!"

"OK."

"Are you thick with me?"

"No."

"Are you sure?"

"Yeah," I say. "I think you're right, though. I need to go home."

He slaps me on the back and smiles. "You'll thank me tomorrow."

❇

Xanthe is outside the pub smoking, waiting for me. "Debbie! What the fuck? What is wrong with you?"

I grab her by the elbow and pull her away from the crowd

of smokers. "Sure there's nothing wrong with me. You've hogged all the problems—all the misery."

"Are you making fun of . . . you're the only person I told about my mental illness."

"You're the only person I told about my mental illness," I mimic her, waving my hands around.

She looks at me like I'm a different person.

"You couldn't *wait* to tell me about your mental illness," I say. "But it's just another way for people to take money off you! You paid a doctor to tell you that you're special. That you're sad and edgy. You're so full of shadow and light, Xanthe. So complicated. So many layers. Not just a pretty girl."

"Being depressed isn't a lifestyle choice, Debs," Xanthe says in a wobbly voice.

"Oh fuck off, you already have everything and you're still not happy. I don't care how much money you spend making yourself miserable. You're a fucking snowflake, Xanthe," I say, backing away from her. "A snowflake."

❆

Between the snow outside and the drink inside me, the world seems surreal. I don't feel cold yet, even though I've left my coat on my seat in the snug. I trudge home leaving the noise of the pub behind me. The Twelve Pubbers have turned the snow on the road to brown sludge.

Jacob comes to greet me at the gate and I push him away from me. I fumble around in my bag for my key. We never used to lock the door but recently Mam has become obsessed with security. I try the key in the lock but it won't budge.

"Come on," I moan.

✳

I go around the back. The caravan is locked. It's never been locked before. Billy said he'd get a lock when there was something worth robbing in it. Now I feel like he's done it on purpose to piss me off.

I scramble my way onto the roof, and lie on my back. My eyes get heavy. I'm starting to feel the cold. It's spreading up my legs and into my belly. It reminds me of walking into the sea—sunlit zone, twilight zone, midnight zone, abyss . . . the hadal zone of Persephone, the winter queen.

Inside

The caravan coughs underneath me. There's a rattle. Something must have fallen inside. My fingernails scratch the ice on the roof. I stare at my hands. They look very red but I'm not cold. I feel like my entire body is floating in a snow globe of white wine. I stand up and try to adjust my wonky view to the horizon. Stare out across the fresh blue-tinted snow. Cherish the glorious moment of defiance where drink triumphs over reality. It's worth it, I think: drinking. Just for this.

I'm thirsty. I jump off the caravan and put some snow in my mouth. It burns my tongue so I spit it out.

The caravan is still making noise. I remember the hedgehog. Maybe it's after escaping from the box. The door is still locked, so I scrape the ice off the window and peer through a gash of clear glass—enough so that I can see one of Billy's tweed coats swaying back and forth. I make the gash bigger and back away from the window. I can see a hand.

It's Billy's hand. He's hanging from the ceiling. Off the ground. Swaying back and forth, back and forth.

"BILLY!" I bang on the window. "BILLY!"

I look around for something to break the glass. I'm shaking. There's nothing. Nothing.

And then Mam comes sprinting around the side of the caravan with a hammer. She tries the door.

"It's locked!" I shout, but she is already running over to the window.

"Stand back." Mam smashes the hammer into the window. She breaks through one layer of glass and then two, until the hole is big enough for her to crawl through. She launches herself forward and tries to push through the shards of glass, cutting her hands and face. She hauls herself in, stands up, and cuts the rope. Billy falls to the floor.

"I'll call an ambulance!" I shout.

"They won't come in the snow."

I call Shirley but her phone goes straight to voicemail.

"Don't come in," Mam says.

"Is he alive?"

"He'll be fine."

"Don't lie."

I'm halfway through the window but she pushes me back out. I try again but this time, she grabs hold of my hands and squeezes them until I can feel them. We're both shaking. She looks at me, her bottom lip over her top, her chin wobbling. "I said, don't come in."

So I stay outside.

I walk around in circles. Jacob is jumping up and down on me, yelping. He knows that something is going on. I can't stay still and I can't think. Think. I look across the fields and start running.

※

A disgruntled Shirley unbolts the pub door.

"Billy!" I'm hysterical. "He's after hanging himself! He's dying. He's dead."

Shirley and Mark come running back over the fields with me. Shirley is asking questions but I can't answer them.

She keeps saying, "But the ambulance won't get here in the snow," and I keep saying, "I know, I know, I know."

※

The door of the caravan is open. We rush inside and Mam is helping Billy into his armchair.

"Jesus and Mary and Joseph. What are ye doing here?" he croaks.

"You're OK!" I go to hug him, but he swats me away.

"Sure why wouldn't I be?" he says, looking past me to Mark and Shirley. "Lads, you're looking well."

Shirley is in her nightie and Mark has a pair of boxers and a coat on. They both look at the broken glass on the ground, the rope on the floor, and the welts around Billy's neck. He pulls his jacket collar up to cover the marks.

Mam mumbles, "I'll leave ye to it," and edges her way past Shirley out the door.

"Are you all right, Billy?" Shirley ventures.

"I'm grand, sure I was only pulling her leg and she goes wakening the whole parish." Billy's voice is shaking. His face is purple and he can't stop coughing.

There's an awkward silence. Mark and Shirley look at their feet.

Billy claps his hands together. "Sure now that we're all here we may as well have a party."

"Billy, we should probably call an ambulance to make sure you haven't done yourself any harm," Shirley says, taking out her phone.

"There's a bottle of whiskey in the press there and some mugs up top." Billy nods to Mark, who proceeds to get the whiskey out.

Shirley turns to me. "Are you OK, hun?"

"I'm fine." I put my hand on Billy's shoulder. "Billy, for God's sake, let us help you."

Billy looks at my hand on his shoulder and starts to laugh. "You know what? I don't even know how we're related. You're some drama queen."

Shirley puts her arm around my shoulders. "Come on, pet, let's get you inside."

"She must have had a bad dream," Billy says.

I scramble out of Shirley's grasp and box him in the face. It's a satisfying punch. I see a flash of truth in his eyes. "How fucking dare you," I say, and turn to Shirley. "I'll make my own way inside."

Nelly

I knock on the Tabernacle door. Mam flings it open and hugs me.

"I'm sorry that you had to see that," she whispers, rocking me in her arms.

"How did you know?" I ask. "How did you know he would do that?"

She frowns. "Will you do me a favor? Will you wait until after I finish writing and then I'll explain?"

"Ah Mam—"

"Please? It's important."

"OK."

She sits cross-legged on her chair and scribbles away in her Aisling copybook.

My head is beginning to pound. The sound of her scribbling soothes me. I lie on the bed and stare at her wall of words.

Mam used to tell me that the reason she kept sticking pages to the walls was to make them thicker to hide her secrets from Nelly who lived behind the wallpaper. Nelly was my grandmother's invention. She claimed that Nelly stuck her nose out of the wallpaper at night and crawled into our thoughts while we slept.

There's a new poem on a piece of newspaper that Mam has smoothed onto the wall. It's called "Raglan Lane." It's a Brendan Kennelly poem, written in response to Patrick Kavanagh's "Raglan Road."

"I saw Brendan Kennelly on a bench in Trinity once," I whisper to Nelly.

Mam sits on the end of the bed and begins to rub my feet. Her hands feel like fire. "Did you say hello to him?" she asks.

"No. He had dandruff on the shoulders of his jacket—lots of it. It looked like his head was creating its own climate—making it snow in September."

Mam wriggles her fingers in between my toes and rubs the spaces in between.

"Mam, tell me what's going on."

She's pulling my toes out one at a time, turning them slightly and waiting for them to crack before moving on. My little toe snaps like a broken wishbone.

"How did you know to check on him?"

"Why do you think I sleep so much? Billy says that he doesn't dream. That's not true. His dreams come to me. I keep an eye on them. When I woke up from this one, I just had a feeling. I knew what was happening."

"You saved his life, Mam."

She shakes her head and hands me her Aisling copy. "I wrote it down. The dream. What I could remember of it. It's contaminated now that I've tried to pin it down with words, but it's the best I can do. Read it. It reads like a child's memory. When Billy dreams about his mammy, he goes back to being a little boy."

I open up the copybook and read the last entry:

Sandman

The baby on the label of the gripe water bottle looks like an old man. When I take the bottle out from its hiding place underneath the sink, Mammy sings the tagline, "Granny told Mother and Mother told me."

Gripe water is meant for babies but his mammy says we're all big babies—even mammies. I am only allowed a thimble but Mammy is allowed to drink a whole glass because she is bigger than me.

It's my job to make Mammy's nightcap in the kitchen when Daddy goes to sleep. I only got the job because I caught her drinking in the kitchen and she didn't want me to tell anybody. Mammy explained that she's not able to fall asleep the way Daddy does. She needs her Sandman. The Sandman is me.

The sand comes in green capsules that Mammy gets from Keane's pharmacy. They're sent from the moon. There's a factory there where the tiny moon people blow moon dust into time capsules to send to Mammy to help her sleep. I tasted the moon dust once and it tasted disgusting. When we come back from the pharmacy, Mammy cracks open the capsules from their foil and tips the moon dust into the fancy sugar bowl we're supposed to leave empty for Christmas. She does it quickly. Her hands are shaking. She slits the foil with her fingernail, opens the capsules, and tips the sand into the bowl.

Every night, I make my special recipe. I pour a wine glass of gripe water and add two bottle-caps of vodka. I stir a spoonful of sand in and watch it disappear like sugar in tea.

Mammy isn't sleeping much these days. And when she does, she says that she has bad dreams. So every night, I add an extra spoon of sand into her drink. Every night, I add one more, just for luck. I stir it in quickly. I don't want to get in trouble like the time I opened up all the doors of the advent calendar and let Jesus out too early.

There is so much sand in the glass that it has stopped disappearing. I swirl the glass around again but the sand sits at the bottom of the glass like fallen snow. Mammy sits down beside me. We cheers— clink thimble against wine glass—and she drinks it—all of it—in one go.

Reason

I go out to the caravan to check on Billy. He is sweeping up the broken window with a dustpan and brush. The shards of glass seem like ice that has broken through the window and Billy looks like winter's janitor tidying up.

"Mind your feet," he says.

"It's OK, I'm wearing shoes."

"Show's over. My audience has left," Billy says. "Thanks for bringing them around."

"I didn't know what to do."

"Well, now we know not to trust you in a real emergency."

"Billy."

He stops sweeping and looks up at me. "Yes?"

"Are we going to talk about this properly?"

He gestures for me to take a seat. "Be my guest."

I sit down and look around at the stacks of old newspapers, his unmade bed, and dingy kitchenette. Billy has changed his clothes. A crumb of glass is on the arm of the chair. I pick it up and roll it up and down the length of my thumb with the tip of my index finger.

"What is it you want to talk about?" Billy asks, emptying the shower of broken glass into a bin bag.

"It wasn't a joke."

"What wasn't?"

"The reason you're wearing that polo neck."

"These are my normal clothes."

"You can pretend all you like, but I know what I saw."

"Do you now."

"Yes."

"So tell me then. Tell me what you know."

I go to the press underneath his sink and rummage around until I find it, hidden at the back. I hold up the empty bottle of gripe water.

Billy laughs. "So this is the shite that your mother has been filling you with?"

"She wrote it down."

"Oh you're helping her to interpret the *dreams* now is it? You're going to spend your whole life bearing witness to these *dreams*? You've finally fallen for her bullshit."

"I know it doesn't make sense when I say it out loud. I hardly believe myself but—"

"But Maeve has been filling your head with shite. I'm telling you, Debbie, once you start listening to her, it's game over."

"Mam just saved your life. She is the only reason you're alive. And this is how you repay her."

"Repay her? What's this? I don't do enough for Maeve, is that it?"

"I don't mean it like that."

"How the *fuck* am I supposed to do more for your mother than I already am?"

"Well she knows—"

"What does she know? Tell me what she knows?"

"She knows why you tried to kill yourself. She knows the reason why."

"The reason?"

"Yes, the reason, Billy."

"You want a reason? You want to know? This has got nothing to do with my childhood or my mother or my fucking *dreams*. *You* are the reason. You. Once upon a time, you were the only thing keeping me going. And I tried my best with you, I really did, but you're your mother's daughter now. I've washed my hands of you. Now get the fuck out."

"I'm not leaving you here alone."

"Get out or I'll throw you out."

※

Mam finds me sitting outside the caravan. My teeth are chattering but I can't feel the cold. I can't feel anything.

She crouches down beside me. "You've a session with Audrey to go to."

"I can't go."

"I think it would be a good idea."

"Why is everyone pretending that everything is OK?"

"It's not OK. That's why I think you should go. You're an hour late but I rang her to apologize. I told her you're on the way over."

Ophelia

Audrey hands me a basin filled with cleaning supplies. Yellow rubber gloves, Windolene, kitchen roll, a green scouring pad, a blue J-cloth, a bottle of Cif, and a bottle of Toilet Duck are arranged like gifts in a hamper.

She holds up a toothbrush. "This is for the tricky corners you can't get at with the cloth."

I nod.

"Take as long as you need. I have the highest of standards."

"I understand."

I expected Audrey to know. I expected Mam to have told her. I expected her to open the door and I'd fall into her arms and she'd hold me and I didn't think past that because I was so sure it would happen.

I survey her perfectly clean bathroom and feel like I'm going to explode. Maybe I could smash the mirror. See if I could stand up in the toilet, balance on one foot, and try to flush myself down. I want her to come back in and see me lying in a bath of blood after cutting myself open—a display gruesome enough to shock Ophelia.

Instead, I decide to play the martyr. I do the most radical, unnatural thing I can think of and clean every inch of Audrey's bathroom.

✳

The tiles in the shower keep threatening to fall apart on me. As I scrub the spaces in between the brown, hexagonal tiles, flecks of white break off in pieces like flecks of shell that I crunch into white sand.

✳

I'm still scrubbing the sand from the tiles when Audrey knocks on the door.

"Debbie?"

"I'm not finished."

"It's just," she peeks in. "It's getting late."

"Oh. Sorry."

"That's all right. Do you want to come into the front room? I'll stick on the kettle."

✳

"Last night, Billy tried to kill himself."

I say it when she's handing me my cup of tea.

Audrey's hand freezes and the tea wobbles. "Is he OK?"

"Yeah," I say, taking the cup from her. "Everyone is pretending it didn't happen."

Audrey is standing in front of the fire, holding on to the mantelpiece.

"I thought Mam would have told you," I say.

"She didn't. Billy?"

I nod.

"That's . . . well, I can't begin to imagine how you feel."

"He said it was a joke—a practical joke. Which is clearly

bullshit. He's not talking to me." I'm crying now. "He's being really mean."

"Oh Debbie."

The tears come harder and louder as I feel her arms around me. I cling to her to make sure she's real, afraid that if I let go she'll disappear.

Lady Bracknell

I wake from a dreamless sleep. I'm not at home. I'm lying on a couch. I think my arm is dead because I can see it in front of me but I can't feel it. The hand moves.

"Ah!"

"It's all right," Audrey murmurs.

"I'm so sorry!" I spring out of the couch. It feels even weirder standing over her.

"It's all right," she says, sitting up and opening and closing her fist. "I tried to move you to a bed, but you wouldn't go. And well, you wouldn't let go of my hand so this was the best I could do. You have an impressively strong grip, even in your sleep."

"I am mortified."

"You're grand." She claps her hands together. "Now, breakfast."

"Oh no—"

"Don't argue with me. You're not leaving here without something to eat."

She skips out of the room and I wonder if I should follow her or stay. My clothes stink, my hands are chapped, and I smell like cleaning detergent. It feels like I'm after sleeping with my old piano teacher.

I creep into the kitchen. It's small but homely and smells like baking. Audrey slaps rashers onto tinfoil and sticks them under the grill. There is a collage of memorial cards on the side of her fridge. The more I look at their serene faces, the less morbid they seem.

"I hope you eat meat," Audrey says, tossing sausages into the frying pan.

"Oh yeah," I say. "Can I help at all?"

"Actually, if you don't mind, you can feed the hens for me."

"Of course." I'm relieved that I don't have to stand in awkward silence. "They are doing well to survive the winter."

"Oh, they are a hardy bunch. The bag of feed is just outside the door. Fill up their bowl—you'll see it when you're out there." She takes a jacket off the crook and hands it to me. "If you wear this and put up the hood they'll think it's me. That way they won't make strange with you."

A fresh layer of snow has fallen last night, but there is only a light dusting on the path that has been cleared from the back door to the coop. The bag of feed is heavier than I thought. I end up dragging it behind me. I can see a matronly hen outside the coop standing on one leg and holding the other up in disgust, like an old woman who just stepped in a puddle.

I'm remembering the game we used to play in primary school. There was a gap in the fence that separated Audrey Keane's garden from the school playground. We used to sneak in to play a game called Catch the Chicken at break-time. If you were lucky enough to catch one you threw it up in the air and it went berserk. We felt it in our guts that the game was cruel, but it was so much fun. The hens would tremble if we even looked at them. And they looked so funny trying to run away, squawking for help.

I pour the feed into the bowl. One by one, the other hens pop their heads out of their boxes. A brown one comes running over neck first, fluttering her feathers.

"There you go." I try to pet it, but it jerks away.

※

The table is set with Delft cups and saucers. Billy has the same set of Delft gathering dust in the caravan. I remember I used to trace the blue willow pattern while he told me the legend of the two doves. The morning sun glints off the silver cutlery. There is a plate of rashers, sausages, and grilled tomatoes and a basket of fresh scones, with pots of jam and cream. I smile at the side plate of white bread soldiers for dipping into our soft-boiled eggs. Audrey makes a pot of coffee and pours us each a wine glass of orange juice. I feel fancy holding it in my hand. I have the urge to hold my pinky finger up while I take a sip.

"How are the hens?" she asks.

"Grand. There's one out there that is disgusted by the snow. She seems really posh. She turned down her beak at the feed like she was disappointed it wasn't caviar."

"That would be Lady Bracknell," Audrey says.

"Do they all have names?"

"They do. There is Lady Bracknell, Lord Goring, the Duchess of Berwick, Algernon, Gwendolyn, and Bunbury. I used to have more but the fox got them."

"'Be yourself. Everyone else is already taken,'" I quote.

"Yes. It turns out hens and Oscar Wilde characters have a lot in common. They are a bunch of neurotic lunatics."

"At least they're original. It's hard to be original these days." I immediately regret saying something so clichéd.

"I think people can be original, they just don't always have the courage to be who they really are. It's courage we need. Courage is as rare as hen's teeth."

"How many teeth do hens have?" I ask.

"Hens don't have teeth."

"Oh."

"Hence the saying."

"Yeah, I get it now." I laugh half-heartedly.

"Tough crowd," she says.

"I remember your hens from school," I say, tapping the top of my boiled egg with the back of my spoon.

"And I'm sure they remember you. You were one of the ones who used to chase them."

"We wanted to see if they could fly."

"I remember seeing you from my kitchen window throwing my Lady Bracknell up in the air. I felt like slapping you into next week."

"Why didn't you give out to me?" I ask, feeling myself blush.

"You were one of my piano students. I didn't want to scare you away."

"The poor things were terrified of us."

"I know! Sure you tormented them so much that they stopped laying eggs."

"What?"

"And then the teacher rang me to ask if she could bring the class to see the hens. I had to run to the shop and buy eggs to put under them."

"I remember that! They didn't lay those eggs at all?"

"Not one. And the little heads on you running around like butter wouldn't melt checking underneath their shaking feathers and shouting, 'Another one, another one!'"

"They were popping them out like vending machines!"

"Except they weren't!" She laughs. "It was all an act."

"Ha!"

"It was pure and utter madness. Me bursting into the shop to buy a dozen eggs in time for you all to come around. The eggs weren't even under the hens that long. They were still cold from the refrigerator."

"Thank you so much for doing that for us," I tell her. "And I'm sorry again."

"You were only a child," she says. "And you turned out OK."

❄

Audrey gives me a carton of eggs when I'm leaving. "You can come back tomorrow and finish the bathroom, if you like."

"I will."

"I'll give you a dustpan and brush and you can use that to sweep the shower. You dug up most of the grouting yesterday."

"Oh God. Sorry."

"I would have smashed a mirror if I were you. If I'd known the day you had, I wouldn't have made you clean the bathroom."

"No worries," I say, taking my jacket from the radiator. "Do you think it will ever stop snowing?"

"Who knows? They were saying on the radio it's the worst snow in twenty-five years."

"It was minus twelve degrees in Donegal yesterday."

"Jesus." She opens the front door for me.

"Thank you for everything."

"No problem. Listen, do me a favor?"

"Yeah?"

"Try to talk to Billy today."

"He won't talk to me," I say.

"It doesn't have to be a heavy conversation. Just, pop in and check on him. I'd say he could do with the company."

"I wouldn't know what to say to him though."

"Talk about the weather."

I look at her.

"I'm serious," she says. "We're Irish."

"Starting a conversation with Billy about the weather is like talking to Met Éireann."

"That's even better. He'll be in his element."

I grunt.

"Promise you'll try?"

She doesn't close the door until I say, "OK."

Snowflakes

The caravan door is locked so I go to the broken window. I push in the sheet of corrugated galvanized steel that Billy has put inside to keep out the world, the cold, and me. It clangs against the piano and I squirm my way in. It's like stepping into a mausoleum. The cheery décor of Billy's bric-a-brac only adds to the eeriness. He's in bed facing the wall, either asleep or ignoring me.

I give myself orders. Check that he's still breathing. Boil the kettle. Fill the hot water bottles and wrap them in tea towels. Put one at his feet; rest his hands on the other. Go to his wardrobe and take out a pile of sleeping bags. Open the zips of their cocoons and put them over him. Go back into the house and bring out two electric heaters. I try to drag the second one through the garden by the lead but its wheels won't budge in the snow. There aren't enough plugs in the caravan so I bring out an extension lead and a bag of supplies.

Open up the laptop. Go to Spotify. Play "The Pilgrim" by The Gloaming. Twist on the gas oven. Crack one of Audrey's eggs into a bowl. Olive oil, honey, and buttermilk. Whisk. Sieve flour into white mountain peaks. Wholemeal, baking soda, salt, sunflower, and pumpkin seeds. Pumpkin—a Polish girl on the train's favorite English word. When I overheard her tell her friend, it made my day. The dry ingredients in the bowl look like the inside of a colosseum. I flood it and work the sticky mixture with my fingers, watch as it falls in slow motion into the tin.

Close the oven door. It smells warm already. Open up an Internet tab. Google "weather" and descend into the vortex, ready to arm myself with information.

There's just so . . . much of it.

Close the laptop again and put frying pan on hob. Turn on the gas. Sausages spit. Rashers hiss. Pat the grease off them with kitchen roll, towel them dry like children coming out of a swimming pool. Crack more eggs. Yolk wobbles, white spreads and crimps crispy around the edges. When it's ready, lift the fried egg out of the pan. Gently.

＊

I shake his shoulder.

"Billy."

Nothing. I sit down on the bed and try to balance his breakfast tray on my lap. I inspect the fry arranged on a china plate from the good press.

I try again. "Billy."

A seismic fart rips through the mattress.

"Jesus Christ." I cover my nose. "You scumbag."

He rolls over in the bed. "Is this for me?"

"Yeah," I say. "You don't have to eat it."

He sniffs. "What's that smell?"

"Your Guinness farts."

"No, nicer."

"It's bread."

"Oh," he says, sitting up. "Thanks."

I hand over the tray. He looks sheepish. "Listen, Debs, I didn't mean . . ."

"I don't want to talk about it," I say.

He looks at the plate of food. "This is lovely."

"You don't have to act so surprised."

"Well I am. Listen, what time is it?"

"Dooley is coming in to milk with Mark. I already rang him."

He looks at me.

"I told him you were hungover."

"I'm grand."

"You're not well."

"I'm grand."

"I'm going to book you in to see the doctor."

"Who, Skeletor?" he says through a mouthful of egg.

Our local GP is so thin that we all suspect that she is anorexic. "She might just be naturally thin."

"She's death warmed up. I'm not going to see a bag of bones. She can't even look after herself."

"Well, I'm booking you in anyway."

"Fire away."

He eats the rest of his breakfast in silence. I open the laptop and Google the name that popped into my head. I find what I'm looking for and turn the screen around to Billy.

He reaches out and takes the laptop from me. I take his plate and leave him to flick through the gallery of snowflakes.

"Where did you come across these?" he asks.

"There was a guy selling prints of them in George's Street Arcade. I took his business card."

"They're beautiful."

"They look like glass, don't they?"

"Half a century ago, we landed on the moon. We can edit genes and clone sheep, but we still don't know how snowflakes grow. They're perfect." He closes the laptop and looks out the window.

"I remember when you were born. You were so perfect I didn't feel fit to look at you. It was the happiest day of my life. And I didn't expect it. I didn't see it coming, not a bit of it. I was too busy being thick with Maeve for getting herself pregnant. And then there you were. A tiny, pink miracle. And so perfect. I didn't want the world to ruin you."

"Well, now it has."

"I didn't mean what I said," he says.

"You can't control what happens to me, Billy."

"I know that."

"I don't think you do. You've been white-knuckling it for such a long time. You're always trying to make sure that Mam's OK and that I'm OK, but you forget yourself."

"Ah that's bullshit, Debs."

"It's not bullshit. You live in this crappy caravan with barely any heating and drink yourself silly. Why don't you look after yourself?"

"Because I killed my mammy." He says it in a small voice.

"That was an accident."

"I've spent all of my life trying to fix it . . . but I knew that I wasn't fixing anything. I was just waiting for another accident to happen."

I wrap my arms around him and let him cry. His sobs shake the bed and shake me. He cries until my clothes are wet with his tears. When he wipes his eyes with the tissue I give him, I see a little boy who wanted to help his mammy to fall asleep.

The Curiosity Cabinet

Audrey is a diligent notetaker. She scribbles away while I tell her how it went with Billy. I stop talking and she scribbles some more before she stops and looks up at me looking at her.

"I have to take notes because otherwise I forget. I would like my memory to be more of a hoarder but it insists on throwing things away."

I want to ask her why she thinks making notes about my interactions with Billy will help in any way.

"Well, he won't go to the doctor," I continue. "I booked him an appointment and told him I'd make him go but it's not going to happen."

"He seemed to like the snowflakes though."

"Yeah, that was jammy."

"I think you could be on to something." She stands up from the armchair and goes over to her drinks cabinet. She pulls a bottle of wine out of the cubbyhole and hands it to me. The bottle is empty, except for a tiny model of a grand piano with sheet music and a lady with silver hair.

"Oh my God!" I say. "It's you!"

"Yes. I have a lot of time on my hands."

I stand up and go over to the cabinet and pull out more bottles. Each bottle is filled with something different—another tiny, silver-haired woman sitting in her armchair knitting, a miniature Leonard Cohen poem on an easel, tiny ice-skaters twirling in a winter wonderland. Some of the bottles are filled to the brim with feathers, daisies, butterflies, and seashells.

"They're amazing," I say.

"When I gave up drinking, I missed my drinks cabinet. I missed the ritual of taking out a bottle of wine, uncorking, and pouring myself a glass. The relief of it. I emptied the cabinet but I was so sad whenever I looked at it. It was like looking at an upright coffin. So I took a Ship-in-a-Bottle evening class in town, along with other old folk. I never liked boats, so I decided to put in things I liked instead. I call it my curiosity cabinet."

"I love it," I say, inspecting the different bottles.

"I have to argue with the voice in my head that says I'm pathetic and reminds me it would be an awful lot easier to use the cabinet for its intended purpose. Drinking allowed me to feel sorry for myself. To go easy on myself. I had a hard time trying to relax without a glass or bottle of wine. I'm still trying. But drinking didn't make me feel alive, not really. It made me mellow, or bitchy, or giddy, or numb. I drank so much I didn't have the attention span to concentrate on anything."

She takes out a bottle of a model father and daughter pointing to a bird in a tree.

"My mother passed away when I was ten. When we visited Mam in the graveyard, a robin would come and perch itself on the headstone. Sometimes, Dad brought me bird watching. Whenever I'd see a robin, I'd say, look there's Mammy."

"That's lovely."

"Dad had Alzheimer's for years before he died. He wasn't himself, in the end. I'm terrified of going the same way. Losing my memory. My mind. But even if I do, at least someone can open this cabinet and show me the things I love, and who I used to be."

I nod vigorously, not knowing what else to do or say.

❄

"I think you might be on to something with Billy and the snowflakes," Audrey says. "Don't be afraid to learn more about them. A shared curiosity is very useful."

Dandelion

Xanthe said that we shouldn't message too much. She would prefer to talk face-to-face. She's left her apartment door on the latch. I knock on the open door and squeeze into the narrow hall. I have to climb across her bicycle like it's a gangly bouncer who doesn't want to let me in. The indoor plants that she got before Christmas are wilting. There's a weird smell coming from the kitchen.

She's sitting up in bed, wrapped in a sheet of imperial yellow Egyptian cotton, the folds of fabric falling like an Oscars dress. I recognize it from the website she ordered it from when we were in a lecture on Virginia Woolf. She has a spot on her chin, and greasy hair. It's the first time that I've seen her with a misbehaving fringe.

"Hi," I say.

I sit down on the edge of the bed. "Is Orla still in Clare?" I ask.

"She's not coming back," Xanthe says.

"Oh. Why?"

"She dropped out."

"Oh."

"Yeah, it turns out that she was pretty miserable here. She hated it. Found it hard to make friends."

"I feel bad," I mumble.

"What would you have done differently?" she scoffs.

"Nothing probably."

There are bowls of cereal on the floor. I recognize the buckwheat flakes with almond milk. It's the only kind of cereal that Xanthe allows herself to eat. One has been overturned. The beige mush has thrown up and dried into the carpet.

"How's—"

"We broke up last week."

"I'm sorry."

"I told him that I wasn't over Griff, which is at least a little bit true. And I'll never be good enough for Griff, unless I grow some testicles and a third leg."

"I'm not sure it works that way." I spot Lorelai and Rory frozen in an embrace on her laptop. "What season are you on?" I ask.

"I'm on the season where I realize they're narcissistic pieces of shit. Both of them."

"OK." I breathe out.

"My mother doesn't ring me," she says. "I'm always the one who calls her. So I stopped calling her to see if she'd notice. We haven't spoken for a week and a half now. Nothing. Not a message to ask if I'm still alive."

"I'm sure she's just busy."

"And my dad—he's never called me. If he rang there would have to be something seriously wrong. I don't even know what we'd talk about. It would be so awkward."

"I imagine it would be the same with me and Billy."

"It's not the same. I have no relationship with my dad outside of the direct debit that goes from his bank account into mine every month."

"I'm sure that's not true," I say.

"I got a tattoo last week. I wanted to get something that would mean something." She turns around and pulls her hair to the side to show off an upside-down dandelion—the stalk growing from the nape of her neck and bending toward her left shoulder. "Remember the story you told me about going outside to the caravan and paying for Billy's bedtime stories with dandelions?" she says, turning around. "Look at the things on my shoulder, the seeds that are blowing away."

I inspect the blobs of black that sweep across her shoulder. "Cool."

"They're supposed to be snowflakes."

"Look, I didn't mean to call you a snowflake," I say.

"What do you think of it, though? Honestly."

"It's lovely."

"You can't lie for shit," she says.

"I mean, the reason you got it creeps me out a bit."

"We're not getting into this again. I didn't get the tattoo because I fancy Billy. It's just . . . not everyone gets to grow up guided by a magical uncle who plays with you and tells you stories, OK?"

"Yeah, but getting a tattoo that symbolizes my childhood?"

"You don't own dandelions, Debbie. Get over yourself. Not everything is about you."

"I don't think it is!"

"Really? I'm pretty sure my whole relationship with my ex-boyfriend was about you too."

"Fuck you, Xanthe," I say, getting up from the bed. "I don't fucking need any of this."

I trip over the bicycle on my way out. "And FUCK THIS FUCKING BICYCLE," I shout and slam the door.

Gloria

The more I clean Audrey Keane's bathroom, the more there is to clean. I'm getting at the tops of the skirting board with a toothbrush. The radio is playing through one of the retro speakers that Audrey has around the house. I wish we had those kinds of speakers at home. I'm always uncomfortable leaving the kitchen when the radio is on. I feel bad that it's rambling away to an empty room. I'm also afraid I'm missing out on something, like the voices will say something interesting, or bitch about me when I'm out of earshot.

Desert Island Discs is on. It must be a podcast. Billy assures me that we don't get BBC around here, unless you're a Protestant and can mentally tune into the airwaves. I smile at the voice of Kirsty Young. She's Billy's ideal woman, and the reason he caved in to listening to the BBC on the laptop in the first place. He figured if the Scottish could infiltrate the BBC, then so could we. I walked in on him knocking great craic out of the Seamus Heaney episode, shushing me and laughing away to the thought of Seamus Heaney stomping around his desert island in a pair of yellow Doc Martens.

Kirsty's dulcet tones introduce her guest, Gloria Steinem, whom I've only vaguely heard of. I like her name. One of my favorite words is glorious. I like the way it feels in my mouth.

The first record Gloria Steinem chooses is Mam's morning song—"Downtown" by Petula Clark. Her father was a dreamer. He had a caravan and they moved around a lot. Kirsty coaxes her into talking about how her mother used to be a badass journalist, but had a nervous breakdown and spent time in a sanatorium. Much of Gloria's childhood was spent looking after her mother, who was often off in a dream world, talking to unseen voices. And then Kirsty reminds Gloria that she once said that she was living out the unlived life of her mother.

I put down the toothbrush and lie back on the cool tiles of the bathroom floor. Tears collect in the corners of my eyes and roll down my temples into my hair, tickling like wet feathers.

⁂

Audrey has given me a diary so I can plan my week. I make lists of things I want to do in the next month. I've booked an appointment at an STI clinic, which makes me nervous, but that's probably the easiest thing on the list. The other tasks seem impossible. Apologize to Xanthe. Don't drink alcohol. Don't kiss people I don't fancy.

"It's important to remember that if you do drink alcohol or kiss a stranger, it is not a disaster. The likelihood is that you will do these things again. You're only human. And you're a college student, which means you should cut yourself even more slack. But you should be proud of yourself for recognizing that it may be self-destructive behavior."

"I don't know if I should tell Xanthe about Billy," I say. "I don't think Billy would want me to. And it would only make her feel bad."

"It sounds like you've made your decision," Audrey says.

"I don't have to tell her?" I ask.

"Debbie, you don't have to tell anyone anything."

"OK."

"Does that make you feel better?"

"Yeah," I say.

"We haven't touched on the dreams. In our first session,

you said that was something you most wanted to address." Audrey flicks back through her notebook. "You said, 'I'm afraid of going the same way as my mother. I'm afraid of being stuck at home forever, not being able to deal with reality. And if I don't talk to someone about it soon, I feel like it will kill me.'"

"I can't remember saying that."

"Do you feel ready to talk about it?"

"I thought you said I didn't have to tell anyone anything?"

"And I mean it. If you're not ready to talk about them that's fine."

"It's not that I'm not ready," I say. "I feel like I'll never be ready. I can't describe it. And I'm afraid that you won't believe me."

"Is it important that I believe you?"

"Are you joking?"

"Why does it matter whether I believe you or not?"

"Because I don't even believe myself. They make absolutely no sense. My whole life I've been told that the dreams are bullshit and my mother is crazy and I've never really questioned that. So yes, if I put the work in to try to explain them, it is important that you listen to me without immediately thinking I'm bonkers. It's important that someone, anyone, believes me."

"OK." Audrey closes her notebook and sits forward. "I'm listening."

"Well, it's not fair that you just put me on the spot like this. I don't know where to start."

"How are you feeling, right now?"

"Angry. I'm angry you can't see inside my head and know what's going on. I'm angry that I have to explain myself."

"I can see that. Have you ever thought about trying to write it down?"

"The dreams?"

"Yes, and how they affect your waking life. Your mother writes a lot. I think it helps her to cope."

"Mam's writing is terrible."

"So, in your opinion, it's OK to write, as long as the writing is 'good'?"

"I'm not saying that."

"But you would like your writing to be 'good' and not 'bad.'"

"Well, yeah," I say.

"How do you know if the writing is 'good' or not if you haven't written anything?"

"It's all right for Mam because she doesn't care what people think."

"That sounds liberating. Not caring what people think," Audrey says. "But perhaps that comes with time."

"Well . . . if I try to write about it, it comes out all wrong. It sounds like I'm lying. I don't expect anyone to believe me. I suspect that in a few years, I won't believe myself. Telling a story—even if it's just talking about my life—requires some kind of hindsight. I'm eighteen. I don't have a whole lot of hindsight. And I can't really say, once upon a time, this happened to me, because it's still happening."

Audrey looks at me as though the solution is obvious. "Then don't say once upon a time."

The Diviner

When I was younger, Billy was always going to see a man about a dog. I used to get excited until I started copping that I was getting fairly few dogs out of these appointments. Whenever James gave out to Billy for getting my hopes up, Billy shot back with: "Good. It will teach her not to expect anything from anyone. A healthy dose of skepticism never did anyone any harm."

Sometimes, I asked if I could go with him and he'd shrug and mumble, "If you want," in a way that let me know that he didn't want me to. Then he'd flat-out pretend he forgot about me wanting to go. He'd tear out of the driveway with me running after him.

So I'm surprised when Billy comes into my bedroom and wakes me up by throwing a bunch of car keys on my duvet.

"Come on," he says. "We're going to see a man about a dog."

"What?"

"Do you want to come or not?"

"Yeah."

"Good, because you're driving."

❋

I have to turn off the radio to concentrate. My heart is going ninety, but time is floating along quite nicely. I'm getting lucky. The crossroads are quiet and there aren't any confusing intersections. I'm following Billy's directions.

"Left, turn left."

I turn on my right indicators.

"Your other left."

❋

We go down twisty roads until he orders me to pull into a driveway with high stone walls and big fuck-off gates. The place is called Ballymore Manor. There's a smaller sign that advertises HAPPY FACES MONTESSORI and PLAYSCHOOL— NOW ENROLLING!

The electric gates open. I get Violet into gear and we trundle up the avenue. Billy instructs me to drive around to the back of the house. The back door opens and a woman waves as we approach.

"Pull up here and don't run her over like a good girl."

He reaches into the back and picks up a massive stick.

"Ah here, Gandalf, where are you going with that?"

"I'll need it," he says, putting the branch of a gnarled old tree between his legs.

We get out of the car and shuffle over the gravel driveway toward the woman, who is wearing a fluffy dressing gown and slippers. The traces of sleep are still in the process of disappearing from her face.

"So you're the man with the stick?" she asks Billy.

"I am, indeed. And this is my apprentice," he says, putting his hand on my shoulder.

"Well, I'll show you around the place then," she says.

She leads us over toward the garden. There are several flowerbeds and a well-kept lawn. The apple trees are old and smell funny. The fruit is rotten and crawling with insects and flies. There's a hut made out of sticks—an impressive teepee with plastic mugs and plates inside. One of the mugs is filled with mushed flowers. It reminds me of the time I used to make dandelion perfume that smelled like piss.

Billy is wandering around the garden with a stick. He holds

it at the top where the branch splits into two parts like a wish-bone. The woman watches him like she's trying to work out what he's doing. He isn't actually doing anything but walking around, stopping every so often to wave the stick about.

"The children go home crying to their parents," the woman says. "And you know how word spreads. People don't want to leave their children here. You'd swear I was doing all sorts of awful things to them. It's a nightmare. We've lived in this house for four years and there has never been anything like this. Ever. We've had visitors over to stay for summer holidays and their children loved the garden—that's where the idea for the Montessori came from. I've always loved having children around. There's just this weird feeling over the place. So many freak accidents. I've had five broken bones in the past year—*five!*"

"This house used to belong to the owners of the stud over the road," Billy says.

"Yes, that's right."

"You bought it off the son. He inherited the property."

"Yes, Michael Corcoran."

"You extended the garden recently."

"Yes, for the Montessori."

Billy is using the same voice he adopted when he told me stories as a kid.

"This used to be a field—part of the stud. The man who sold you this house, the Corcoran man. His sister . . . when she was a little girl, she fell off a horse here. She was about seven or eight. She broke her neck."

The woman gasps. "That makes so much sense."

"Before you extended the garden, am I right in saying those apple trees were healthier than they are now?"

"Yes! I used to make apple tarts. Children always loved

playing in the orchard but now they don't go anywhere near it. How do you know this?"

"The land tells stories. All I do is listen. Now, I'm no John the Baptist. I'm a bit rusty. I haven't done it in a while. My father used to divine, and he tried to pass his skills on to me but I thought it was a load of shite, excuse my language."

The woman laughs. Billy has charmed her already.

"I can neutralize the ground for you, which usually clears the tension. The extension into the garden has brought up a lot of bad energy surrounding the death of that little girl. Children tend to be very intuitive. They're very good at picking up on energy. I have a feeling that is what is causing the broken bones."

The woman nods. "That makes sense."

"I can't make any promises, but I have a feeling that once the land is healed, the trees in your orchard will yield ripe fruit again."

"Thank you, so much."

"Hold your horses now, I haven't done anything yet."

"Whatever you have to do, go ahead. How much do I owe you?"

"Oh, nothing at all."

"I have to pay you."

"No, you don't. I can't guarantee it will work."

The woman looks uncomfortable. "Well, come in for a cup of tea at least, when you're finished."

"Of course. Now, if you'll excuse me and my apprentice."

"Oh right. Well. Good luck," she says, backing away and giving us a thumbs up.

"Come on," Billy says to me and walks back toward the car. He opens Violet's boot, takes out two long steel poles, and hands them to me.

"What do we do with these?" I ask.

"Stick them in the ground. It's kind of like acupuncture."

He takes out four more poles and a hammer. We walk back over to the lawn, toward the fence at the back. Billy instructs me where to place the poles and hammers them into the ground.

"How did you know all of that?" I ask.

"I don't know," he says.

"But you did know."

He stops hammering. "It's hard to explain. I don't know how I know. That's why I haven't done it in a while. I feel like a con artist."

"But you were right."

"Thank Christ."

"So you've done it before? When you were a kid?"

"Yes. My father used to bring me."

"Why did you stop?"

"Because I didn't believe in it. Couldn't believe in it."

"So why are we here then?"

"Because I want to get better. And someone told me that if I started doing this, and helping other people, it might make me feel better in myself."

"Oh, right. Well that's good?"

"Yeah."

"Why did you bring me?"

"Someone told me that it might be a good idea to let you in on what I was doing. Because, well, you seem to think you're mad. There are lots of kinds of madness that run in the family."

"Are you going to tell me who this someone is?"

"Audrey Keane."

"You went for a session?"

"She came over to the caravan one day out of the blue and asked me around to hers for dinner. I didn't want to be rude and I know that she was a big help to Maeve so, I said yes."

"Oh. So you just went around for dinner."

"I did."

"Just the once?"

"Well, she's a good cook and I felt bad her going to all the effort. I wanted to repay the favor so I took her out to dinner, as a kind of thank-you."

"Where did you go, the pub?"

"No."

"Where?"

"I'm not telling you."

"What did you wear?"

"Clothes."

"And she got a lot of chat out of you?"

"She did. Well, we went to school together. And her father was good friends with mine. They used to go bird watching together, and Dad told Keane about the divining. That's how she knew."

"She's a lovely woman," I say.

"She's a lady."

"Are you going to take her to dinner again?"

"I took her to dinner once. As a thank-you."

"Understood. She *is* a lovely woman though."

"She's a lady."

Amuse-Bouche

We're still on Christmas holidays, but I'm going to the library to do some reading for essays that are due when we get back. The campus is quiet. The only people I interact with are the security on the way into the Berkeley. I spot Griff coming out of the turnstiles as I'm going in, but he's too busy fixing his hair to notice me. My phone vibrates in my pocket. It's a message from Xanthe.

Hey. Do you want to meet my parents?

She sends me an address and says to meet them at seven.

The restaurant looks more New York than Dublin. There are red-bricked walls and plants that could pass for trees. I think the waiter assumes I'm lost, wandering in in a tracksuit with a school bag on my back. He is a man in his fifties who is already sick of my shit and over this shift, but he smooths on a smile because tips are his trade. He leads me to an out-door seating area with heaters and fairy lights. Xanthe is sitting there sipping a glass of white wine. I'm nervous, but she seems relieved when she sees me.

"Hi," we say.

The waiter pulls out my chair. I take off my schoolbag and sit down.

"Anything to drink?" he asks, already beginning his retreat.

"No thanks," I say.

Xanthe waits until the waiter is gone. "Listen, I'm so sorry—"

"Don't. There's no need. I was an arsehole too."

"OK. Good." She takes a deep breath. "I don't think Dad is coming and Mum is running late."

"It's only five to seven."

"I told them dinner was at six."

"Oh."

We sit in silence for a while until we hear footsteps. I turn to see a woman walking toward us in a navy blue suit. Her hair is blow-dried. She seems to take delight in the sound her stilettos make on the restaurant tiles.

"What's the occasion?" she asks Xanthe when she gets to the table. She has a posh radio voice, the kind that is difficult to situate. I notice the frames of her glasses match her suit—they are the exact same shade of blue. I wonder if she has different glasses for different outfits.

Xanthe stands up and introduces us. "Mum, this is Debbie. Debbie, this is my mum, Jean."

Jean shakes my hand and looks me up and down, taking in my greasy hair and tracksuit. "Oh God, you're not going to tell me you're gay, are you?"

I shake my head vigorously.

"What if I did?" Xanthe asks.

I look at Xanthe and back to her mam. "I'm not gay," I say, pointing at myself to make things clear.

"Why would that be an issue though, Mum?" Xanthe sits back down, crosses her legs, and leans her chin on her hand.

Jean smiles at me and takes a seat. "Xanthe likes to shock me. She likes the shock factor." Her eyes widen every time she says shock. "I'm surprised she didn't bring her dad along to this meal."

"He was invited."

"Of course he was."

"He just texted me there to say he's running late."

"If your father shows up I'll sign over the deed to my house to this man here," she says, patting the waiter on the arm.

The waiter gives her a tight smile. "Would you like anything to drink?" he asks.

"Can we see the wine list?" she asks.

"The selection of wines are on the back of the menu," he says, turning the menu over for her.

"Is that all there is?" she asks.

"Yes," he says. The way he says it, he might as well have told her to go fuck herself.

"We'll just have water then."

"Still or sparkling?" he asks.

"Tap is fine," she says.

The waiter leaves and Jean looks at me as though she's registered me as a person for the first time, rather than an extra on the film set of her daughter's life. "I never caught your name."

"Debbie," I say.

"What are you studying, Debbie?"

"English."

"At Trinity?"

I nod.

"Where are you from?"

"I live on a farm in Kildare. It's a dairy farm," I add, for something else to say.

The waiter comes back with water and fills our glasses individually.

"Can we have some bread and olives for the table please?" Jean asks him.

"Of course." He takes the wine glasses off the table. They make the sound of the bell ringing at mass as he clinks them together.

"How many cows do you have?" Jean turns her attention back to me.

"Oh, I don't know. I've never counted," I joke, but Jean doesn't smile. Billy has me prepped to answer this question. If he were here, he'd say, "The taxman wouldn't even ask me that." Asking a farmer how many cows he has upon introduction is like asking someone you've just met how much money they make in a year. Most people don't realize that.

"I grew up on a dairy farm," Jean says. "I milked cows before I went to school, and again in the evening when I was home. I hated it."

"Oh, wow." I get the impression she doesn't usually give out this information freely.

"I decided that I was going to be a doctor when I was three years old."

"Wow," I say again. "Fair play to you."

"I didn't have any other choice," she says, pursing her lips.

I want to ask her why she felt she had no choice other than to make a career decision as a toddler. Being in Jean's presence for two minutes is already making me stressed. I know her type. She's one of those people who interview you about your future and can sense when you're bullshitting.

"Are you going to sit these"—she waves her hand in the air searching for the word—"scholarship exams next year, Debbie?"

"I don't know," I say, trying not to blush. The way that she's looking at me, it's like she can tell I got a 2.2 in that essay I wrote at the start of the year. "I'm not sure I'm smart enough, to be honest."

"She is," Xanthe says.

"You don't know that," I say. "Xanthe should go for it, though." I nod at her across the table. "She'd get Schols."

"I know," Jean agrees. "Still, it doesn't guarantee you anything, does it? An English degree."

"I suppose not. Sure we always have the dole," I say. I have just become the type of person who laughs at my own jokes.

The waiter appears with a basket of bread and a plate of tiny, slick pink rolls filled with green stuff. "We have no olives, but the chef has prepared some amuse-bouche."

"No olives?" Jean looks baffled.

The waiter's jaw clenches and he directs his words to the legs of the table. "I'm afraid not, but these are avocado and salmon bites with lemon and deep-fried quinoa."

"Do we have to pay for these?" Jean asks.

"No."

"OK."

※

Dinner continues to be a painful affair. Jean sends back her main course. The waiter offers her another dish on the house but she refuses. The chocolate soufflé dessert is complimentary. I thank the waiter profusely, which seems to annoy him even more.

I don't learn much about Jean other than she thinks duck confit can be overdone even when it's still bleeding. Xanthe appears unfazed by her mother's antics. When Jean gets up to pay the bill I sneak a twenty-euro note under a tea saucer. Xanthe gives me a funny sideways smile and says, "Do you want to come back to mine?"

❋

Jean appears uncomfortable outside the restaurant. She asks Xanthe if she's OK for money. Xanthe nods.

"I'll leave you to it so. Let me know if you need anything. Nice to meet you, Debbie."

"You too, Jean."

We watch her turn and walk away, her stilettos clacking against the pavement.

Xanthe asks, "Well?"

"Well what?"

"What do you make of her?"

"She's some woman is Jean."

Xanthe laughs. "I love my mother, but . . . I find it difficult to like her."

"I can tell."

❋

We walk back to Xanthe's apartment in silence. I'm in a bit of a daze. I'm glad when we get there, relieved at the thought of sitting down. She opens a bottle of red wine and takes two glasses out of the press.

"Just water for me," I say. "I'm trying to take it easy."

I'm waiting for her to raise her eyebrows or say something but she doesn't. I take the glass of water and curl up on the leather sofa, pulling her patchwork blanket over my knees.

"I just don't understand how you . . . came out of her?" I finally say. "Are you adopted?"

"I think we're very alike, actually."

"No you're not."

"We are." Xanthe takes a seat beside me and the sofa sighs

under the weight of both of us. "I'm just more of a people-pleaser. That's something I admire in Mum actually. She doesn't feel the need to endear people to her. It's a rare quality in a woman."

"But she actively pushes people away. That waiter was fit to kill her. You're not like that. People love you."

"Do they though?" Xanthe looks into her wine glass and swirls it around. "Or do they just like how I present myself? Mum came from a big family with very little money. When she decided to be a doctor at three years old"—she rolls her eyes—"she rejected her family and everything they represented. She was completely on her own."

"An independent three-year-old," I say.

"She wasn't joking."

"I can imagine her in her navy blue romper and matching specs."

"Exactly." Xanthe takes a sip of wine and scrunches her nose. "This wine is rank."

"Is it corked? Will we ask Jean to send it back?"

Xanthe doesn't laugh.

"Sorry," I say. "I feel bad, slagging your mother off."

"Mum just . . ." She repositions herself on the sofa and tries again. "Mum's a perfectionist. We both are. It doesn't make me better than anyone. It paralyzes me. It limits everything I do."

"It kind of does make you better though," I argue. "You're the only one in our year who got a first."

"I only got that first because I bullied myself into going to the library every day. I wrote six different drafts of the same essay. You want to know how to get a first? Give out to yourself. Constantly. Be disappointed in everything you write. Tell yourself you're worth nothing if you don't get over seventy percent. I actually *like* hating myself. It's my comfort zone."

"Do you imagine the rest of us go around loving ourselves?"

"That's why I'm so obsessed with your family. You're all so—"

"Fucked up?" I offer.

"Yeah. And beautiful."

I hold out my hand and she looks at it.

"Shake it," I say.

She takes my hand.

"That's a good handshake," I compliment her.

"Almost perfect."

"Welcome to the club," I say.

The Yellow Bookshop

It's the first week of Hilary term. Xanthe and I have spent the last ten minutes standing outside the sunny, yellow exterior of a bookshop. We peer through the window display past our own reflections to see if he's working today.

"We can't go in now. We've stood outside for too long. It's too weird."

"Of course we can," Xanthe says. "Now, what are you going to do when we get in there?"

"Em, browse?"

"And?"

"Maybe buy something?"

"You can't buy anything. That's cheating."

"I'll still talk to him."

"But then it won't be a conversation. It'll be a transaction."

"Can I just point out the irony of you telling me not to buy anything?"

※

We've visited the yellow bookshop regularly since I moved into the apartment with Xanthe. She won't let me pay rent, which Billy says suits him down to the ground. We've been scouring charity shops to do the place up. We got a vinyl record player and we're compiling a pretentious collection of classical music and jazz. We're also building up our collection of secondhand books.

The yellow bookshop is only a fifteen-minute walk from our apartment. It's like being in someone's sitting room.

There's a rug and a rocking chair with a blanket. They take good care of their plants. I fancy one of the guys who works there—the Italian in my Theories of Literature class.

❋

The bell above the door tinkles. He looks up from his seat behind the counter, grins at us, and continues to read his book. Xanthe heads over to the Classics corner. I run a finger along the book spines. Browsing in a bookshop is a lot like collecting shells on a beach on a really good day. I want all of them.

I have a hard time distinguishing between the books I've bought and the books that I've read. Xanthe says that she's the same. We don't want shelves full of books we haven't read, so we have agreed to make a "To Be Read" list. We're not allowed to buy a new book if we haven't got time to read it. It's an attempt at self-improvement.

"Am I allowed to buy this?" Xanthe asks, holding up a copy of *Infinite Jest*.

"Are you joking?"

"Sorry, Mam."

She's waiting for me to strike up a conversation with the guy. I continue to browse, ignoring her.

Xanthe gasps. "Oh my God! Debbie!"

I turn around. She's on her knees pulling a tome out of the Classics section. She turns the cover around.

"Oh my God!" I kneel down next to her.

Lorelai and Rory smile up at us from *The Gilmore Girls Companion*.

"The holy grail."

"The ideal coffee table book."

"We don't have a coffee table."

Xanthe is flicking through it, handling the pages like it's a copy of *Planet Earth*. "There's a whole section on Emily!"

"Emily?" The guy has stopped reading his book and is looking at us like we just offended his mother. "Emily is the absolute worst. I mean, all of the characters are morally dubious, apart from Lane. Lane is the best."

"Team Dean or Team Jess?" Xanthe asks.

He considers this. "Team Leave Luke Alone."

Xanthe nods. "I respect that."

"Don't get me wrong," he says, double-bagging the book for us at the counter. "I didn't want to watch all of *Gilmore Girls*. I was supposed to be writing an essay on *Ulysses* and boom—it just happened."

"I can sympathize," I say.

"You're in one of my tutorials," he says to me.

"Oh yeah! Theories of Lit?" I answer, pretending to recognize him for the first time.

"Yes. I can place you now. Debbie, isn't it? You're the funny one."

There's an awkward silence while I process whether that is an insult or a compliment.

"We should have a *Gilmore Girls* trivia night," Xanthe says.

"Sounds good," he says.

"Nice to meet you . . ."

"I'm Nic," he says. "Lovely to meet you too. See you around."

❄

"It's more than likely that he fancies you," I say on the way home.

Xanthe stops walking and crosses her arms. "Look at me. You have to stop doing this, to me and to yourself."

"I'm just telling the truth."

"No, you're not. You're beating yourself up. And even worse, you're imagining me as something that I'm not."

"You are though."

"Debbie, the only compliment I want to hear is that I'm an OK human. Do you think I'm an OK human?"

"Yes."

"Thank you. Do you think you're an OK human?"

"Em."

"Look in the reflection of that window and tell yourself that you're an OK human."

I look at my reflection.

"Say it," Xanthe pleads.

I look at the girl in the window. There's an easy expression on her face. She's not frowning. Usually, my face is all scrunched with worry, but I've done my makeup nice today. I had a good sleep last night. The dreams are still there, I'm just able to let them come and go. Xanthe bought me a bag of Guatemalan worry dolls that I keep under my pillow. Mam gave me a framed quote to put in my new bedroom, to remind me that we all live in each other's shadows.

> *Ar scáth a chéile a mhaireann na daoine*

I'm dressed in someone else's clothes that I found in a charity shop last week. I find it comforting to wear clothes that already have a history of their own. "I'm really happy," I say to the girl in the window. "I'm really fucking happy."

Silver Island

Mam won a poetry competition. We spotted it in the local paper a few weeks back and I told her to apply. The prize was only twenty euro, but Audrey suggested that she should do something to celebrate. Mam wanted us all to go to the island together. I asked if I could bring Xanthe. Then Mam suggested we ask Audrey to come.

Billy was skeptical of the whole arrangement.

"That poor woman has enough of us," he said.

"Ah Billy, sure we're only asking her as a way of saying thank you."

"I think, as a way of saying thank you, we should leave her alone."

"Well, I've already asked her and she's said yes."

"Fucking wonderful."

"I'm glad you think so."

❋

Mam and Billy used to go to the island as kids. There's a thatched cottage out there that has been in the family for gen- erations. Our ancestors hailed from there. We can trace them back to the 1920s—James and Bridget O'Donnell headed the top of my family tree in primary school. I remember getting a gold star for how much effort I put into doing it. Mam did it with me. She was always really into our roots and where we came from.

She tells me that she brought me to the island as a child, but I can't remember it. I can't remember the last time we went on a holiday. Billy isn't usually able to get away from the farm, but Mark and Dooley said that they would cover the milking and look after the place until we got back.

Mam has been meticulous in her planning of the trip. She wrote to her second cousin Judy to ask her where the key to the holiday cottage is hidden. Judy occasionally writes letters to Mam on a typewriter and encloses a tarot card in every wax-sealed envelope. She wrote back to Mam straightaway and told her that the key was kept in the decapitated Buddha in the garden.

Audrey arrives to the house fully kitted out in hiking gear. I'm waiting for Billy to slag her but he doesn't. He waits until Xanthe comes to look around him during an awkward pause in conversation and says, "Blessed is he among women."

It's a four-hour drive. Billy offered to share the driving but I want to prove to myself that I can get Violet there in one piece. Billy sits beside me in the passenger seat and Mam, Xanthe, and Audrey are squished into the back.

"What am I putting into Google Maps?" I ask.

"Money Island," Mam says.

"Cha-ching! Is that the name of it?"

"Yeah. It comes from a bad translation of the Irish. It used to be called Inis Airgead. Silver Island. But *airgead* also translates as money so, Money Island it is."

"Nice bit of trivia there. Thank you, Maeve," Billy says.

"I'm going to call it Silver Island," I say.

As I pull off, Billy orders Xanthe to start the sing-song. She obliges with a rendition of *American Pie*. As Violet crawls up Clock's Hill, I watch the village disappear in my rearview mirror. Billy leans back in his chair and whispers, "What a song."

✳

We get to Tipperary before we realize that Google Maps has taken us the wrong way. Mam wants to stop in the shop for supplies and the rest of us just want to get there.

"There's no shop on the island," she insists.

"Mam, last time you visited the island was during the Stone Age. I'm sure that it has come on a long way."

"Well I don't think we should go if we're not prepared. You can let me out here and I'll walk home."

"From Tipperary? It's a long way to go."

"I'll get the bus. Or hitchhike."

"People don't do that anymore, Mam, it's dangerous."

"God help the poor fucker who stops to pick you off the side of the road," Billy mumbles. "Get more than they bargained for."

"I actually think Maeve has a point," Audrey says. "It would be nice to arrive prepared."

A silence falls over the car while the rest of us process Audrey siding with Mam.

"There's a SuperValu on the way," Billy says. "We can stop there."

✳

It has taken us eight hours to get to the island. It's pitch-black and raining. The wind rattles Violet and I squeeze the steering wheel to try and calm her down.

"Do we have to get a boat out to the island?" Xanthe asks in a small voice.

"No, there's a bridge connecting it to the mainland."

"Thank Christ," Billy says.

The headlights shine on the treasure trail of grass in the

middle of the *bohereen*. We give a tentative cheer when we cross a bridge. We're still not sure we're going the right way, but Mam is adamant that this is the place. It's only when I navigate Violet around a hairpin bend that Billy confirms the house is at the top of this hill.

"I told you," Mam says. "I fucking told you. No one ever believes me."

❋

It's so dark by the time we arrive at the house that it takes us a while to locate the keys. We're out in the lashings of rain, shining the torches on our phones into the wet black abyss.

"How big is the Buddha?" Billy asks.

"She didn't say," Mam says.

"How are we supposed to know that it's a Buddha if it doesn't have a head?"

"By its man boobs?" I suggest.

"Why couldn't she have left it under a flowerpot?" Billy roars.

"Too obvious."

"Whereas a headless Buddha in the garden is not suspicious at all."

Audrey is the last person to get out of the car for a look. She hasn't been feeling well all journey so we insisted that she stay put. As soon as she steps outside the car she says, "I have it!"

The Buddha was around the side of the house, next to a bag of firewood.

"Audrey, you're a legend," I say.

She gives the key to Mam, who puts it in the door. It takes a few attempts to turn the lock the right way. It's a glossy yellow door that opens in two parts like in a fairy tale. Mam opens the top part and is able to open the bottom from the inside.

"Billy, bring some firewood inside so it can dry out for the morning," Mam says.

He does what he's told. The rest of us pile into the house with the bags, relieved to get out of the rain.

"Oh wow." Audrey is the first one to really notice the place. We're in the part of the house that was originally a one-roomed cottage. The focal point is the fireplace. There is a big brass box filled with coal and old newspapers. The fire utensils gleam on their stand like the dangling jewelry of giants.

There are wetsuits hanging inside the door. They smell like summer. I look at the collage of photos that are framed on the old stone walls. Happy faces, full of devilment. Kids building sandcastles, standing with their ankles in the sea. A posed family photo with a little boy acting the eejit, sticking out his tongue to the camera.

Billy appears beside me and points to the little boy. "Do you recognize the cow's lick?"

"Oh my God! It's you!"

"Once upon a time," he says. He points to another photo of him looking more like his old self, pushing a child in a wheelbarrow. "And that's you."

"I can't remember ever being here," I say.

"No one ever believes me," Mam says, kissing me on the cheek.

"No, I mean, I just thought I'd remember it, even vaguely."

"Well you were three."

"Three and a half. I remember you kept telling everyone you were half past three."

"You were such a gorgeous chubster," Xanthe says.

"I look like a Cabbage Patch doll."

❋

There's a bit of awkwardness as we sort out sleeping arrangements. Mam insists on sleeping on the single bed in the kids' room and Xanthe and I bagsy the bunk beds. Billy says he'll sleep on the couch but Audrey is having none of it.

"I've brought my own mattress. I'll sleep on the floor."

"You won't sleep on the floor, you're the guest and you'll take the bedroom."

It sounds like Billy is threatening her. Audrey shakes her head and stands her ground.

Mam claps her hands. "So that's settled, Billy's on the couch and Audrey has the other bedroom."

"I feel uncomfortable taking a bedroom to myself," she says.

"Well I'd be uncomfortable sleeping on anything other than a couch," Billy says. "I'm already out of my comfort zone. Don't make me sleep in a bed in a house."

"Fine," Audrey gives in, graciously conceding defeat.

❋

We're hungry and too tired to cook, so we have cereal and crisp sandwiches.

We sit around and wait for Mam to say aren't you glad we stopped in the shop but she keeps quiet, smug in the knowledge that we're all thinking the same thing. We all agree we should go to bed. It's freezing. Mam discovers a pile of dressing gowns in a wardrobe. They smell of must but they're warm so we wrap them tight around us. I forgot my toothbrush so I use an ancient one that feels like straw on my teeth.

Xanthe takes the top bunk. I push my feet against the steel net that supports her mattress.

"What the fuck is that?" she asks.

I drop my feet and the net squeaks down again. "Sorry, it was just me."

"Are ye two still awake?" Mam whispers.

"No," we say in unison, feeling like bold children.

"Go to sleep."

❋

I wake up to the sun shining in through the white shutters and the smell of a fry. Mam and Xanthe are still asleep. I traipse out of the room, my bare feet slapping the floor. I'm embarrassed that Audrey is the first up and figure I should help with breakfast.

The radio is playing "Jack and Diane." Billy is standing over the frying pan in a pink dressing gown, pipe in his mouth, dancing along.

I lean against the doorframe and watch. He doesn't notice me until I say, "Do your best James Dean."

He almost throws the sausages out of the frying pan and clutches his dressing gown. "Jesus Christ," he says.

"No, it's just me," I say.

"Good morning, Debbie," he says.

"Good morning, Billy. Where in God's name did you get the pipe?"

"It's my holiday pipe."

"Are you trying to impress us with your culinary skills?"

"I was hungry. I'm not hungover for a change, and there's not a cow in sight. I had to do something. I tried to start the fire but it wasn't having any of me."

"I could try and google it?"

He laughs. "Wait until your mother is up. They call her Hestia out here."

"Hestia—the firstborn of the Titans," I say.

"Swallowed by Kronos in the end. She is an awfully underrated character. Goddess of the hearth and home."

I look at the fireplace. "This place makes me want to have a fireplace when I'm older."

"County councils won't let you build chimneys nowadays."

"Don't be telling me that. This house is so great," I say, touching the old walls of the sitting room. "They don't build them like they used to."

"It's like Padraic Colum's house."

"Sure that wasn't his house at all. It was the old woman of the road's."

"That's true."

"Why did you stop coming out here?" I ask.

"Ah just, fell out of the habit. It's hard to get away from the farm."

"From the pub, you mean."

I spot a map of the island marked in Irish, but the terms are translated at the bottom. "There's a map out here," I shout. "Some of the names of things are hilarious."

Billy comes out of the kitchen and stands beside me.

"Oileán na nGamhna—island of the calves," I say, pointing to one of the smattering of islands off the main one.

"Now that's less of an island and more of a rock in the sea," Billy says.

"Loch na Reillige—lake of the graveyard."

"I know where that is," Billy says, stroking the stubble around his chin. "We used to do treasure hunts out here."

"I'd like to scope some of these out. Oileán na Luchoige—island of the mice."

"Oh yes. They have a rodent-only immigration policy," Billy says. "Have you seen the conservatory?"

"There's a conservatory?"

"Well, it's tiny. It's out through that door, past the bedroom."

I twist the doorknob gently, afraid I'll wake Audrey. When I sneak into the sunroom she is sitting cross-legged in the middle of it, meditating.

"Sorry!" I whisper.

"No, come on in!" She laughs.

The sunroom gives a panoramic view of the island. I sit down on the couch and breathe out. There is a small commune of holiday cottages alongside us. You can see the beach past the hills, the sleek black roads, and our small, wonky front garden.

"Had you a nice sleep?" I ask.

"Oh, I slept like a baby."

Her face is shining and her hair is wet. "You'd a shower already?"

"I had a swim in the sea."

"What?!"

"It was glorious."

Mam and Xanthe burst into the room. Mam throws her hands out to frame the view.

"Oh my God, it's amazing!" Xanthe squeaks.

"Audrey has already been in the sea!" I say.

"You mad bastard, Audrey!" Mam says.

"Oh, we're all mad here." Audrey winks.

"What time were you up?"

"Sunrise. It wasn't that early. Seven o'clock."

"I was just rolling over for my second sleep," Mam says.

"I can't wait for a swim," says Xanthe.

Mam gasps and bends down to pick up an old button accordion behind a rocking chair. "I can't believe this is still here."

"Is it yours?"

"It was my grandmother's. She used to play in a marching band. She only knew the one tune. Hang on." Mam winces as her fingers try to find the memory. She slowly begins to play the song.

Billy comes into the room in his dressing gown with a tray of tea. I help him carry in a plate of cremated sausages and toast.

He slaps his hands together, delighted with the feast. "Get it into ye Cynthia. We've a long day ahead."

❋

We get a grand tour of the island. Maeve and Billy are sharing the role of tour guide. First up is the abandoned house. When we peer in through the windows we're able to see furniture and decor from the seventies, religious iconography, and, bizarrely, a calendar of Mariah Carey stuck on July.

We stand on top of huge rocks on the wild side of the island and look out at the wind-whisked sea. There are huge fringes of foam on the waves. The wind picks them up and they fly past us like snow.

❋

We go to Brian's Beach—the one we can see from the conservatory. I put on my swimsuit underneath my clothes but I'm not sure if I'll get in.

"Why is it called Brian's Beach?" I ask Billy.

"Brian was the name of the guy who parked his caravan at the top of it."

"Did Brian inspire you to take your first step on the caravan property ladder?"

"God no. He was a terrifying old fucker."

Xanthe and Audrey strip off down to their swimming suits straightaway and run into the waves. Mam hangs back with me and Billy. We walk the beach, picking up shells that take our fancy. I'm going for the whitest cockles I can find. I'm looking forward to seeing what shade of gray or beige they will turn when they dry.

"I feel like your shells wouldn't be friends with my shells," Mam says.

I inspect the injured razor and moon shells in her palm. "You've a bunch of rejects."

"Well, aren't you a snob," says Billy.

"Trinity has changed me."

"It's a morbid hobby, really," Mam says, looking at her collection. "Why not study mollusks? They're the ones that make the shells in the first place."

"They're rotten though," I point out.

"Exactly. They're slippery, slimy yokes. We prefer to wait until the little life dies and disappears, leaving an empty, clean skeleton. That's all shells are. What if we collected human skeletons the way we do seashells?"

"Why would you even think like that?" Billy asks.

"I'm just saying."

"I don't buy that. Shells aren't skeletons." I point to the center of the cracked moon shell in her hand. "They have belly buttons."

A surprised cackle escapes Mam. "That's so true."

"I've never seen a belly button on a skeleton," I say.

Mam traces the navel of the shell and hugs it into her chest. "They symbolize birth, not death."

"Oh Jesus, here we go." Billy throws his eyes up to heaven but I can tell he is relieved as well. Mam is skipping through the sand dancing with the shell in the palm of her hand like it's her tiny lover.

Billy and I stand back and watch Mam dance around in the sand. "They found traces of calcium carbonate on Mars," I tell him. "Shells are made of calcium carbonate."

"She can't hear you now. You can stop showing off." But then he laughs and shakes his head. "Shells in space. Imagine Maeve in space."

"She already is," I say.

He grins at her. "Our very own space cadet."

❋

We trawl through clumps of rushes on the sand dunes. Billy uses his penknife to cut some reeds to make St. Brigid's crosses later. He brings them back up to the house with him when he goes to check on the fire. Audrey and Xanthe come out of the water shivering and run back up the road for hot showers.

"Are we going in?" Mam asks me.

I take a deep breath. "OK."

I bend down to take off my trousers and turn around to see my naked mother bouncing up and down to keep warm. We both start laughing at her boobs going everywhere. I look down at my black Lycra. I feel like I'm cheating, but I can't bring myself to take it off.

The tide is out, but the water rushes to meet us. The first touch of cold water shocks me back into myself. I squeal and turn to walk away but Mam takes my hand. She's being very patient with me. My chin starts quivering. My hands are red. I have the complexion of a plucked turkey.

We wade into the water. It feels like we've been walking for ages, but the water is only up to our thighs. The sea stretches before us, glistening like mercury. The clouds are fluffy, tinged with purple and blue. It's like we're walking toward heaven, only it's a test and I'm failing miserably.

"Relax," Mam says.

"I'm really sorry, I don't think I can, Mam."

"Just keep breathing," she says. "Breathe with the waves. Stop where you are now and listen. Notice how the water is breathing."

"My breath—keeps—catching—in my chest."

"Your body will adjust." I'm glad to see her teeth are chattering. I feel like I'll never be warm again. "You're OK. Now, duck your head under the water."

"No thank you."

"Come on, we'll do it together."

"I'm not ready."

She walks in and recites her faithful lines. "Sunlit zone, twilight zone, midnight zone, abyss and—" She dives under the water.

"Hadal zone, the territory of Persephone, the winter queen," I finish it for her.

She emerges from the water a few seconds later. "I feel so much better."

"Good for you."

"Come on."

"Stop talking to me. I just need a minute."

I spot a wave on the horizon and watch as it comes toward us. As soon it reaches me I'll surrender, I think. It looms toward me. Passes me.

"For fuck's sake," I say.

"Try again."

"Stop looking at me."

I wait until something inside me breaks. I bend my legs and kneel into the sea, surrendering. A wave comes and my head goes under. Mam is cheering. The water sleeks my hair back off my face. My nose is running. I taste salt. I'm so stupidly proud of myself.

Mam splashes me. "Doesn't it feel better?"

"No," I insist.

"Keep moving."

I start to move differently under the water. The waves pull me this way and that so that it feels like I'm stretching beyond myself. Mam holds my hand and kicks her legs out from under her. I follow her lead until we're both floating on our backs and sky is all we see. Mam squeezes my hand. I squeeze back. Water floods into our eardrums. For a moment, the only thing connecting us to the world is each other.

❋

I'm shaken awake in the middle of the night. There's a hand over my mouth and I moan in panic.

"Sshhh, don't wake anybody," Billy whispers. "Come on outside. Bring your duvet."

I lie in bed for a moment, considering the likelihood that this exchange has taken place in a dream.

I go outside anyway, suspicious of reality. Billy is waiting for me.

"Where are we going?" I ask.

He produces a dandelion from behind his back. "There's a full moon out tonight. Come on."

There's a gentle wind stroking the island, rocking it to sleep. We shuffle toward the sound of the waves soothing the shore and stop at one of the flat rocks on Brian's beach. Billy rolls out his sleeping bag like it's a red carpet and shimmies his way into it.

"This is where I started noticing them."

"The stars?" I wrap the duvet around me and lie down on the rock beside him.

"I used to come out with Mam when she wasn't able to sleep," Billy says. "We'd both sneak out of the house and lie down here. She'd pick a star and tell me a story."

"About the Greeks?"

"Yep."

We listen for a while to the sounds of the beach.

"I don't like thinking about them," Billy says.

"The Greeks?"

"No, the dreams. Even as a child, when Mam would tell us about them. Maeve lapped it all up but I was jealous of them. They took my mammy away from me. I saw what they did to her. She was an angry person. She had a temper, but it was made worse by the lack of sleep. She never left the house. I thought it was easier to ignore them. After she died, I stopped believing in them. I told myself it was all in her head. And it was all in her head. Look at Maeve. It's still all in her head, that's the problem. It's too much for any one person to handle. It's all just . . . too much. So I worry about you—about what they're going to do to you."

"I've been thinking about the dreams, and aside from the fact that people would think I was crazy if I ever brought them up in conversation, I don't think they're the strangest thing I've ever experienced," I say. "Like, there are polar bears in the world. They actually exist. That's much more of a statistical impossibility than me slipping in and out of dreams, regardless of whether or not they belong to me. I'm not sure anything belongs to me, anyway."

"Debbie?" he asks.

"Yeah?"

"Tell me a story."

Acknowledgments

Thank you to everyone who made this book possible. There aren't enough words to thank my agent, Marianne Gunn O'Connor, for believing in me and the story I wanted to tell from the moment we met. Thank you to my secondary school English teacher, Sarah Butler, who offered me encouragement and guidance when I needed it most.

I owe a debt of gratitude to Paul McVeigh, who judged the Seán Ó'Faoláin Short Story Competition and is responsible for starting a chain of events that completely changed my life.

A good chunk of *Snowflake* was written during a six-month workshop facilitated by Seán O'Reilly and *The Stinging Fly*, which was enormously helpful. There, I met the members of my writing group. I cannot thank that group enough for the chats, laughs, free therapy, embarrassing sentences, and the best feedback.

Thank you to my amazing US editor, Emily Griffin, for her razor-sharp eye and invaluable input. It has always been a very quiet dream of mine to have a US publisher based in New York. Being published by Harper is beyond my wildest expectations.

Massive thanks to Padráig O'Meiscill, Colin Walsh, Sophie Stein, Marcus Bradshaw, and Mark Kelleher for reading early drafts and for listening to me ramble on. Thank you to Ciara Conlan, and to Lisa, Colm, Ollie, and Jackie Conlan for all of their support. Thank you to my extended family and all of my friends for keeping me going through tough times. Huge thanks to Mary Ellen Nagle for agreeing to be my friend at a short story festival in Cork, and good luck with ever getting rid of me. Thanks to Laura Sheary, Niamh McCann, and Emer McGuckian for providing me with sea swims, soul food, and some of the best days of my life.

A special thanks to Cappagh GAA and Camogie Club, especially to the team of 2019 and Niall Williams, for always keeping us tuned in.

Finally, thank you to my family for putting up with me. I had to come home to write this story. To my mam and dad, Michael and Stephanie, Catherine and Cathal, and Sarah, Paul, and Sophie. This book wouldn't exist without you. Le grá, Lou x.

About the Author

LOUISE NEALON is a writer from County Kildare, Ireland. In 2017, she won the Seán Ó'Faoláin International Short Story Competition and was the recipient of the Francis Ledwidge Creative Writing Award. She has been published in the *Irish Times, Southword,* and *The Stinging Fly.* Nealon received a degree in English literature from Trinity College Dublin in 2014 and a master's degree in creative writing from Queen's University Belfast in 2016. She lives on the dairy farm where she was raised, and *Snowflake* is her first novel.